Topsy Turvy

k i n d a   l o v e

ZDrake

ZOEY DRAKE

Topsy Turvy Kinda Love
Copyright © 2020 by Zoey Drake
All rights reserved.
All rights reserved worldwide.

May contain sexual situations, violence, sensitive and offensive language, and mature topics. Recommended for age 18 years and up.

Print ISBN: 9798531711168

Editing: Jenny Dillion
Proofreading: Yvette Deon
Formatting: Champagne Book Design
Cover Artist: Book Cover Kingdom

Other Titles by
ZOEY DRAKE

Sweet and Sexy Standalones
Second Chance Rescue

Moonshine Springs Novels
Written in the Sand
Written in Love Letters (Coming Fall 2021)

425 Madison Avenue Series
Melting Wynter

Dedicated to those struggling this year.

To those who persevere when things get tough.

To those who still fight even though it seems useless.

To faith and hope that things will get better.

To love and those who love us.

To compassion for those who need it.

To those who lend a helping hand when they don't have one to lend.

To those who need a voice.

To those too afraid to give love a chance.

To You…

For continuing to read my words time and time again faithfully.

Playlist

Crush by David Archuleta

Heart Attack by Demi Levato

Kiss Me by Ed Sheeran

Harder (with Bebe Rexha) by Jax Jones

Bad Guy by Billie Ellish

Into You by Ariana Grande

Living Proof by Camila Cabello

As You Need by Alex Aiono

It's You by Ali Gatie

Sex on Fire by Kings of Leon

If We Never Met by John K

"Your love is like alcohol. Life threat."

—Yatish Jottings

Brooks

I ran under the cover of darkness with only a duffel bag to my name.

Once you leave the compound, you're spiritually dead, outlawed, excluded.

I wanted more to live outside of everything I'd ever known.

What I found was Mia.

I can see my ring on her finger.

Her heart in my palm.

Her name on my lips.

My child in her belly.

And I'll do just about anything to get it, even sex lessons if that's all she'll give me.

Mia

I'm your average bartender with a bad little habit.

I won't deny it, I like a little weed while I paint.

Creative juices and all.

My life is just fine until I meet him.

He says he only wants sex lessons, but I know that's a lie.

He wants me,

To wear his ring.

A white picket fence and two point five kids.

But I'm not sure how to love and I'm not sure I want to try.

We'll see if Brooks is up to the challenge of calming this cotton-candy haired badass.

Topsy Turvy

kinda love

Z Drake

Prologue

I'd always wondered if one solitary moment had the potential to change the rest of my life. One single second that could create such an occurrence that every life event after it would differ, just slightly. As if one small particle may change my whole outlook. Standing here, I finally believe it.

Shadows of bright cotton candy colored hair trace along the curve of her shoulders as I watch her hips sway with the movements of each step. My eyes can't seem to part from her as she approaches. I'm drawn in, entranced from where I stand waiting beside the bar. An erratic beat hammers against my ears and for a moment I wonder if I'm still breathing. Is it possible to breathe without a heartbeat?

The bar is loud, but all I can see is her. The other noise filtered out by my thoughts. She's been starring as the main act in most of the daydreams I've been having for the last week and I can't seem to turn them off. Not that I want to. She caught my eye the day I interviewed with Eddie and since then it's been non-stop. All my senses are out of whack—thoughts fluttering in a mad rush to go somewhere—but I can't pull my eyes away, and the instant replay is available with the snap of a finger.

"Maybe you should just take a photo, handsome," she says with a wink as she passes by me carrying a tray of drinks.

"What?" I mumble, shaking my head to clear my thoughts.

"You know, there's this thing called a camera. They're these devices that take pictures... A picture lasts a lot longer than just staring. Just saying. Oh, and you can even use it to jerk off if you want. I wouldn't mind you thinking about me while you stroke it, sexy. Now, are you ready to get some work done or should I swing around again so you can get another look?" I barely hear her over the drumming in my ears and the drop of my jaw.

I shake my head, clarity finally spotlighting each word. "What?" My mind spins, trying to process the words that spilled from those red lips.

"The name's Mia. I'm assuming you're my trainee for the night?"

I nod my head briefly because words still elude my brain like I've been drugged and can't form them. My lips feel thick like they're numb. Silence drifts between us like the lightest feather before she speaks again.

"What's the matter, cat got your tongue, handsome?" She laughs and my ears rejoice at the sound of it. How smooth it flows from her lips. Those bright red lips that beg for touch. "Okie do-key then, you'll be working behind the bar with me tonight. Over there is Zara. You'll meet the waitresses when they pop back over for drink orders."

She points behind her to the other bartender. Zara's tall with jet black hair, nails, lips, piercings, and dark eyeshadow. My mother had warned me about people that looked like her. Like they worshipped the devil. One of those demonic cults. Sorry, mother, you're not here to warn me off this time. I let my eyes wander over the bar and notice a theme. It's like the island of misfit toys—hippies and piercings galore.

The one she calls Zara pipes up before I can respond. "Damn, he's a weird one. Where'd Eddie find this one?" she says it as if I'm not standing right there, listening to every word.

"You're one to talk." Mia smarts back at her.

I shrug my shoulders, letting their words slip into the air between us and disappear. It's not the first time someone has called me weird, and I can guarantee it won't be the last. I'm finding out that things, where I came from, are definitely different than they are around here.

The compound I grew up in didn't allow for many visitors and the rules were strict, so to say that I'm socially unaware wouldn't be an understatement. Once a year, they'd have a fair, but it was only for the compound families. The main events every week were church related. We were founded on strict beliefs about life and faith. Both things I couldn't see myself adhering to for the rest of my time on this earth. I wanted out, but once you did, you were outcast, shunned.

Today marks the first day of work at my new job. Topsy Turvy is located in a college town. One where everyone buzzes around and most days Main Street is packed. There are endless things to do– karaoke, coffee shops, diners, bookstores, ice cream shops, various knick-knack stores, and candy shops. One of these days, I plan to actually walk around and see what all this town has to offer. But today isn't that day.

Mia moves to make her way behind the bar when a gust of cotton candy fills my nose as the front door sweeps open. This new aroma makes my mouth water, begging for more of that sweet candy flavor. It's not the first time this scent has intrigued me, tortured my senses. It took over for the first time just one week ago.

She starts fiddling with glassware and I can't help but admire the ease she has as she moves.

The bar is getting louder as more people pile in through the front door. Everything fades away to the back of my mind as I watch her. The voices and laughter get increasingly less loud and pronounced.

Her eyes find mine, her smile creeping up to her eyes. She winks and I'm a goner. I let my gaze trail over the pristine features of her face, lost in a fog of pink, blue, and purple colored hair, and vibrant sapphire blue eyes. I should pause my urge to ogle her like a creep, but she's one of the reasons I left the compound. I knew the world held more for me—dating who I wanted to and marrying for love.

"Okay, you ready to finally get to work? We only have a couple hours before your first night, so I'm going to need you to get your head in the game, okay, handsome?"

The beautiful cotton candy haired temptress waves her hand in front of my face and I blink slowly. "Dude, did you hear me? Hey, are you okay?"

A bell goes off in my brain that I need to speak, but words won't form. They clog in a ball in my throat, cutting off my airway.

What the hell is wrong with me? I swallow once, then clear my throat. "Uh, yeah. I'm good. My bad." Embarrassment floods my face with color.

Her rainbow hair bounces as she cocks her hip, hand falling to her waist. There is no shame in my ogling as my eyes trace along every curve and dip of her body. Satan himself couldn't pull me away from taking in every inch of her gorgeous figure. In fact, he's probably cheering in glee at the unbridled lust raging through me. Her skin is like porcelain and I wonder how soft it is to the touch. How it would taste against my tongue. I want her, and I'd almost, almost sell my soul to get her. If mother could see me now…

4

A smile covers most of her face. "Alrighty, then. Now that we've gotten the awkward part over with, let's start with a blowjob."

I swallow. She wants to do that with me? I look around to see if anyone else is looking; I'm in luck. No one is. I point to my crotch right as she lets off a snort followed by a laugh.

I lean over and whisper, "You said blowjob...didn't you mean..." I motion down south again, and she laughs harder.

"Handsome, I'm down for anything you want to do, but right now. I'm talking about the blowjob cocktail—Irish cream and amaretto. Can you grab those?"

I curl my fist into a ball, embarrassment flushing my skin. I can't believe I really thought that she was going to... Of course, she wouldn't do that with me. She doesn't even know me. But her response confuses me. Does down for anything mean she'd really want to do that with me? Are girls outside the compound really that outgoing?

I sigh, feeling like a moron. I've never had interactions with women that didn't have a chaperone, so I'm not entirely sure how to interpret her words. I know what I want them to mean, but if I'm wrong things could go poorly.

I can't resist her. Something about her calls to me, and I can't quite put my finger on it. A mirror beaconing me to the light that flints over her when the sun hits her just right.

A soft palm falls on my shoulder. "Hey, you sure you're okay?" Her brow furrows.

I give a small nod, too many thoughts overwhelming me right now. She moves effortlessly, and slings drinks like it's second nature, while I fumble over my damn words like a petulant child. I want to learn more about her. She's my complete opposite, and it intrigues me.

I also need her to like me. To want to get to know me. But not just because she's my trainer.

I've taken entirely too much time staring at her and not enough time getting the mix for the drinks she requested just a few minutes ago. Moving quickly, I grab the amaretto and Irish cream.

"So handsome, tell me your story? All those dark and dirty secrets. Why do you blush when I say something naughty? Why did you decide to work at a bar with no prior experience?"

I keep quiet because I have no idea how to respond. So I just stand there sunbathing in her attention, like a lizard who basks on a rock in the hot summer sun. For some reason, I'm speechless again. It's starting to become a problem. I am glad that Eddie was willing to offer me this job without any experience. I got lucky. Everyone I'd asked before turned me down on the spot.

I open my mouth to speak up, but she speaks first. Mia is clearly not like the meek girls we have back home.

Her gaze catches mine briefly in between grabbing items. "You just move here?"

"Yep, sure did."

"You're a man of few words." I nod because it's true. I have no clue what to say to her.

"Okay, so we need a shot glass, shaker, an ounce of amaretto, and an ounce of Irish cream. Grab some ice for the shaker. Measure and add in your amaretto and Irish cream. Then you shake and bake it, baby. Strain it into your shot glass, leaving just a little bit of space for whipped cream. And voila!"

I watch the simplicity of her movements, each as smooth as the last -the curve of her pour, the accuracy of knowing how much to use. I wonder if eventually, I'll get that proficient with my skills. I can only hope.

So far, I haven't figured out why it's actually called the blowjob, but I'm sure she'll tell me when we get there.

"So, handsome. Want to know how to drink this bad boy?" I nod. "Well, it's kinda like bobbing for apples. You go down slowly, and then you shoot it back quickly." She leans down and grabs the drink between those pretty dark lips, before quickly shooting it back into her throat. I watch her swallow like it's the best porn I've ever seen.

"And there you have it. A blowjob."

I swallow harshly, words lodge inside me. Probably for the best.

For the next hour until the bar opens for the evening, I watch the skillful talent of Mia making all these drinks. It's like she's magic. Gliding here and there grabbing bottles, pouring, making drinks. I have a notebook and make notes as we go. I may look like a nerd, but if that's what I need to remember these drinks, then so be it.

College students file in slowly throughout the night. Mingling, dancing, eating, and drinking. Mia delegates me to grabbing people beers and straight liquor. Someone whistles over the bar, and she signals to them that she'll be with them in just a minute and turns back to me. "You going to be alright for a minute? Zara is down the bar if you need her..."

My head spins. Probably not, but I'll do it anyhow. "But what if..." The words start to spill from my lips finally.

I look up at her, but yet again, words fall flat, my sentence incomplete. "Hey, look. It's only beer, Zara's doing the hard stuff. You've got this. I believe in you, handsome."

I simply nod. I don't know how to respond. She smiles, shaking her head. "Alright, you. Go grab a beer for the guy at the end of the bar." Walking to drop off the beer, I ponder to myself as she walks away to help another customer. I've never seen anyone who looks like her before, and I'm drawn to her instantly. She's unlike any other woman I've met, and I can't help but want to know more.

My, prominent leader of the compound, father would tell me that my thoughts about her verge on the side of sinful, but they're not here to do anything about it this time—no preaching to me about the ways of the devil and lust. No beating me with a belt and demanding I repent.

Back home, there was a zero staring policy when it came to women. If you looked too long, it was considered lust.

The shift has flown by, and my feet ache from being on them all night but doing this feels right. Supporting myself, doing what I want to do for the first time in my life. I'm not dragged down with rules or smacked for doing the wrong thing.

The best part is her.

Mia comes over to cash out a patron's tab and I watch her delicate fingers push buttons on the cash register. I've got a lot to learn, and I'm not afraid to put in the work.

"Good work tonight, handsome. Same time and place tomorrow." I nod my head and start to walk away.

She hollers at me, "Hey, Brooks."

I spin around, my eyes landing on those sapphire blues. "You'll be making sex drinks in no time." She winks at me.

I never expected someone like her and now that I know she exists; I'm going to do whatever I have to do to make her mine. Even if that means damning my soul to hell forever. Hell, I'm already spiritually dead, what's another notch.

One

Brooks

One year later

"**H**ey man, hold up for a minute." Wyatt walks up behind me while I'm in the kitchen. It's a small space so we take up most of the room. The coffee pot makes sputtering noises as I wait for it to finish.

I nod our usual hello. "What's up, Wyatt?"

"Need to talk to you about something."

"Alright."

"So, you know Kaylen and I haven't been dating long, but I think she's the one. We've decided to move in together. I know this is short notice. I'm sorry about that, and I'll pay for the next month, but then I'm out." He looks down; I don't know if it's out of embarrassment or he's worried that I'll be mad, but I don't hold it against him.

My eyebrows raise. That is not what I was expecting. "Oh, you're right. That does suck. Good for you though, man." Reaching out I pat him on the shoulder.

His eyes grow wide like he wasn't expecting that response from me. What did he expect me to do? "Wow, so you're cool with this?"

I shrug my shoulders. "Dude… not much I can do about it. Lives change, people leave, things happen."

"I really appreciate it, man." He pats me on the shoulder before leaving the kitchen.

"No worries." It's what I say, but my real thought is… fuck… what do I do now?

There's no way I'll be able to pay for this place without help. After work, I get fliers printed up and ask Eddie if I can put them up around the bar. Roommate needed. I'm not sure what good they'll do, but it's worth a shot at least.

Within several hours I get multiple calls inquiring about the room for rent. A few mingle into the bar to meet me, but no one fits what I'm looking for yet. It's not as easy as I thought it would go. Beggars can't be choosers.

"So… you're looking for a roommate to take over your friend's lease? How's the search going so far?" I look over to find Mia looking back at me with those bright blue eyes, her hands grazing one of the fliers I'd hung up.

I sigh. "It's basically non-existent these days. No one's responded to the dang things, other than a few crazies." I cringe thinking about all of the people that reached out to me. I'm pretty sure half of them would either murder me in my sleep or get super creepy with my underwear drawer. "It's been a couple of weeks since I put them up and still nothing promising…"

"You're still looking though?" Her eyebrow lifts as if it's a question and I resist the urge to say duh.

I nod. "Yep, Wyatt's moving in with his girlfriend Kaylen. I'm gonna need someone to help out with the rent and bills. Place is too expensive for just me on my salary."

She shrugs. "Well, I've got a spare room if you're interested." She goes back to pouring shots for some guys from the football team at a booth in the corner. They're celebrating the big win tonight or something like that.

I can't believe that she's offered me her second room. My heart is on a rollercoaster as it climbs the first hill, ready to speed off down the other side in a blaze of glory with useless breaks.

"Brooks? Earth to Brooks?" she says, snapping her fingers.

I deadpan. "Uh, yeah. Are you serious?"

"Of course I am. Why would I even offer if I wasn't?" I watch as she reaches up and pulls a liquor bottle from the shelf behind the bar and a sliver of skin peeks out to greet me. I can't tear my eyes away from her. My fingers itch to reach out and take a quick swipe. What I wouldn't do for just one touch.

I shake my head. See, it's thoughts like this that make me believe moving in with Mia wouldn't be in my best interest. If I can't tamper down on these lusty thoughts just working together; I certainly won't be able restrain myself living under the same roof as her. It may take all of my willpower, but I won't pass up the opportunity to be closer to her. Call it whatever you want—a crush, an obsession—but I can't get her out of my head.

She's strung me in her tangled web of rainbow-colored hair and I can't find it in me to care.

"So, where do you live?" I ask because I honestly have no idea.

Mia jerks her finger behind her. "Right down the road. It's a two-bedroom flat on the second floor of the building. You'd have your own room. Let me know if you're down for being roomies, and I can show you around if you'd like? I get off in a couple of hours." She stares at me, waiting for an answer, and I clear my throat.

"Yeah, that would be awesome." I'm excited at the prospect of seeing her home. The place she spends most of her time when she's not at work.

I hang out at the bar until Mia's shift is over. The two blocks to her apartment go by faster than expected. The streetlights illuminate our path. My feet thump on each step as we climb the lit stairs to her apartment, and I stand patiently behind her as she opens the door. I'm glad I was able to walk her home.

A cotton candy scent mixes with vanilla and- is that weed- hit my senses as I follow her in. Maybe I'm just imagining it. Taking in the room, my eyes scan over every single corner of it. It's exactly how I pictured it to be—mostly darker colors with the occasional pop of color.

Dark walls enclose light grey sofas, and a cream-colored faux hair rug lines the floor. A fireplace takes up a corner of the room, and a large flatscreen hangs above it. A black metal coffee table sits in the middle of the room. The walls are covered in abstract paintings, signed MP. Bookshelves line one wall and I notice random statues in pops of color woven throughout the room.

I look over at Mia and notice her chewing on her bottom lip nervously. It's weird because she's never acted nervous before now. Maybe it's because I'm actually in her own space, invading her bubble, not just at the bar. Her long blue, pink, and purple hair hangs in curls around her face.

Bright ocean eyes find me, and she smiles a sweet smile.

"I gotta be honest. It's exactly how I pictured it would be," I say with all sincerity. She stares at me, almost as if she's not sure how to respond.

"Really? Huh." She quirks an eyebrow.

My eyes make one more pass over the room. "Well, yes and no. It's like the clothes you wear– mostly dark but with bits of color scattered here and there. Everything is in the right spot. Perfect like it's meant to be there. But I didn't know that you were an artist." I spot a gothic style painting hanging on the wall and walk toward it.

I turn my body to face her, pointing at the painting. "Did you paint this? It's really good."

Her mouth goes slack jaw right before she composes herself. "Stop it, it's honestly not that great."

"Don't lie to yourself, Mia. This looks like gallery level art." I watch her roll her eyes, but I don't miss the smile that peeks out. I have no idea if the painting is really good or not, but I'd say just about anything for another one of her smiles.

"Look, I'm just being honest," I murmur as her eyes find mine.

We're caught in each other's gaze. One tiny moment turns into several more moments. Deep blue eyes peer into my soul, while my own eat into hers, grasping for more. My ears feel like they're on fire and my breath is stunted. The air levitates between us.

So many things pass without any words ever being expressed. I don't know what's happening but it quickly dissipates when Mia blinks and I'm instantly thankful for the loss of connection. I walk over to the bookshelf and check out her books. Mostly drink books, art books, and a few paranormal fiction reads. I expected to see romance, but there were none. Instead of bookends, she uses statues- all abstract works, dark in color.

All of a sudden, it's like she remembers why I'm in her home. "Well let's get the room situation squared away. I'm sure you want to see that, right?"

"Sure," I say, but my feet remain planted to the floor. I'm

unable to move simply watching her walk away. A few steps later, she stops and turns. "Hey handsome, you coming or what?"

My brain begs my feet to move. To follow, and finally, they seem to listen. My central nervous system is back up and running messages to and from the body parts that should be making me move. She stops at the first door on the left down the hallway. I stop just steps behind her, her cotton candy scent entwining with my airway. "This will be your room."

Stepping aside, she allows me to check it out. Dark walls with light trim. It's a large room, and I can see my furniture fitting in here perfectly. Where the bed will sit, the dresser, the nightstand. She's quiet as she steps up behind me. "Not entirely sure what your furniture sitch is… but I don't have an extra. The couch is free, or you can bunk with me for a day or two until you get things figured out."

We step back into the hall, and she speaks again before I even have a chance to respond. "My room is the one down the hall," she says pointing to the closed door in front of us. "Over there's the little boy's room, or girl's, when I'm using it." She chuckles and I can't help but smile. "I'm not entirely sure what self-imposed boundaries you have on sharing a room with a girl, so…?"

A smirk curls the sides of my lips as I watch her word vomit into the air helplessly. "You're finally taking me up on that, being ready for anything offer?"

Heat snakes up her face, her creamy skin turning a shade of pink. She opens her mouth, but words never part with it.

"Anyhow, I'll take it. The room that is." I smile.

'Well, I'm going to ask you to sign a contract. Nothing personal, just like having things in writing. Plus, you've gotta take my word that I'm not a serial killer or anything."

"I trust you, Mia."

"Why?"

I shrug. "You haven't given me a reason not to."

"Where are you from, handsome? It's clear you aren't from around here because no one is that trusting. People don't just shack up with people they don't know."

"Maybe you just ain't found someone worthy of your trust. The way I see it, we've been working together for over a year, Mia. We may not know each other as well as I'd like yet, but I think it'll work out just fine. Plus, you know your way around the bar, and maybe if I moved in here, you could show me some of the crazy bar tricks you have."

"You want me to teach you how to sling drinks like some fancy mixologist, Brooksy?"

"I'll take whatever training you're willing to offer."

"Don't ask for things you can't handle, Brooks."

"Um..."

She laughs and sticks out her hand. "Alrighty, then. Guess you've got yourself a new roommate."

My hand moves to shake hers, but when we touch, a current of power zips through us. Shocking us to the core. "Wow. You got some magical pixie powers or something."

Heat creeps up her cheeks and she clears her throat. "So, we're good?"

"Yep, as long as you're good, I'm good." This is the craziest thing I've ever considered, but I'm all in—any chance to spend more time with the real life pixie standing in front of me.

"So when do you want to do all this? It being close to the end of the month and everything." My mind still can't comprehend that she's okay with me just moving in here.

"When does it work for you?" I ask heart in my throat. I can't believe this is actually real. I'm giddy in a way I've never felt before, and I'm hoping my face doesn't betray how overly eager I am to be in her space. That would definitely freak her out and send her running. She gives off the runner vibe for sure.

"Well, if I remember correctly, we're both off this Friday. So, how about then?"

My mouth drops open. "That's soon. You sure you don't want to like, wait a week?"

"Brooks, you second-guessing it now?"

"No, just want to make sure you're ready."

"Already told you before, handsome, I'm ready for anything."

"Uh, okay, then. Friday it is. You sure you're okay with this?"

Her gaze darts to mine, light blue colliding with chocolate brown. "You keep asking me that I'm going to forget the whole thing and take back my offer."

"Nope. We're good." I'm backpedaling fast. I don't want her to take away my chance at spending more time with her than just in passing as we changed shifts at work. She nods once, and I let out the breath I've been holding.

"Wait, one more thing..."

God, I hope she isn't going to take back her offer now.

"Yeah..."

"You don't have like, a crazy girlfriend or anything, right? I don't need some psycho coming in and fucking up my place because you decided to move in and not tell her."

A sigh rumbles from my lips and I breathe out again. "Um. Nope. We're good on that too. No girlfriend here."

"Okie dokey then, Brooks. Looks like you got yourself a new roomie. And this doesn't have to be the regular friends only type roommate's situation either. I'm open to anything. You're single. I'm single... endless possibilities." With a wink she's off again.

I watch her as she walks away and wonder what she means by that statement. There's something about her that seems closed off like she's putting up a façade for the world to see without ever really letting anyone in. I'm going to figure Mia out, and I'm going to keep her. Just need to find a way in...

Two

Mia

I lift the joint to my lips, inhaling the fragrant aroma of weed. I sigh when the all too familiar taste of bitter citrus hits my taste buds. There's just something about marijuana that makes me feel good. Yes, it's more than likely its little friend, THC, but I'll take it. I lean back as the smoke trails from my lips, evaporating into thin air.

Anytime I need to chill and shut down my brain for a while, I smoke. More often than not Zara tags along on my high. My smoke and chill sister from another mister and my coworker at Topsy Turvy.

"Girl, I'm still confused about why you agreed to let him move in with you…" Zara says to me with a quirked eyebrow. Truth is, I'm not one hundred percent sure why I did it. Normally, I enjoy the peace and quiet of my own space, but for some reason, I enjoy hanging out with Brooks even if it isn't that often. He's different from the regular guys I pick up. He doesn't have arm sleeves of tattoos and piercings in every orifice of his body… not that I've seen every orifice.

I have a terrible habit of picking the cheaters, the liars... one's just like my father. My attraction to him is something different.

Some part of me feels like he's safe. Another part of me can't quite figure him out, and I'm intrigued. Most people show you who they are in the first half an hour of talking to them. I read people, and for some strange reason, I can't get a good read on Brooks. Maybe I see him as a challenge, one I've happily accepted. I want to discover the bed of secrets he's hiding. No one is that pure. I take another hit on my joint and sigh.

Ignoring her question, I reply, "How do you always manage to get your hands on the best weed in the city?"

"I've got good connections, and hello, it's a college town." She signals around us from the front window.

"That's what I'm saying. College towns always have shitty weed, but you manage to find the best strains." She finishes hitting the current joint and plops down on the cushy chair next to mine.

"What can I say, I have good connections... I'm not giving away my source if that's what you're asking. Oh, I almost forgot..." She gets up and leaves the living room.

"Huh, alright then."

Strolling back into the room, she plops down on the couch, a new baggie of weed in her hands. Quickly rolling up another joint she hands it over. "Here... try this new hybrid I just got in. It's called Purple Platinum Cookies. Amazing for relieving stress. Sixty percent indica, forty percent sativa. It's a cross blend between Purple Haze and Platinum Cookies."

"Yes, please." I could use some stress reliever in my life right now. I hit the joint, and my taste buds rejoice at the fruity, sweet flavor of it. Reminiscent of my favorite OG strains.

"So... Brooks?" Clearly, she's not giving up on this grill session when all I want to do is chill, so I decide to appease her.

"He's hot, okay? I think he'd be an excellent lay and what better way to get in his pants than to let him move in with me?" It's only a partial truth, but these days no one gets the whole truth. Why bother telling people anything when chances are, they're only going to hear what they want from what you've said. People are fake. A shell of who they really are on the inside. They're drunk on fun, debt, money, gambling, or prostitutes.

The truest person I've ever met is probably my best friend, Macy. She's married to the love of her life now so I'm on my own. Occasionally she graces me with her presence, but it's never enough.

My gaze turns back to Zara and I notice her lifted eyebrow. "What?"

"Where are you at today? Seems like you're not here with me."

I roll my eyes. "I'm high. I'm never here with you, Zara."

She lifts the drink she procured while getting up to roll the last joint. "Touché."

I feel like she's still waiting for me to spill my guts so I decide to give her a little more information. "Look, he's just looking for a new place to live. His roommate is moving out soon and it just so happens that I have an extra room available. Somewhere in my brain, I decided that it would be a good idea to invite him to live with me, so I asked him. He couldn't say yes fast enough."

"And he didn't even want to see the place first?"

"Oh no, he saw it, but I don't think he needed to. He didn't seem to be paying attention when I gave him a tour. He just kept staring at me." That thought alone gives me weird vibes. He's willing to put his complete trust in me. Yeah, we've worked together quite a few shifts over the last year, but it still baffles me. How can you trust someone you don't know?

She snorts. "Clearly, he's not from around here..."

"I know, right? At least he doesn't have a girlfriend. You know what that means?"

She seems to think about it for a minute before responding. "I got nothing."

"It means I don't have to be confined in the friend zone. He's single, I'm single. I wanna see what he's packing down below and I bet he'd be down for it."

The look on her face makes me feel like she isn't really following anything I'm saying. "Hey, Mia. I think he's into you more so than just an "as friends" basis."

"I don't know, maybe he's just looking for a hookup. He was totally into me the first day I trained him. When I said the word blowjob, his eyes lit up like a Christmas tree, and he even put his hands to his pants button like he was going to let me. He's got some nice artillery down there and it was more than happy to try and poke its way out. My hot pocket definitely wants to play with his crotch rocket."

She sticks out her tongue at me. "Thanks so much for the visual."

"Please... you're far worse than me any day of the week," I say through a giggle. "Do I need to remind you of all the dirty details from the sex club you went to last week?"

"God, it was so fucking hot. I still can't believe it. You should try it sometime. Let someone tie you down and dominate you like a helpless little submissive who will do anything for the big dick that belongs to your master."

"Wait... you let people tie you up?" The thought of a sex club intrigues me. It's something I'd always wanted to try but was never that bold. Don't get me wrong; I love sex... somedays more than life itself, but I've never really been one for exhibitionism. Plus, I'm not sure I could give up that much control.

"I've only ever done it once. It's definitely an experience. I, personally, prefer to be the one in charge." She winks at me, and I wonder what she means. I've read about sex clubs in books. Zara definitely seems to be more of a dominatrix than a submissive. Or at least that's how she is in real life.

"You wanna go some time? I can get you in..."

"Um. Yeah, thanks for the offer, but I'm going to pass for now."

"Your loss...ever change your mind, you let me know. So back to Brooks. I think he's into you, girl." I roll my eyes at that, but she keeps going. "Look, I'm serious. You don't see the way he stares at you as if you're an angel that's fallen from heaven just for him."

I look up at the ceiling, prickles tingling up my spine. "Gah... no, he doesn't. He's just never seen a rainbow-color haired chick that bartends before now. I'm like one of those things that you can't stop looking at yet can't turn away from either."

"Well, if you don't see it, then I guess you're blind. All I'm saying is that you need to be careful with him if things get to the point of between the sheets play. I mean he already tells you that you're a pixie. Like he thinks you're a magical creature or something."

"Zar..."

"Look, all I'm saying is that things are about to change for you. You're Mia, this badass. The, I bring home guys, fuck them, and then run when the feelings get tough. How do you think he'll feel seeing and hearing you with other men? The guy has a huge crush on you."

She sighs. "I'm just saying that him moving in changes things. Whether you want to believe it or not. I think you better think long and hard about all of this stuff. He may be your main dick for a while, so I wouldn't want to do anything to jeopardize that. Cause going without dick for months on end... the agony. And ain't no one got time to hit up a hotel like a prostitute."

"I guess I hadn't really thought about it."

"Well, now's your chance. Don't get me wrong, it seems like a match made in roommate heaven. Mr. Hottie McHot Pants moves in. You get dick on the side... but don't count your chickens before they hatch."

"I'm not dating him, Zara. I'm letting him live with me. If we hook up occasionally, then we hook up."

"Mia let's be honest. Brooks is very transparent in his feelings about you, and you can deny it as much as you want to, but there's more there than you're letting on."

"Great, thanks." Our previous joint is long gone. The mood between us sober as the high wears off slowly and the thoughts I'd been pushing away start to creep in again. Before they can fully take up residence, I'm rolling up another joint and bringing it to my lips.

What would happen once he moved in? Would it really be as easy as I thought it'd be? Regardless, I need to clean up some areas, like the living room with my paint and brushes littering it, dump out my ashtray, and pick up the clothes littered throughout my house.

I get up and slowly meander my way toward her front door. I need to get away, and I hope my retreat isn't noticed. But Zara being her know it all self, reads it all for what it is.

"You're heading out already?"

"Yeah, got some errands to run before Brooks comes."

"Yeah, definitely do it before he comes." She laughs with a wink.

"Don't be gross, I just have some things to do."

"Lies, you're off to go clean-up for the new roomie, aren't you?"

A shiver runs through me and I let my imagination about what happens next run wild. "So, sue me." I don't even bother hiding my smile about it this time.

Three

Brooks

It's been a slow day. A few college kids started filling in around lunch time and grabbed some food. In the afternoons, the bar is quiet. Study sessions are held in corner booths. Chatter is continual. Zara's been working with me today. We don't talk much because I'm not sure how to take her. She's a lot like Mia, but she also isn't afraid to go down the perverted train. It's still weird talking about such things out loud without reproach from anyone.

The hum of the music bleeds through the speakers, and I whistle along with the song. My eyes find the clock and I can't help but think about how a certain someone will be coming in to work soon. I've been messing with drink recipes and ideas but haven't come up with anything that jives just yet. I reach for another shot glass and start filling it, thankful that after a year, I've finally managed to learn how to make decent tasting drinks. It was an uphill battle, but I'd say it paid off.

I don't even realize I'm overpouring the shot until Willie, an old bar patron, clears his throat across the bar. "You're wasting all that good alcohol on a bar that ain't gonna appreciate it as much as I will."

"Uh…" I look down and realize that the shot glass is in a puddle of whiskey. I'd over poured so much that it was spilling off the side of the bar and onto the floor. "Shoot." I grab some napkins and try to soak up the alcohol. When did he get here?

I catch Willie's laugh. "You got a girl on your mind?"

"Yeah, you could say that." He caught me thinking about Mia.

"Wait, you into that weird haired chick that works nights here, huh?"

"How'd you know that?"

"I got eyes, boy. Your eyes follow her around like you're in dire thirst, and she's going to provide the rainstorm you so desperately need. I get it. Used to be that way myself a long, long time ago. You get to asking her out on a proper date yet?"

"Nope, not yet. I'm actually planning on becoming her roommate, so I'm not entirely sure where that leaves us." My eyes dart between Willie and the bar top.

He whistles. "Woo-wee, you got some balls, son."

My eyebrow quirks. "Why ya say that?"

"She's a fiery one, that girl. She'll chew you up and spit you out before you even get a chance to breathe. Very much an act first, talk later type of person. You don't seem as outgoing, boy. Haven't had a chance to talk to ya much. Not sure where you grew up, but it's clear it wasn't around here. She's going to need a man that can stand up to her. That ain't afraid to tell her what you think. Someone that doesn't easily bend to her every whim. She's got a fine ass to go with all that sass. I'm just thinking you need to be ready."

"So, what do you recommend I do?"

"Well, where do you stand with her? Is this a roommate's only situation or do you think she wants more?"

I shrug my shoulders because I have no idea. We haven't talked about it other than her mention that we're both single. "I'm not sure."

"Do you want to rock the boat by dating your roommate where if things go wrong, your potential home could be in jeopardy, or do you want to play it safe and wait on the sidelines pining for her and hoping she doesn't find someone else to love?"

Charlie snorts loudly, clearly eavesdropping on our conversation. "Kid called dibs on her the first day he saw her. You here that day, Willie? Man it was a sad sight for sore eyes... He wants to rock the boat."

I don't dispute any of it. She's been mine for over a year, except she doesn't technically know it yet. I get a bitter taste in my mouth when I think about how much I want her to be mine. What am I going to do? I want to move in with her to be closer, but I have no idea where this leaves us. We're both single, and she's hinted she's down for whatever, but sometimes I can't tell when she's bs-ing me or not. I feel like I know nothing about the woman. That's probably because it's true.

Willie nods. "Sure was, and he's still entranced by her, it appears."

Charlie chuckles. I kick the bar in front of me, not wanting to think about the truth of it.

"It's okay, son, I think she likes ya. If she didn't, she wouldn't sass you so much. What is it they say... wouldn't pick on ya if I didn't like ya?"

Charlie pipes up. "Yep, that's it. No doubt about it."

"Yeah?" A flicker of hope lights up that one tiny word. It's a weird feeling thinking about her. I get tingles under my skin that radiate. Take my man card now.

Willie shoots the shot I re-poured earlier after the spill and wipes his mouth. "Give it time, she'll be all over ya. Treat her like a lady, turn on that swoony charm I know you have. Bada Bing. Bada Boom."

I look away, trying not to let my nerves get the best of me while I ask my next question. I open my mouth to speak, but a laugh erupts from Charlie's mouth, interrupting me before he points toward Willie. "Wait, you really trying to seek advice from this old guy?"

"And you're any better?" Willie looks pointedly at Charlie, clearly offended.

"Oh, hell no, but I also don't pretend to know things like you do, old man." His accusing stare fixes on Willie.

"Eh, bastards probably right. I don't know left from right some mornings," Willie replies.

I look between them trying to get any other tips that I can. "So what? I just wait and see what happens? Let her make the first move?"

"Good lord, son. Have you not been listening to anything that's come out of my damn mouth?" Willie mutters. "Do that and you'll likely never get laid."

A blush creeps up my face and I can't help my embarrassment about being a virgin at this age. My patience is slowly waning with these two old guys, so I take a deep breath. "What do you think I should do then?"

"You looking for true love, a ring, two point five kids or you looking for a hookup? That's the question you gotta ask yourself." Charlie cuts in.

I open my mouth once and then close it again. I'm not exactly sure how to respond. This seems like a private topic of discussion, and one maybe I'm not ready to share.

"I'm looking for…"

Willie looks over at me with a lifted brow. "I know that look. He's in love with her. He wants to keep her forever."

"The lot of you are saps. Complete saps." Charlie says before he strolls off to chat with an older lady down the bar.

Willie raises his brow. "So, Mia Preston, huh?"

"Yep, the one and only." I dip my chin slightly so he doesn't see the double meaning I have behind that comment.

"So, you're moving in with her in just a couple of days from now?"

"That's the plan. Honestly, I could use any advice you'd like to give me."

Willie rubs his jaw. "Son, I could give you all the advice in the world, but it seems like every relationship is different. It depends on the people. What I can tell you is to not take it for granted. Follow her lead. You can rush into things all you like, but love is built on trust and respect. Take it slow, learn her heart and her mind. You'll figure out what it'll take to break through to her as you live together. Maybe that's physical upfront, maybe not. You'll know."

My pulse is pumping faster, thinking about invading her space, maybe getting physical with her. If it were up to me, I'd already be moved in, but I don't want to rush anything. We've got all the time in the world.

"But what does that mean exactly?"

"You'll figure it out. This whole experience is more than likely going to be new for you. I'm assuming you've never lived with a female other than your momma before, and I'll be the first to tell you that some days it's a battle of wills. It won't be a picnic. Some days it will try your patience. You'll want to yell and scream and throw shit. She'll say something that you don't understand. You'll fight but remember to always apologize and never go to bed angry. Never said love was easy and some days you may have to fight for it."

"You sound like you seem to know a thing or two about it... Have you been in my situation before?"

"We aren't here to talk about me and my shortcomings... we're here to talk about you and your lady friend. But to answer your question, yes. I made that mistake once. Don't ever see myself doing it a second time. Old ticker won't survive another woman like her."

Willie shakes his head and sighs loudly. When he's facing me again, he looks me straight in the eye. Boring into my soul. "Now saying all this… I want you to be careful with your heart. I've known Mia for a while now. Never seen her with a guy. Doesn't have many friends. She doesn't trust easily, and it takes her a while to warm up to people. Once you're in her inner circle, she's loyal to a fault, but also guard yourself."

He pauses briefly. "Look, you seem like a good kid. Got a solid head on your shoulders, and I'd hate to see that change over a woman. Many men have been crushed by feelings over a woman. The last thing I want to see is you get hurt over this whole situation."

Anger rises at the idea that Mia would do anything to hurt me, but I know he's just trying to be open minded and make me think about everything. Since starting at Topsy Turvy, Willie has been nothing but the best giver of advice and support. In the end, he means well, but I'm probably not listening to any of his suggestions. I'm all in as far as I'm concerned with this girl. White dress, kids, picket fence… the whole ten yards…

"Thanks for the advice."

He knocks on the bar top before getting up, and an echo rings out across the bar. "You have yourself a good night and good luck. I'll be seeing ya."

His words replay through my mind the rest of the night while I continue making drinks and refilling beer. Maybe it will be the story of a lifetime and maybe it'll all go down in flames. Regardless I'm not backing down from the challenge.

Mia comes in five minutes early, like always by the telltale sign of her perfume. That cotton candy smell I just can't get enough of these days- an alluring scent filled with possibilities and what's to come.

"Hey, Brooks. How's it shaking?" Her lips part into a gorgeous smile with that quirky tilt.

"Slow start this morning, but things have been picking up this afternoon. About twice as many people here now as there were earlier."

"You all packed up yet?" I watch as she moves to her station to get her well set up for the evening. She seems so at ease and natural in her environment. Like she's been doing this for years. It's mesmerizing... well, she is.

"Nah, finally getting around to it tonight. I don't have that much to move. Anything else you need help with before I head out tonight?" I get my station cleaned up and shut down for the night.

"Nope, I'll see you tomorrow."

"Sure will." I smile once more before turning to leave for the night. I have things to pack up and get ready at home. Wyatt moved out earlier this morning, so it's just my stuff in our apartment. He'll be back on Friday to help me move over to Mia's place. A thrill of excitement shoots through my veins at moving in with my crush.

Four

Mia

I paint another stroke over the same line I've been going over for the last fifteen minutes, and my hand shakes. My nerves are out of control today. I take another hit of my joint, hoping it'll take the edge off. I allow my eyes to crawl across the room. Although I've already cleaned up, I know there's still a few things out of place. He probably won't even notice, but I know they're there, so it's going to bug me. Dust on the bookshelves. Artwork littered throughout my apartment. I'm sure there's a bra or two stuffed somewhere…. Maybe a thong out of place.

Taunting me.

This is the first roommate I've ever had. I still can't believe I offered. My hand trembles again, and I shake it out. A shaky hand is the worst thing for an artist. It really fucks with a straight line. Why the hell am I so nervous?

A knock on my front door pulls my attention away from the stubborn black line in front of me. Brooks is here… to move in with me. He's patiently waiting just beyond my front door, waiting for me to open it so I can invite him into my home. I saw him earlier this week, but it's a different feeling. Like I'm going to vomit. I would call them butterflies, but I don't believe in that or anything love related.

My heart jackhammers an uneven rhythm in my chest and not even weed can calm it right now. If anything, my senses are heightened. Breathing is the hardest thing I can manage. I snuff out my joint against an ashtray and put my paintbrush in a cup of water beside the canvas—something to come back to later.

I give myself a pep talk. There's no reason to freak out. I make my way to the mirror in my living room, fixing my hair. I make eye contact with myself. *You are Mia fucking Preston and you are a badass. You got this.*

Brooks is hot as fuck, I'll give him that, but I'm not down for a relationship right now... or ever. I do one-night stands and casual hookups, that's it. Fulfilling my sexual desires and needs, it's just physical.

I've been preparing for this moment. I don't understand why I'm so thrown off, but then again, I do. Letting him move in with me is the most intense thing I've ever done. I've never lived with a guy or even another roommate before. We've worked at Topsy Turvy together for the last year. Boundaries will need to be set right up front, but what the hell, I've never had boundaries before... I'm very much the do first, deal with the consequences after type of girl. But nonetheless, boundaries need to be set even though I know I'll be continually tempted to blow through because as much as I like sex, I know he likes me for more than just friends-with-benefits. And it's not fair to drag him along. No matter what I say to Zara. Brooks will never be a meaningless fuck.

Another knock comes at the front door, and I curb my mental pep talk.

"Coming!" I yell as dirty images and thoughts creep into my

mind of us doing just that. I mist some air freshener around where I was smoking to cover the weed smell and straighten out my clothing, worried about wrinkles like I'm going on a first date with a guy I'm into.

Get it together! I tell myself.

I whip open the door, and words get caught in my throat at the sight in front of me. Brooks looking hot as shit in a black t-shirt and grey sweatpants stands awkwardly outside my door. *Damn that man lingerie.* I have to check myself to make sure the drool isn't falling out of my mouth because hot tamales, that is a dick print if I've ever seen one. I just can't look away, and I know I should.

"Damn, son... you packing some serious heat down there. Didn't your momma ever tell you not to go out in public looking like a slut?" I blurt out, the filter between my mouth and brain clearly turned off.

A blush covers his cheeks. "Um... what?" he says, looking down at his outfit. I continue my ogling, eyes roaming over wide built shoulders and down bulging biceps that I swear are getting bigger as I stare. The black cotton tee molds obscenely well to the washboard abs and chiseled pecs he's packing just below it. Bro works out, for reals. Now, if only I had some water for a wet tee shirt contest.

Stop it.

"Oh...nothing. Sorry." I brush it off as if I wasn't ogling him like a total pervert just now. I'm not really sorry at all. I've never been that blushing virgin who takes peeks as sexy men. No I openly ogle them like a pervert. My brain is screaming at me that all those before mentioned boundaries have fallen to the wayside. It's the Titanic, and I don't have a lifeboat or a lifejacket. Looks like I'm going down with the ship tonight.

"Hey, Mia," Brooks croons and I'm dead, well... not literally, but that voice. It oozes with sex and naughtiness. *Yes, please!*

I finally tear my gaze away from those sinfully low, dick print showing pants. Trailing up his body, I catch the amusement on his face as he notices my obvious perusal. Embarrassment flames my cheeks and so I do the only thing I can think of. "Oh, hi." Heat swamps my cheeks, embarrassment evident. Damnit Mia, stop acting juvenile. *What the fuck is wrong with me?* I internally roll my eyes at myself.

The intensity of his stare gives me the chills, and I want to shrink away because this feels too close. Too intimate. Too much. Combined with that sexy as hell grin and the two dimples lining his mouth, I'm starting to melt into a puddle.

I need to move away from this conversation. *Be strong.* I tell myself. He's just a full-blown man, wrapped in a delicious sandalwood scent with scruff I'd like to feel down under who needs a place to stay. I'm being a good human being.

He's showered recently because I can smell the cologne he used. Not too strong, but enough to make my mouth water and my nose crave more of that aroma. Is it weird that I almost want to smell his armpits just to get more of that freshly showered scent? I want to do delightfully depraved things to him, but I can't. I've already told myself no.

I gather myself. With a newfound control, I smile and widen the door, so he can get past me. "Well, what are you waiting for? Get in here sexy."

I glance behind him, confused. "Hold up, where the hell is the rest of your stuff? You literally have a single duffle bag and a toiletry bag with you... where's the bed, chairs, furniture, etcetera... Or are you planning on just sleeping with me?"

A blush creeps up his face before he speaks. "Um, no. Wyatt will be here in a couple of hours with his truck. He offered to help me move in since he feels bad about leaving before our lease is up."

Now that he's closer, I take in his appearance more. Dark brown, almost black hair covers his head and stops just above the tops of his ears. It still looks damp. Another little tidbut that tells me he's recently showered. Eyes the deepest brown I've ever seen. God, I've never realized how sexy he is before this exact moment. I'm more than mildly lusty over my coworker, even if we do work different shifts. No shame here.

I'm off work tonight, so we hang out for the next two hours chatting about things at work. When he tells me about Wyatt and Kaylen moving in after dating for just three short months I scoff on the inside.

Love?

Great. Insert internal eye roll here. Another couple supposedly bitten by this love bug that everyone seems to believe in. Here's the thing... just because P goes into V does not automatically mean you're in love. I'd know this well because I've had a lot of P in V.

Another thing... love doesn't exist. Yes, I'd told Macy I believed in it, but I didn't want to break her delicate emotions by telling her how I really felt about it.

Love is a sham. How do people even fall in love? Do they believe falling in love is similar to Alice in Wonderland falling down the rabbit hole? Yeah, that's dumb. People who run around with their crazy notions of hearts skipping beats and butterflies are nuts. Newsflash, if your heart really skipped a beat, you'd be dead. How's that for love? Death by love. I laugh at my own joke.

He looks down at his phone, and a frown furrows his brow.

Just as I'm about to speak up and ask why the furrow, there's a knock on the door. Brooks gets up and walks to the door, opening it to unveil the mysterious roommate, or who I assume is Wyatt. If not, it's hella weird that there's a random guy at my front door. He's tall like Brooks but skinnier with blonde hair. He has muscles, but not my type. Dark green eyes and a clean shaven face. He really shouldn't stand beside Brooks because there is no comparison on the hot meter.

Brooks moves to the side, allowing his friend to come inside as I silently stroll over to where they now stand. "Mia, this is Wyatt. Wyatt, Mia." He nods his head at me with a polite hello. His eyes trail over my space, and I wonder what he thinks about it for a brief moment.

Having someone occupy my space is different, but it doesn't feel awful. It's a little uncomfortable now that Wyatt is here, but he'll be leaving shortly.

Maybe it's the fact that it's Brooks, and I can admit I'm mildly attracted to his chill demeanor. I don't know where he'd come from a year ago, but he seemed to fit into our Topsy Turvy crew fairly well.

"Okay, well. Wyatt and I are going to unload his truck. We'll be back." With that, they both slip out the door and spend what takes like forever before they return, even though it's only a few minutes.

A knock sounds on my door again as he and Wyatt let themselves back in. I cock my eyebrow at Brooks. "Why did you knock?"

"Um, don't really know…"

"Dude, this is gonna be your home too now. There is no need to knock on your own place… "

He nods, his smile tipping the corners of his lips and reaching his eyes. "Alright." A smile creeps across Wyatt's face as he shakes his head, but he makes no move to comment on the awkwardness of it.

As they trail across the living room, I notice both men are carrying boxes. Brooks is carrying three large boxes, while Wyatt holds one small, simple box. I wonder what the significance of the small box is, but I keep my question to myself. I don't want him prying into my life, so I'll lend him the same courtesy.

A dresser and side table slip through the door next and are placed in Brooks's room.

They disappear out the front door again, and I listen as their boots thump down the ten steps that lead up to my apartment. The door flies open again, bumping and cursing hit my ears, and I jump up to go hold open the door. The top of the ugliest recliner I've ever seen in my life comes through the door, and I feel my face scrunch with displeasure.

Who in the world would own something that ugly? Brown and orange plaid, like something from the seventies.

My eyes find Brooks as he peeks around the back of the recliner. He shrugs or tries to while holding the chair, shaking his head, and his dimples are on full display again. Dear Lord, those dimples are sexy as fuck. "Do you have any idea how ugly that thing is?"

Helping Wyatt set it down, a full belly chuckle erupts from his lips. "Yeah, that's what makes it so great."

"You keep telling yourself that, Brooks."

The chair is left in the middle of the living room and my eyes find Brooks. "Oh, hell no. You're not leaving that out here!"

"Well, I hate to break it to you, but it won't exactly fit in my room with my mattress and other stuff."

"How big is your damn mattress?"

"It's real big."

"Ha! That's what she said." A laugh rips from Wyatt's lips before they leave again.

Brooks and Wyatt return with the biggest box spring I have ever seen. It's got to be a California king size bed, by the looks of it. Like, this thing is HUGE. Like a caveman or a six-person family all sleeping in the same bed, huge. Hell, a homeless family could all sleep on it under a bridge somewhere and still have room for a dog or two.

They leave and come back once again with a mattress just as impressive as the box springs. I strangle the laugh bubbling up my throat as they curse and mutter their complete disapproval of how awkwardly large it is. I hear several bangs against unsuspecting objects—I'm assuming his dresser and side table—as they try to fit it in my second room, followed by curses. He wasn't joking.

Luckily, I have huge rooms in this apartment, so it's not an issue at all. I wonder if there is more furniture coming, but when Wyatt shakes his hand and says goodbye, I'm stumped.

"Wait, that's all?"

"Yep, had a couple more pieces, but I didn't think they'd all fit here and I never really used them, so I donated them."

Huh, interesting.

"I'm sure we could have made it work, Brooks."

"Ehh, it's okay. I'm not worried about it now." He heads back into his room and shuffles the dresser, nightstand, box springs and mattress until he gets it in just the right place.

I decide that while Brooks is getting his room altogether, I'm going to pour myself a drink. 11:00 AM isn't too early for wine, right? I determine that it's not and continue on my way; liquid courage and all. I walk over, pick up the paintbrush again, and get back to working on that stubborn black line.

I'm finally getting it smoothed out when Brooks reappears from my—his- room, a flush covers his face, and even with a sheen line of sweat beading his forehead, he still looks fine as hell. I'm losing my damn mind.

The smile on his face is infectious, and I want to bask in it. I've seen him smile before, but this one is an 'I just caught my first fish' or a 'kid in the candy store' smile. "I always forget how big it is until I have to move it."

I lose my shit. I laugh so loud I think it shocks him. "You've got to stop doing that, Brooks."

"Doing what?"

"Giving me the chance to make that's what she said jokes."

He cocks his head. "What's that mean?"

My jaw goes slack as I stare at him. "You mean you've never

heard that phrase before… in your whole life?"

"Um, no. Should I have?"

"Oh… never mind…" I say, shrugging it off.

He holds out his arm stopping me from turning away. "No, hey, wait… I want to know what it means."

"It's a sex joke, Brooks. Basically, someone says "man, that thing is huge," and someone responds with that's what she said… ya know, like, damn his dick is massive. Like… that's what she says…"

He shakes his head. "I don't get it."

Oh boy. Where did he come from? "You never heard of a thing called a sexual innuendo?"

He deadpans. "No."

"Where'd you say you were from again?"

"Somewhere you wouldn't be able to find on a map. Do people really talk about that stuff? Guys dick size and stuff?" He looks so serious when he asks, and I bite down the laughter that threatens to break free.

"Yeah, girls talk about stuff like that, Brooks."

"Is it something you wonder about me?"

"Wait, you know how big you are?"

Embarrassment flames his cheeks. "Well, I mean, I've compared it to objects that I've found laying around my old place if that's what you mean…"

"What kind of objects?" I say. Now, I'm dying to know. I mean, the dick print on those grey sweatpants was showing off a lot, but I'm just downright curious.

"Let's see… my phone, my roommate's girlfriend's penis shaped toy…"

"You mean a dildo? Your roommate's girl left her dildo just laying around for you to compare your dick too?" Laughter bursts from my lips, unable to keep it in any longer.

"Yes…Look I don't know much about girls or…dildos. Where

I come from, the girls were separated from the guys unless there were chaperones, or your parents had announced your pending nuptials." The hurt look on his face makes me feel bad. Obviously, he isn't comfortable talking about this sort of thing, but the fact that he is gives a new light to the Brooks standing in front of me.

He looks around the room and sighs. "You know, maybe this was a bad idea after all. I'll call Wyatt back and have him take the stuff back to my other apartment."

He turns to walk away, and my arm reaches out uninhibited and stops him from going any further.

"Hey, I'm sorry. It's just this living with someone is new to me, and I have a huge tendency of putting my foot in my mouth before thinking... Just... don't go yet. Okay?"

A smile creases his mouth, "Okay."

"One more question?" I ask because I still want to know.

"Shoot." A question crosses his face like he isn't entirely sure what's going to come out of my mouth. To be honest, I'm not sure either.

"Were you bigger than the dildo?"

His eyes widen as he looks at me, uneasy. "Yes... That a good thing?"

"Hunny, that's gonna make any girl smile," I say with a wink, and he smiles again. I'm going to earn every one of those damn smiles.

"So..." he says with a finger pointed over his shoulder. "You wanna check it out?" Excitement sparkles in his eyes, and I can't say no. Plus, I'm curious about the monstrosity currently residing in my second bedroom. I walk into the room, and a gasp falls from my lips. It's enormous, and there's barely a walkway between it and the dresser he brought. The room is stuffed to the brim.

The fluffy white pillow top makes me want to lay down and sleep for hours in its comfy-ness. To get lost in it. The pristine white

ZOEY DRAKE

is a clear contrast to the dark grey walls surrounding it.

I whistle. "If you even plan to have a slumber party, this is the perfect size bed for one."

The corner of his lip curved into a smirk. "That a suggestion?"

"Hunny, I don't think you could handle all this…" I wave my hand down my body.

His smile dims, and I feel like a royal asshat. Brooks stabs his fists into the pockets of his sweatpants, and I try not to drool over the fact that he just tightened the front of his pants again, enhancing my view more. He rocks back on his feet, looking embarrassed. "That's probably true, but it doesn't mean I wouldn't like to give it a try."

Five

Brooks

I'm glad Mia let me borrow a comforter and pillows. Obviously, I had managed to lose the set I had. I looked through the box three times with no luck. "Thanks for letting me borrow these," I say to Mia as she walks out of the room.

"If you need help ordering some of those custom fitted one's this week, let me know. I'm not entirely sure this little college town will have… what is it… California king size sheets."

"I'm terrible at this shit. I have no idea what happened to the ones I had." My somber tone halts Mia from leaving the room, and she turns around.

"No worries. It happens to all of us at some point. But hey, your super big comfy bed—that I'm totally jealous of—is here now. If you need me, I'll be in the living room." I watch as she glides past me and props herself up on the chair in front of her easel.

My feet stay planted for a few minutes just watching her. She lights up a joint, and for a moment, I wish I was that close to her lips. Mia picks up the brush, and it glides smoothly over the canvas.

I wonder if it's something she knows she's going to paint or if she just paints to paint. How long has she been painting? When did she start? I want to know every single detail. I take one more look before I head back into my room.

She isn't in the living room when I come back from getting things somewhat set up in my new room. It's weird to call it that, mine, but at the same time exciting. I'm finally going to be occupying the same space as Mia on a regular basis, and I won't have to look like a creeper doing so.

I find her in the kitchen, but she hasn't noticed me yet, so I take a minute to let my eyes take her in fully. Long waves of purple, blue, and pink cascade down and curl around her shoulders. Jean cut-off shorts cover her perfect, heart-shaped ass. She's wearing her normal cat graphic t-shirt and combat boots—a trademark outfit for Mia Preston. Every part of her draws me in, and I'm a goner. I continue my perusal before her voice brings me back to the present. "There you go again, hot stuff, checking me out. You sure you don't want a photo? I promise it'll last longer."

Her bottomless blue eyes sparkle more than any I have ever seen in my life. She highlights them with the same colors she uses in her rainbow-colored hair. I want to know what her regular color is under all that fake dye.

Mia makes me feel like I've been living in a hole in the ground. She's so out there with her sex talk and her flirting—so far out of my league, it's not even funny. It doesn't make me want her any less, though. I knew exactly what she meant by that's what she said earlier today, but I like the way she explains things to me. Watching as her tongue dips out to lick her lips between words.

It was a little awkward with all the penis talk, but I wasn't planning on holding anything back from her. If she wanted to know how big my dick was, then I was going to tell her. My answer seemed to please her. My mind wanders to other things that may please her just as much.

I should feel guilty for all these primal thoughts and feelings toward her, but the opposite is true. She makes me feel alive for the first time in my life. Father and the compound taught us to believe that sin was death, the worst kind of evil. To look at a woman for too long was lustful and wrong. But how could something so simple be so evil?

How could one thought, or touch send someone to hell for eternity? Simple—it can't. I'm choosing to ignore all the lessons I was taught growing up. Lord knows mama would have a heart attack if she knew what was going on in my mind or life. One look at Mia, and she'd start praying for my soul immediately. It didn't matter though, because I hadn't looked back once since I'd left. Not that I'd be allowed back even if I begged. I take another greedy look at Mia.

She moves effortlessly in the kitchen. I watch the dance her hips do as she walks. The red of her puffy lips as she holds it between her teeth like she's in thought. The sliver of creamy skin that peeks out when she reaches to put the dishes she just washed away. I should offer to help, it'd be the gentlemanly thing to do, but I can't seem to stop standing here.

It's hard to believe that she's real and standing right in front of me. The one thing I keep picturing is her being with me. Being mine. Growing old with her. Maybe it's more of an obsession than a silly crush after a year, but I can't help how I feel.

I shake my head to rid myself of those crazy thoughts.

What the hell is wrong with me?

I just moved in, no need to think about that now. She's my

endgame and I have all the time in the world to win the girl and build that white picket fence.

My brain is drowning in everything Mia, and clearly, it's affecting my other thoughts, like buying sheets for my new oversized bed. The same bed I'd like to see Mia in… completely naked.

Stop.

I tell myself before I get yet another boner that I'll have to figure out how to discreetly rid myself of.

I close my eyes and focus on the sugary sweet aroma of her apartment. It smells like a mixture of weed and cotton candy. The lit candles are probably the reason for at least one of these amazing smells, but my brain seems to think that it's mostly her. Why am I wondering if she tastes just as sweet?

"I feel like this afternoon calls for celebration," she says as she walks toward the back of the kitchen. I follow behind her, admiring the view.

What meets my eyes has me sucking in a breath. A full bar sits at the end of her kitchen—every type of liquor you could imagine plus wines.

"What kind of drink do you want? And don't say blowjob… we know how that went down last time." I laugh at her joke, embarrassed. Mia reaches for two lowballers in the cabinet above her, and her shirt rides up just enough to tease me again. A tempting sliver of her skin, a little more than last time, taunts me, and my legs move of their own volition, forgetting my place. I close my mouth stifling a groan from escaping. Desire stirs within me, sending all pertinent blood to the member below my belt.

Not good. Mia has always called to me, but this is another level. One where I feel like my need for her is only going to grow at this point. Well, my need isn't the only thing growing for her.

What the hell am I going to do? I find myself thinking about this statement a lot lately. Shaking myself out of my own head, I ask already aware of the answer. "So, what do you normally do on Saturday nights?"

"You know this better than anyone, work. I'll be leaving here shortly. Just because you're off today doesn't mean the rest of us are." She winks at me before handing me a glass, of what, I'm not sure.

"But I thought you were off?" Confusion laces my question.

"I was, but Eddie called and asked if I could come in. Someone called off. I imagine it's Sabrina."

I nod. "So, what is this?" I say, sniffing the beverage.

She laughs. "It's a dick sucker."

I can't hold in the moan that escapes my lips as I think about her doing that exact thing to me.

"So Brooks, I'll need to leave here in a little bit. But first, I think we need to set some ground rules for you living here. You've had a roommate before but living with another guy is a little different than living with a girl." Her flat tone leaves me almost worried about what's going to come out of her mouth next.

"Um... okay."

"First, you can't come in here looking like sex on a stick and expect me to just do things for you. I'm not your girlfriend or your mom. Basic manners are a must. I need you to do your own laundry and help with dishes. I expect you to put the toilet seat down when you pee. If I walk in there one time and my bare ass is greeted by cold porcelain, we're gonna have an issue. Like me yelling at you super early in the morning."

I laugh, but she continues. Picturing it in my mind is fucking priceless. "If the toilet paper roll is empty, replace it. Don't just leave it on top of the toilet paper holder. I may tend bar, but I won't be tending to you. Unless... you ask for it. And by it... I mean sex. There are rules about that too, but we'll swing back to those."

She sighs. "I don't cook, so don't expect it. Just cause your momma made you homemade meals every night doesn't mean I'm going to do the same. And eating out daily will certainly kill that boyish figure, so I don't recommend that either."

My chest rises in a laugh and my dick twitches at her insulting tone. "Hunny, there ain't nothing about me that's a boy anymore."

I'd love to know how much, she mumbles under her breath. I roll back on my heels, my attempts at flirting crashing and burning miserably. I take a minute to take in the room around me more intently. It's completely Mia in a nutshell.

Sketches line the black coffee table, and though I try to resist the urge to walk over and snoop, my feet lead me anyhow. Her easel sits in the corner with a half-painted canvas, another abstract piece. A joint sits in an ashtray to the side of her brushes, and I wonder what it's like to get high for a minute. I have—well- had friends that smoked back home when we were out from under the watchful eye of our parents but never tried it myself.

The thing I find most interesting is that there are no photos of her with her family in any place that I've seen so far. It makes me wonder if her relationship with her parents is strained much like my own. I take one more glance around before realizing how comfortable I feel in her space. Like I'm meant to be here. I want Mia to feel the same way.

"You know, this is not what I expected when I met you. You being an artist with a penchant for smoking joints."

She quirks her eyebrow. "What exactly did you expect?"

"I'm not entirely sure… not saying that I don't like it by any means, but it's…" A weird look flashes across her face and I kill my thoughts instantly. "I'm just going to stop talking now." The last part comes out as a mumble as a smile forms on her lips.

"I like clean lines, black and white, yes or no. There is no in-between and blurry colors mixing up things in real life, but with paint, I can let it all explore."

My eyes immediately go to her hair, and I raise an eyebrow. Her eyes follow the path mine have just led and she smirks. "This doesn't apply. I'd rather look at colorful hair than dull blonde hair."

"Well, I think you'd look great in either."

Her eyebrow lifts. "If I didn't know any better, Brooks, I'd say you were being sweet to get into my pants or something."

A smile forms across my lips. "Nah, just raised with manners. What I really want to say to you isn't appropriate for the situation." I want to say all types of things to her about how gorgeous she is and how I want to make her mine. Not to mention all the dirty things I want to do to her, but I refrain.

"Sometimes, manners are really the pits. Don't you ever feel like breaking out of those dreadful bonds of politeness every once in a while? Letting the truth spill from your lips like the softest velvet."

I want to. So badly, but my brain won't open my mouth to process the thoughts I truly want to let slip.

"So..." I say, trying to get my mind off those certain things, which will ultimately lead to an unnecessary tenting in my pants. "Where did you come up with the idea for a black, white, and grey interior design like this?"

"Oh, um... Pinterest. I pin things entirely too much. My friend, Macy, got me into it a couple years ago, and I've been doing it ever since. To say I'm obsessed is probably the understatement of the century."

I blink at her. "What's a Pinterest?" We have the internet where I came from, but I've never heard of such a thing and I want to know everything that I possibly can about Mia.

She giggles. "It's like this site with a whole bunch of picture ideas on how to design, what recipes to cook, crafts, and so on. You can basically pin things you like which means saving them to a list to go back and look at later on. Sometimes I find inspiration for paintings and sculptures there too. I lose myself for hours on end, just looking at pictures." I've noticed a few sculptures spread throughout the room. She pulls out her phone and quickly shows me what's on her own Pinterest. It doesn't seem like my thing, but if she likes it then so be it.

She puts her cell phone back in her pocket and looks up at me. "What do you like to do in your spare time?"

"To be honest, I'm not really sure what I like to do. When I was growing up, I fancied working with wood pieces. It was one of the few things where I didn't have everyone around. I'd go out to our shed and whittle away the afternoon once my chores were done. I could turn on my music and get lost in the craftsmanship of making something out of nothing, I suppose."

"I totally get that. Taking something so simple and creating a design or a sculpture that you made with your own two hands without the help of anyone else. It's about feeling oneness with your creation. I guess it's a weird thing to explain out loud, but I get what you're saying."

I nod.

"So… where are you from? You're pretty closed lipped about it. Is it a secret or something? Wait, are you in the witness protection program or do you like… work for the CIA?"

A chuckle slips past my lips before my thoughts run cold, dark. Thinking about that place gives me the creeps. The leaders were in charge of who you hung out with, how you lived, what job you would have within the compound. They chose who you would marry, who would be best suited to make a stable life partner—whether you wanted one or not. I fight the urge to curse it, like every time I think about it. I grit my teeth. "Frazier's Creek, Tennessee."

She purses her lips. "Where is that?"

"It's in the middle of a nowheresville mountain range."

"How in the hell did you end up in Ithaca, New York?"

"Honestly, a dart on a map." Thinking about it makes unease creep into my chest. The compound has a group of guys that work as security, looking for anyone who might try to escape the clutches of their reach. Anyone who might share the secrets and inner workings of the assembly. It's why I ran in the middle of the night with just a duffel bag to my name.

But at this point, I'm a lost soul, spiritually dead. I no longer have the Lord's protection, and I'm supposed to have a life of misery. I'm gone to the outside world of sinners and non-believers. I didn't leave a way to trace myself. Plus, once you leave, you're shunned for good. They've disowned me.

"So, it's just you?"

"Yep, family and I cut ties a while ago." I don't tell her the real reason.

"Huh," is the only thing that comes from her mouth. I'm glad that she doesn't continue to question me about it. I feel like maybe she'd feel the same way if I started asking her questions. We've both worked at Topsy Turvy for a year, but I still feel like I don't know anything about her life, which is obvious. I had no idea that she was a painter or a sculptor. I didn't know either that she was amazing at it. It makes me wonder why she works at the bar when she's got this much talent.

"So, what about you?" I ask getting the attention off of me. "Have you lived here your whole life?"

Her small smile lights the corners of her face. Happy memories blooming, hopefully. "Nope, I moved here for Cornell and ended up staying for my best friend. I love it here."

Her words give me a sense of hope. A sense that this life could be mine. That I could fit into a place that is as supportive and charming as this college town. It'd be something I've never felt—the feeling of belonging and being one with a group of people.

My confidence since I got here has definitely grown. Back

home, I was taught what to say and what not to say and if you spoke out, chances were you'd come to regret it. So, I'd learned to stand back and not say anything. People here speak their minds and say what they want. I feel like I've started doing it more than I used to, except for when it comes to Mia. I certainly stumble all over myself with her.

"I'm glad you fit in this town, Mia. Topsy Turvy would certainly be lost without you. Eddie wouldn't know what to do without his best bartender."

"Psshhhhhh…. I think you give me a run for my money, Brooks."

I shake my head and smile. She fits in here like a glove and thinking about gloves makes me think about wanting her mouth fitting around me like a glove. I feel like such a pervert being around her so much. I'm afraid that if we ever slept together, my inner caveman would come out, and I'd say things I couldn't take back. Mia makes me feel like a teenage boy again. Like I'm ready to explode at any moment.

"So," she says, her voice bringing me out of my sick thoughts and back to the present. "Why bartending?"

"Believe it or not, many people don't want to hire someone who has little more than a high school diploma. I have zero past work experience. All my education was done within the compound, so no schooling records. Eddie was the first guy that offered me a job and I figured it seemed like something I could pick up easily."

Her eyebrows furrow. "Do you not like bartending?"

I shrug. "I like it. The tips are good, decent, but I don't think I want to do this for the rest of my life. At some point, I'd like to be able to support a family, and you know what they say, knowledge is power."

"I get it. I probably won't work at Topsy Turvy forever, but I'm not sure what else I would do."

My eyes fly again to the painting on the wall I'd studied earlier. "I know what you would be really good at... have you ever sold your art?"

"No, didn't think anyone would ever be able to appreciate it as much as I do. Each piece of art is a part of my soul and selling it would be like letting go of my child, especially if the person that bought it one day decided they didn't like it. It would break my heart."

Mia glances over at the clock. "Shit, I gotta go. First, more ground rules," she says and taps her chin. "Use whatever you want. I'm not super picky about my stuff. Um.... What else?" She snaps her fingers before continuing. "Hmm... Oh, if you decide to have people over, a heads up is appreciated. If you're getting jiggy with it, put a sock on the door. Please only masturbate in your room and if you do, at least close the door. Or don't. If I come home and you're jerking it with the door open, I'll assume it's an open invitation to join you."

My eyes grow to the size of saucers as I look at her, confused as to whether she's shitting with me or actually being serious. I bark out a laugh, and she pauses giving me a weird look. "What's funny?"

"The fact that you think I'd have a party and not invite you... or that you think I would be getting jiggy, not sure what that means, with someone else."

Her creamy white cheeks blush. "Well, the option is definitely open."

I nod my head. "Duly noted."

"We work opposite shifts, so the likelihood of us bumping into each other is slim. It'll be like having your own place most of the time."

My heart sinks. The whole point of this arrangement was to be near her. I rub at the hole in my heart, forming in my chest cavity and stare over her shoulder. Maybe I could ask Eddie to switch my shifts with someone, so we could at least work together.

"Hey, what's wrong?"

Her question breaks through the disappointment I'm feeling. "Nothing, it's just that I kind of like having you around," I admit it out loud.

"Awww, that's sweet. I'm sure you'll eventually get sick of me. Tell me that you don't like my painting, or you can't stand the fact that I smoke weed or.... I don't know. I'm sure you'll think of something. It happens more than you think."

I scoff. "I highly doubt that."

She ducks her face, however, I don't miss the grin that spreads across it first. "Okay."

"Anything else I need to know before you leave?"

Mia runs her hand through her brightly colored hair and looks around. "Oh, you're going to need this too," she says, dropping a key in my hand. "You know, in case you want to go out." The weight of it in my hand feels significant. Her fingers tickle my palm as she pulls away, and I'm saddened by the loss of heat when she fully disconnects.

"Thanks for putting your trust in me to not snoop through all your stuff before you get home. And for everything."

"You're a good guy, Brooks. Even if you do snoop, what are you going to do? Go through my underwear drawer? Wear it on your head? You know the terms of jerking off. Just be warned if I see it, I'm joining in."

"Don't tempt me, woman." I blink, confused about where that comment came from... She doesn't say anything else but gives me a smile and a wink.

I'm glad that she trusts me with this. I feel like I'm making a huge deal out of this, but I've been into Mia since the first time she offered me a blowjob (not literally). Mia will be in my proximity all the time now. Well, not always her, but her stuff. I sound like a creep in my own mind, but I don't really care.

"What's that look for?" Her question pulls me from my dirty musings.

I cough to cover up the arousal clogging my throat. "Just thinking about later." *When I can jerk off in the privacy of the bathroom and think about you while I do it. Screw my bedroom only.* I think to myself.

"Oh, big plans?"

The biggest.

"Apparently, I need to go shopping."

The baby blue eyes sparkle with amusement. "Lucky you. I will try super hard not to be jealous that you're out shopping for normal people stuff while I'm dealing with drunkards."

"Well, if you want, I can wait until you can come with me. Ya know to make sure I get everything I need? Say sometime this next week between our shifts?" I want to erase the comment she had earlier about not being around most of the time. I want to be around her constantly.

She seems like she's debating it, so I feel the need to put on the pressure. "Look, I am a grown-ass man who is just asking for some guidance, please."

She still hasn't agreed so I decided to pull out the big guns. "Pleassseeeee." I stick out my bottom lip, imitating a child, but when her eyes glance to my mouth, her look is anything but child-like and sexy as hell. I don't mind it one bit.

She rolls her eyes and then mumbles, "Okay, fine. I guess I'll go shopping with you, weirdo. If you insist."

Blood pumps through my veins and I want to dance with glee, but that wouldn't be very manlike, so I shrug. "It's a date then!"

Her jaw drops with a garbled exhale. "Yeah…no."

I'm pretty sure this attraction isn't one-sided by far. Unless I'm blind, Mia is giving me tiny hints and comments that show interest.

They sure as hell make my dick twitch. I dig her naughty eye language and her inaproapriate conversations.

As if reading my dirty thoughts, she reaches up and runs her fingers through her long strands of rainbow-colored hair, the movement causing her shirt to rise up. I'm given a brief flash of a pink stoned belly button piercing, and I have to immediately adjust my semi. Shit, just a brief glimpse and I'm treated to a sexy little piercing that turns me on faster than I can swallow.

"It was a joke. Just a joke, geez." I put my hands out in a non-offensive manner. Her reaction is a jab to my gut, so I look away. I don't want her to see my face.

"Uh huh," she says, eyeing me suspiciously.

"Alright, one adult helping another adult, that's it." I tell her honestly because I'll take what I can get. I'm not entirely sure where the boundaries are with us. I'd like to know, but I'm also not sure if I want to know.

"This is a friend and roommate, possibly benefits thing..." She points between us, and even though it makes me sad I get it. Obviously, something caused this reaction in her and even though I want to get to the bottom of whatever that is, it won't happen today.

"It's all up to you, Mia. Your apartment, your rules," I say, motioning around us.

She smiles. "Now that's something I can work with, but it's our place, not just mine anymore." On that note, she does one more solitary glance at the clock. "Okay, I really gotta go this time. I'll see you on the flip side."

"Have a good night at work, roomie!" I holler after her as she runs out the door. Now to find something to do to occupy my time...

Six

Mia

Holy sex god, Brooks is hot as fuck. The forgetting to wear a tee shirt. The grey sweatpants. The freaking dick print. Lord have mercy, you don't even understand…

And don't get me started on that sweet personality and charm. I almost can't handle it. There must be something wrong with me because I've never been this attracted to someone that isn't a glorified asshole.

I mean, look at any one of the flings I've had. My type is much more tattoos, drunk sex, and getting high. Sneaking out of bed before the other person wakes up in the morning. Not knowing the name of the person you slept with the night before. I've been drooling over Brooks since he stepped into Topsy Turvy a year ago. The shit thing is that I have no idea where we stand. We set boundaries and rules but haven't actually talked about what happens if something goes down between us. What happens if we rock this boat, get a little freaky between the sheets?

My nether regions are begging me to turn this into more than just a roommate's thing. No mercy full on begging. To va-va-voom him. I've given up the facade of turning away when he catches me looking. Yep, I'm not even trying to keep my eye ogling to a minimum. Every morning he glides past me, bare chested. Arm muscles, abs, and pecs on full display for my wandering eyes.

Man candy Monday has turned into an everyday occurrence. And, somehow, my mouth always speaks before my brain can function enough to tell me no. Nope, my lips open and just flap unconsciously about how sexy he is. I used to tell him to buy a camera and now it's me questioning it. He just waggles his eyebrows and walks away. It's really unfair how attractive his face is... It should have zits or something...

I want to know who's playing a joke on me. Guys like Brooks just don't exist in the real world, and if they do, I've never met one. Maybe he's really an invisible friend and if that's the case I should be really nervous about the state of my mind.

The broad arrows that point to the happy trail that lines his stomach and dips below his pants makes my mouth water and me light-headed.

Damn, I'm in so much trouble with this one. Like lock me up now because I'm yelling timber, it's going down.

Brooks seems to be just as into me as I am into him, yet I wonder why he never seems to make a move. I haven't exactly told him no to other things happening, but for some reason, when things get too intense, he always backs away first or breaks the silence. He's told me he doesn't have much experience with women, but that can't be right because look at him.

Who wouldn't want to ride him like a stallion? Or maybe, he's a virgin and needs a little nudge with the suggestions.

Avoiding the lingering stares, he caresses my body with is very... hard. Yeah, there's no hiding the effect I have on him. I secretly high five myself every time I see him adjust himself. He's not a man of many words, but his actions tell all. Knowing he shares in these feelings makes me want to know why he holds back from me so much. Does he turn into a caveman? I bet he goes all Dom.

God, why does that make me want it even more?

I'm trying to focus on being unfazed by him and failing miserably. Brooks is calm and collected with this confidence that I've never seen before. Me? I'm a blubbering mess of an individual. It's funny how our personalities change over time.

I used to think of myself as this badass, tattooed chick who smokes weed and paints on the side. Now, I find myself more like I have a crush and can't hide my fangirling over him type. Which is a problem in itself. I've never let a man affect me this much. Maybe eventually, I'll drive him bonkers and he'll realize that moving on is better than sticking around with the basket case that is currently me.

But I can't think about that right now while we're strolling through Suzie's Discount Mart. We should have gone a week ago, but time flies when you're having fun.

It's my favorite store in this town—filled with odds and ends. Everything from painting supplies and crafts to home goods. All the things any college student would forget at home and have to buy. It's my happy place. Brooks walks quietly beside me as I ooh and aah over tiny things along the way. A display of new oil paints stops me in my tracks. I never purchase anything other than black, but I like to look anyhow. Maybe one day, another color will speak to my soul, requesting to spice up my life just a tad.

"What color would you pick?" I ask, turning to Brooks.

He gives me a weird face. "I don't paint."

"I know. Just go with me here. If you were to pick any color off the rack, what would it be?"

"Blue."

I lift my brow. "Why blue?" I'm not really surprised by this color choice, but I'm curious why he picked it out of the multiple color options available. The few tidbits of information I've gleaned from him include a talent for making drinks, being extremely tidy around the apartment, a lover of meatloaf, and always picking something I'm never expecting.

He keeps me guessing. I don't know much about him, but the more time I spend with him, the more I want to know.

"Blue exhibits confidence, integrity, trust, and reliability. Things that I want you to see in me as we live together. Plus, it's my favorite color, and since it's a part of your hair color, I'm guessing it means something to you as well."

SWOON.

I bite my lip, not entirely sure how to respond to that comment. I've never had someone be this nice to me without an end game.

"Would you like me to buy it for you?" he asks, his eyebrows lifted in a question. "I'm going to need a new painting to hang up in my room and nothing I've seen so far compares to what I've seen on your walls at home."

The way he says home makes me wish it were true. A real home. Not just this one in which we play roommates forever.

No, Mia. Stop thinking like that. You've seen what happens when people fall under the influence of love. Love isn't a thing, just a figment of a fairy tale lost long ago.

"We're supposed to be shopping for you."

"We are… I'm just asking you to paint me something. See, it's still for me, but we'll both get something out of it."

My belly dips at the fact that he wants me to paint something just for him, using his favorite color. I've never painted anything for another person specifically, but how can I refuse that sweet request?

An image of him standing behind me, helping me paint in nothing but our underwear flashes through my head, and I mentally clear my throat. I tug at the collar of my shirt, suddenly feeling overheated like a woman in menopause. Is this shirt closing in on my throat? "Um... ah...sure."

"Glad you're saying yes." The smile on his face makes my legs weak, and I take a deep breath to compose myself.

We move onto sheets, and he goes straight for the cheap ones. I'm shocked they legit have the right size for that massive ass bed. "Alright, I think these will work for me."

"Brooks, you need a better sheet count than that. How are you supposed to talk a lady into staying with you overnight if you only have 150 thread count sheets?"

I watch him swallow a gulp and his face blushes slightly as he ponders my statement. I don't really want to see him with another woman, but I have to be realistic about the fact that it may happen. "The sheets are for me... and I highly doubt I'll ever have a lady spending the night with me. Other than you... on the other side of my wall."

I roll my eyes and start to retort his comment, but then shut it. I'd like to spend the night with him. It's obvious we're both into each other. The sexual tension is killing me slowly. I can't stop thinking about him.

Every time he's in the shower, I wonder how the water looks skimming in and out of his ripped abs and muscular arms. I want to drool. I've seen him without a shirt on, and that's enough to drive me crazy. Pretty soon, I'm going to have to issue a "full clothing at all times" ordinance at the apartment, or I'm going to jump him so hard.

I started watching him after he moved in. He's a true gentleman. Brooks is one of those people that continually cares about everyone else first. The first to help someone out at the bar. The first to open the door for you. He doesn't complain when he has to take a cold shower.

His eternal optimism about me is almost hard to deal with at times. He's also forever the last to complain when life is too hard to handle. He sits for hours and watches me paint while I smoke a joint, but never once mentions it.

Little touches here and there. I can't manage to figure him out. He seems like he's never been on his own, but he's lived in his own place for over a year.

I look away, fighting the urge to feel anything for him more than just roommates. I've seen what happens when two people fall in love. I've seen the worst love can do to people. I wouldn't call it love. Love... it's been misconstrued into a fairy tale for so long that people start to believe in it as much as they believe in Cinderella. But the truth is... fairy tales are for children because when real life sets in, you realize that it was all just a lie.

Macy, my best friend, used to talk about her parents and how her father worshipped the ground her mother walked on. That seemed like love.

Not the messed up household I grew up in. My father ruined the fantasy of love when he killed my mother's spirit by cheating on her. The fighting between them was day in and day out. It seemed to always be the blame game. I wondered why one of them didn't just leave. They didn't seem to care what it did to me either. Do you think any child wants to grow up in a household like that? I sure as hell didn't. Or maybe it was the guy my sophomore year of college that told me he loved me and then ripped my heart from my chest after taking my virginity.

Whenever I bring up Brooks' past, he brushes it off. I get it. We all have our own skeletons to bear. He may be reluctant to share with me, and for now, I'll allow it. Lord knows I don't want him digging up my past either. Those graves should stay filled.

"Alright, well, we've successfully gotten everything on your list. Anything else you need? Toothbrush, toothpaste, deodorant, condoms..."

"Nope, I think I'm good."

"You sure?"

He quirks an eyebrow at me. "Yes… is there anything you need while we're here? Tampons, body wash, deodorant…"

I give him the side-eye. "Why did you list things off?"

A smirk graces his face. "I thought we were comparing notes on what men and women use as toiletries?"

"Touché, my friend. Touché." Brooks has sass. Who would have thought?

I bounce on my toes, trying to not feel so awkward about the silence that follows. "So, what now? More shopping? Or something else?"

His eyes met mine and his smile grew even wider. "What are my options for something else?"

Cheeky bastard.

"Food? I'm starving actually."

His dark chocolate eyes sparkle. "Whatever you want, Mia."

We step outside into the sweltering heat that is mid-August. My shirt is sticking to me, and I can feel a bead of sweat tracing its way down my back. Popping my cherry red sunglasses on, I look over at Brooks.

His eyes find mine briefly before he chuckles and slides a pair of bright green sunglasses over his. "Hey, you okay over there?" I can't handle not staring at him for a minute. I don't get it. It's like I'm in a man daze and I can't shake myself out of it. A week later, and it seems like my confidence is slipping like it's trying to run on marbles, and his confidence is building like he can walk on water. It's driving me insane. Brooks touches the small of my back, and I realize I never responded.

"Yeah… um good." I fan my face. "I'm just hot."

"Every single part of you, darlin.'" It's then he realizes my meaning. "Oh, the weather, it's a warm one today for sure." He swallows roughly and turns away. Not that I can see his eyes behind those shades anyhow.

Seven

Brooks

I rise for my day with Mia on the brain and the dream I had about her last night. A shower will do me some good. Mia won't be home yet, so I figure I'll take the opportunity to go ahead and get my strokes in while she isn't around. She told me early on to only jerk it in my room with the door closed, and I want to test those limits so badly. But… I'm not sure if she'd actually follow through with her threat or if I would just be the awkward one sitting with his dick out.

Stepping in the bathroom, I slowly start removing my clothes. My half semi is already tenting my pants just thinking about Mia. God, I'm in so much trouble. I should be ashamed, thinking half of the thoughts that I have about her. If I was still living at home, I'm sure I'd feel downright sinful thinking these thoughts, but if it's about Mia, I'll gladly be a sinner for the rest of my life, no repentance.

I turn the shower to hot, wanting to feel the burn. Hot ringlets of water drip down my body biting into my skin as my hand finds my dick. Soft flesh covers my pipe, and I need some relief. I stroke myself once and then again. Thoughts of Mia sucking me down her throat. Thoughts of touching Mia naked. Her screaming my name as I go down the apex between her thighs. The pressure's building, and I can feel myself on the verge of coming early when the door to the bathroom flies open, and I hear Mia's voice.

"Hey, Brooks. You okay?" Mortification pours off me as I realize I've been standing here thinking about the very person that has now interrupted my jerk session.

"Um… yeah. One sec." I look down at my dick, willing it to go down. But it's clearly not leaving the fully satisfied position it currently resides in. Not even thinking about my grandma is doing it for me this time. My brave thoughts about testing limits earlier are gone in the blink of an eye.

"Brooks, are you jerking it in there? I said, hey, like five times… Dude, what are you doing in here?"

The shower curtain flies open, and my hands jerk to cover the length of my dick. Her eyes go straight to my dick, and her eyebrows raise.

"Well, looks like I walked in on a fun time." She winks at me. "Need a little help with your friend there, Brooks?"

"Um…" It's all I could get to come out of my mouth. My dick wags its appreciation of her offer. I nod my head because words won't come.

She walks over to me and moves my hands from covering my length. It bobs up to her, pleased with itself. Her first touch lights a fire in me. I'm so aroused I can't hardly stand it and Mia touching me is the best version of a dream come true. When she kneels on the floor in front of me, I have to look away. The sight is a fantasy in itself. My eyes find the ceiling. I have to focus on anything other than coming too soon because that's just embarrassing.

When warmth wraps around my dick, I have to look down.

The sight before me is the sexiest thing I'd ever seen. Mia's red lips wrapped around me is sexy as fuck. That's it. I'm a goner. She's literally gone down once or twice on my shaft, and that's all it took for the previous pressure to build back up. I put my hands down to pull her off of me.

"Mia… I'm about to…". She shakes her head and continues on with her ministrations. If she doesn't want to take her mouth off me, so be it. I run my hands through her rainbow-colored hair and gently hold her close to me, pushing myself farther into her mouth. I feel it as my cock hits the back of her throat, and she gags slightly. A tear slides down her face and I pull my hands away. I can feel my orgasm rushing up my spine.

Mia sucks my dick dry and pulls the come from my body. It's the biggest release I've ever had in my life, and for a moment, everything goes black. The desire to pass out is strong with this head rush. Slowly lights and shapes come back into form. Mia's still kneeling in front of me. A smile plastered across her face, satisfaction.

"That was so hot, Brooks. Let's talk about your dick for a minute, shall we. Why have you been hiding this thing from me?"

"You like my dick?"

She points down at my slowly deflating fun stick. "Um… Brooks. That's the biggest dick I think I've ever seen… and I've seen a lot! You should be proud of that thing."

I smirk. "Thanks. I think. Do you want me to…" I nod to her nether region. "I've never actually pleasured a woman… but I'm sure you could teach me a thing or two."

"Hold up. You've never gone down on a girl?"

I shake my head, looking to the ground. You couldn't do that with anyone at the compound. Chaperones were ever present when the females were around us. Even if we were allowed, no one held my interest like Mia does now. I want to do that with her.

"How?"

I shrug. "It wasn't something you were allowed to think about at the compound"

My eyes lift to her again before she asks another question. "Do you want to now?"

I don't know what comes over me as my mouth opens, and word vomit falls from my lips. "I've been thinking about this very long, and I've come to a decision. I want you to teach me how to pleasure a woman, Mia. Like going down on a girl. I want you to... to be my... sexy Jedi pleasure master. Let's fornicate. Get it on Marvin Gaye style. Show me what girls like."

She smirks and shakes her head. "First off... never ever, ever as long as we're friends call it fornication... and do not under any circumstances say that to Zara. I will never hear the end of it."

"Noted," I say simply.

Her eyebrow raises, and she gives me a questioning stare. "Secondly, why do you want me to give you sex lessons, Brooks? I mean, seriously, have you seen yourself and with that dick... I can't imagine anyone would say no."

I lie. I let it slip right through my lips. Mia never gets into anything personal. She never talks about her family life. I've gotten the impression that if I tell her, she's the girl I want to impress that I'd send her running for the hills. She doesn't really seem like the settling down type, but I want her to be.

"You see... there's this girl that I like and well... I have zero experience in pleasuring women, and I don't want to make a complete fool out of myself the first time. I thought if you could show me, then I would be prepared for when we get together."

A cocky smile crosses her face. "Alright, Brooks, you want sex lessons. I'll give you sex lessons."

My heart leaps at the fact that she's agreeing to it. I knew this was my way in—my way into that impenetrable heart of hers. My dick jumps at the thought of all the naughty things I get to do with her. Do I feel bad that I'm not telling her she's the girl for me? Yes. In a way, I do, but at the same time, would she have gone through with it had I told her? No.

My dick perks up again at the idea of finally seeing Mia fully naked. I think about kissing her soft skin and running my hands through her soft, rainbowed colored hair while her mouth wraps its way around my cock. I wonder if her breasts are pink and perfect like I've imagined them to be. Yes, I may be a virgin… but that doesn't stop the thoughts running rampant through my brain when she's around.

The clearing of a throat brings me back to the present, and I realize that I'm still standing there awkwardly naked in the bathroom while we discuss what kind of sex lessons she'll give me. The urge to cover my dick hits me, but I don't give a shit right now. Let her see it. She obviously likes the look of it.

"I'm impressed, Brooksy, full mast again so soon. Tell me. When do you want to start these sex lessons of yours?"

"I can start now. Yeah…" I look down at my dick. "Yep… I'm definitely good with now."

"Okay, lesson one. Never seem overly eager for sex. It makes you seem desperate and creepy."

I shake my head. I bet I one hundred percent look all sorts of creepy right now. My gaze trails the sweet sway of her hips as she leaves the bathroom. Guess my next lesson is going to have to wait.

The light streams through the window, highlighting a bright red tea kettle as it whistles and steams. Right on cue Mia, glides to the kitchen, lured by the promise of a fresh cup of tea. I always thought she'd be more of a coffee girl, but I was wrong.

She looks sleep-rumpled, but it's still sexy as fuck. Hair sticking up here and there. A smear of black paint is prominently displayed across the creamy skin of her face. A stark contrast. Evidence that she hasn't realized she wiped her face while painting yet again this morning. I smile at her lack of caring.

My fingers itch to wipe the smear of paint away, but I haven't been granted the permission for that type of intimacy yet. The sleep shirt she's wearing exposes her midriff, and her shorts are extra skimpy, revealing the slight crease from her leg to her ass cheek.

I want to strip her and run my hands over each dip and curve, yet I also want to cover her with my own shirt. Something that smells like me to brand her as my woman. Damn, I'm losing it over this girl. She's unlike anyone I've ever met in my whole life. Her eyes find mine, and a smile widens across her face.

My mind drifts back to yesterday. The way she gave me head is still a piercing memory in my mind, and I keep playing it over and over again. My dick is raw from the number of times I've jerked off since then, just picturing her red lips wrapped around me again.

My face blushes. I clear my throat and shake my head, clearing the lust fog going on in my brain. "Good Morning darlin'," I say in the cheesiest accent I can manage.

"Morning. The good is still to be determined." *Typical Mia*, I think to myself.

I've started going out for runs in the morning or working out before I head into work. Living in the same space as my crush gives me all this pent up energy, and my dick needs a break. As I head back into my room to change into my clothes, I turn back to Mia. "I'm going for a run, wanna join me?"

She looks at me, startled. "Brooks, I appreciate the offer, but do I look like someone who participates in physical activity?"

My gaze slides up her body appreciatively, and I quirk an eyebrow. What I want to say is that she'd look good doing physical activity with me… but I refrain. Instead, I say, "I hate to break it to you, Mia, but sex is also included in physical activity."

"Duh, I know that better than you do, but at least when I sweat doing that, I'm enjoying the fuck out of it. Not just running to kill myself."

I chuckle and hold my hands up in front of me. "Fair enough."

She takes a long sip of her hot tea, and a satisfied moan passes her lips and makes my dick twitch. I was already sporting a semi, and it did not need any more encouragement than it already had, damnit.

"What would people do without tea? It's a godsend some days."

"I'll take your word for it. Can't say I've ever had a cup of tea."

Her jaw hits an invisible boundary. "How have you never had tea? Seriously, Brooks? Looks like I'll be bringing you pleasure in more ways than one while we have our little arrangement."

I smirk at how awkward her words come out sometimes. That's just my girl. A pain shoots through my heart. She's not mine, and at this point I'm not sure if she ever will be.

I'm wondering if maybe I'm imagining things that don't exist. We tend to tiptoe around touchy subjects like her family and past. She's been coming home more these days than hanging out with Zara, and I choose to believe that's because of me, but maybe she is genuinely just anti-social.

"Hey Brooks," she says, snapping my attention back to those beautiful blue eyes of hers. "What's a Jedi master?"

My jaw literally drops as I gawk at her. "Star Wars? Return of the Jedi? Princess Leah and Luke Skywalker?"

"Is that like a movie or something?"

"New plan. You teach me about sex, and I'll teach you about Star Wars. I'm honestly shocked you've never seen it. Like how is that even possible? I thought everyone had seen Star Wars before…" I shake my head, still in disbelief.

Her eyes lift up to mine, and I'm rewarded with her signature smile. "You have a deal, Brooks." We shake on it like it's some important agreement. A giggle escapes her lips- the perfect cadence of pitch like an angel singing in my ear.

This girl...

I love moments like these where her barriers are down, and I'm given a glimpse of just her, not this wall of goth clothes, rainbow-colored hair, and sass. I don't even want to fight this weird tension we have between us, and I'm falling under this lust-induced cloud we've surrounded ourselves with over the last couple of weeks staying together.

I'm stoked that she said yes to giving me lessons on pleasure. She's my one, but I won't be the one to tell her. Not yet at least. And it's not just the sex, it's her.

I want to date her. To woo her. She's locked in her past, without the key, and I want to be the one that opens that damn door and sets her free. She won't be able to turn me away from her. I've started to pick the lock like a criminal breaking in. I need to remember, though, that once this door is open, there is no turning back. It's fragile territory I'm treading just by turning the key.

She has passion in her eyes, and sometimes I see glimpses of what she truly wants, but I won't do a thing to topple this shaky tower. Something holds her back, blocking her path from whatever this thing is growing between us. I have no idea what it is, and it makes me twitchy with anxiety. I could ask her, but would I? No, absolutely not.

Maybe she'll realize that whatever she built those walls up for in the first place isn't a reason to keep them up permanently. She may act like a total badass when she's around other people, but the person I see when it's just her is simply a girl that wants to be loved.

Eight

Mia

"Wait, he asked you for sex lessons?" Zara sits in Brooks' ugly recliner, a joint between her fingers, a glass of wine in her other hand. The afternoon light slips in through a slit in the curtain, painting the floor with its rays, and I stare at it. The light reflects off a glass piece on my coffee table, and I can't help but admire the kaleidoscope of colors it sprays into the room.

"Yep." I still can't believe it, but it explains a lot of the way he acts in certain situations. I can't even fathom not having sex until I was 22 years old.

She takes a hit, leaning against the back of the chair. "You gonna go for it?"

"Have you seen Brooks? Hell, yes, I'm going to jump on that offer, literally. You should see his dick, Zara. I'm talking long and really thick. If he can figure out how to work it, damn. I'll be one hella lucky roomie."

Her eyes grow wide. "Hold up, when did you see his dick?"

I shrug, a smile permeating my face. My core heats up thinking about how hot it was watching Brooks fall apart in front of me. "When I gave him a blowjob in the shower the other night."

"Ok, I'm going to need you to walk me through that whole story." And I did, not leaving out a single detail.

She wiggles her eyebrows at me. "So, when is this all going down?"

I shake my head and laugh. "Not entirely sure yet. I guess we need to come up with a list, ya know. Like a sex bucket list or something. I'm assuming he hasn't done anything, but I don't know for sure."

"Okay then, sit down tonight and make a list for Brooks. Then at least you know what you're getting into. Who knows, he may be into kink. He may like domination."

"I'm pretty sure he doesn't know what he likes other than getting his dick sucked and thinking about P in V."

"True. I'd suggest sexting. Teach him how to talk dirty. If he looks like that, has a dick like you say, and can talk dirty... damn. He'd rock someone's world for sure."

Yeah, he's going to rock mine. It's the first thought that pops into my mind, but I keep it to myself.

I look over at her as she takes another puff. "Dude, you gonna share that joint, or you just getting high alone?"

"You out already, girl? I was just here last week to restock you..."

I made a noncommittal shrug. "Do you have any idea how much anxiety I have over giving him sex lessons. I've never been with a virgin before... he's not going to be like a girl, right? Like he's not going to fall in love with me just because I take his v-card?"

"You're thinking too much into this, Mia. Just go with it."

I sigh a deep breath. I don't understand the nerves. I've had sex with plenty of men, and I've never been worried about how it would go. "You're right. Enough about me. What's going on with you lately? Any new sex club visits?"

She nods. "Uh huh."

"And..."

71

ZOEY DRAKE

"I met Donatello."

"Who's Donatello?"

"The owner of Pelle."

"So, Pelle is the name of the club?"

"Yep." It came off as she popped the 'p'.

"Italian...nice... and Pelle, doesn't that mean skin in Italian?"

"Hells yes."

"And..."

"He's hot as fuck, Mia. Think six foot five. Older. Dark hair, dark eyes, thick beard, six-pack, ripped arms... He made me drop to my knees and suck him off while he held my hair and fucked my mouth like a God."

I fan myself. "Damn, girl."

"Yep, then we went into a private room where he laid me down on a bed, blindfolded me, tied my hands and feet, and then ran a feather up and down my body. Teasing me until I was begging him to just fuck me already."

I can't help but squirm at the images plaguing my brain, only it isn't the sexy Donatello in my daydream. No, it's a dark brown-haired, chocolate brown-eyed man. The same man I imagine thrusting into me and pulling scream after scream from my body until we're both soaking the sheets with our sweat.

This is going to be trouble. I don't think about guys. I don't picture them doing naughty things to me. I live in the moment, never letting them occupy my mind, so why am I letting Brooks? I need to boil this back down to what it is... sex.

"Damn, Zar. Sounds like you had a real good time."

She giggles. "I can't wait to go back and do it again tonight. So... anyhow. Let's get back to Brooks. Sexting?"

"Ya know, I think it's a good idea. It'll give me a feel for what I'm working with..."

She nods her agreement. "So, what's new at the bar?"

72

"Gah, Eddie's got a new girl starting in a couple weeks. Says she has experience."

"Well, that's good…"

I huff my disapproval. "Guess so, she looks like a fucking Barbie doll. I'm sure all the guys will fawn over her like the last hot chick that worked there before she got fired for being a God- awful bartender."

"You afraid Brooksy is going to find her more attractive than you, Mia?"

"Oh, hell no. I'm hoping he's not dumb enough to fall for blonde Barbie." The words formed on my tongue feel like a lie. Lying to my best friend tears a hole in me. Lying is one of the things I hate most. As if you don't trust someone enough to give them the whole truth.

"Well, you'll be training her. For your sake, I hope Eddie's right about her being trained already."

"Yeah, me too."

Zara leaves me thinking about sex with Brooks. Maybe I'd try this sexting thing.

Me: *What are you doing?*
Brooks: *Working…*
Me: *What are you wearing?*
Brooks: *You saw me this morning before I went to work. A black t-shirt and blue jeans.*
Me: *Mmmm…those sexy blue jeans?*
Brooks: *Um…*
Mia: *Work with me here, Brooks…*
Brooks: *I'm really confused about why you're asking me questions that you already know the answer to?*
Mia: *O.K. Tell me something that will make me wet.*

Brooks: *It was raining earlier when I came into work.*
Mia: *Try again… *winking emoji**
Brooks: *Going outside without an umbrella?*
Mia: **eye roll* What would you do if I showed up at work right now?*
Brooks: *Offer to make you a drink?*
Mia: *That's all?*
Brooks: *Um… yes? I'm really confused by this line of questioning…*
Mia: *You want to try something fun tonight? Something that involves pillows and blankets?*
Brooks: *You want to build a fort?*

I smack my hand against my forehead and groan. This sexting idea is worse than I thought. I need to come up with a plan B on teaching Brooks the art of sexting, clearly. I growl out my frustration, reading through the texts again.

Mia: *Let's try this again…*
Brooks: *Try what again?*
Mia: *What are you wearing?*
Brooks: *The same thing I was wearing four minutes ago when you texted me.*
Mia: *Come on, play along with me. Just invent something that you couldn't possibly be wearing right now, like assless chaps.*
Brooks: *But why would I be wearing assless chaps at a bar… then people would see my ass. Potentially other parts too if I bent over. It just sounds like a really bad idea.*
Mia: *Okay, I'll try. I'm wearing a see-through lace bra and panties and I'm getting wet. What am I doing right now?*
Brooks: *Wait, you're outside in your bra and underwear in the rain? I think that's a really bad idea, Mia. You should probably go back inside.*
Mia: *Good Lord, Brooks. I give up.*
Brooks: *Wait, no. I really want to know what you're doing.*

Mia: *Why would I be getting wet, Brooks?*

Brooks: *Is this the rain again?*

Mia: *I'm sitting here in my bra and panties, masturbating thinking about you.*

Brooks: *Oh.*

Five minutes later.

Brooks: *OH! Tell me more.*

Mia: **winking emoji* I think we should start a sex bucket list. Write everything down that you want to do or learn.*

Brooks: *Yeah, let's do that, back to the masturbation thing. What's it feel like?*

Mia: *Please tell me you've done it before…*

Brooks: *Rubbed it raw.*

Mia: *Then you know.*

Brooks: *Great, now I have a boner.*

Mia: *Stay behind the bar, no one will know. *winking emoji**

Brooks: *I'm going to get you back for this, you know that right?*

Mia: *I'll be waiting. By the way… you fail at sexting.*

Brooks: *Add it to the bucket list.*

The rest of my afternoon consists of laundry, cleaning, and painting the day away. I love my days off. Sitting in a smoke-filled room, getting high, watching the bristle of my paintbrush drag its way across a canvas, covering it in dark colors. The blue paint Brooks had picked out at the store sits on my art stand. This piece is for him. It's still dark. Still black with a pop of blue.

I swirl the paint on the canvas, making shapes and patterns in a random way, a never-ending line. Each line paints a story—something foreboding, something light, something welcoming. It all depends on the shade and the thickness.

I haven't noticed the time until I hear the lock on the front door click and look over to see Brooks walk through. My eyes fall to the window, noting the sky has turned dark, and it looks like rain is coming. It's amazing how I can get lost in my art. Lost in the magic of creating.

Finding Brooks again, I openly ogle him. He looks good in his black tee-shirt and tight jeans. It doesn't show off his package as well as my favorite pair of his grey sweatpants, but I have a vivid imagination even if I can't see it.

"Hey, roomie." He smiles at me, that panty-melting fuck-me smile.

"Hey, Brooks."

"Why does it look like a cloud in here?"

"I was smoking…" I look away, not wanting to see the judgmental look that most people give me when they find out I smoke weed.

He nods. "Oh, what's it like?"

My eyes widen as I take in his question. "What's what like?"

"Smoking weed."

"Oh, it's kinda hard to explain unless you do it."

"Okay."

"You wanna try it?" I say, offering him the joint, but he shakes his head.

"Um… maybe. Not today though. I want to get into this sex bucket list you talked about earlier. By the way… not cool giving me a boner at work."

I chuckle, shaking my head.

"Hey, is that my painting?" He moves around me to take a look at the canvas I've been working on this afternoon.

"Yeah, I started it today. It's not finished yet. I'm not exactly sure where to go with it."

"Well, it looks great so far."

"Brooks…"

"You are damn good, Mia. Accept it."

One single nod. That's all I give him. Images of what Zara and I talked about earlier this afternoon flash through my mind, and heat seeps into my cheeks. He's here now. If I want to try things, we can. He's open to it, but a part of me still says they're sex lessons, so I have to treat them as such.

Scheduled. Bucket list. And when the bucket list is checked off, it's done. He'll go on to find someone else, and I'll keep on seeing other guys.

"Alright, let's grab some food before we get into this. I'm starving."

"Tacos from El Famoso?"

"You read my mind."

Half an hour later we're sitting on the couch, chowing down on tacos, when Brooks speaks up. "I always forget how good these are…"

"Best stoner food ever."

"Stoner food?"

"Yeah, smoking gives people the munchies. Makes you so freaking hungry you can't handle it."

"Huh."

"I'm gonna grab a drink, you want something?"

"Yep, I want a blowjob." His eyes sparkle with mischief. My brain takes me on a flashback to the first night I trained Brooks, and I can't help the laugh that escapes my lips.

"Ha, do you remember that first night?"

A blush creeps up his face in embarrassment. "How could I forget?" He shakes his head and laughs.

"I'll make you one."

One breath.

Two breaths.

Three breaths.

What the hell is he doing to me?

For the first time in my life, I'm sitting and talking with a man I don't just want to have sex with and it feels weird. I mean... I want to have sex with him, but I also enjoy the talking. Finishing making our drinks, I pick them up and walk back out to the living room, noticing that Brooks has changed into my favorite grey sweatpants, and his dick print is on full display.

Damn, that's a nice dick.

"You changed?"

"Yeah, figured I wanted to be a little more comfortable."

"Worried your pants may get too tight if you get another boner?" A smile tears across my cheeks, and I shoot him a wink.

He shrugs in a so-what pose.

Handing him the drink, I remember we'll need something to write on. "Let me grab a pen and paper. I'll be right back."

"I'll be here."

I return a few seconds later, pen and paper in hand. Ready to make this sex bucket list.

"Okay, before we start making a list. I need to know what you've done already. Is there a certain point we need to start, or are we starting at the very beginning?"

"Well..." He looks down as he twiddles his fingers.

"Wait, you haven't done anything?"

He lifts up his left hand. "Nope. I have an active imagination, but that's about it. Well, unless you include the shower stuff the other day."

"Seriously?" I ask exasperatedly. Surely he's joking...

He shakes his head. "I already told you. Wasn't exactly into anyone, and if you had those thoughts you had to follow through with an agreement and marry her. There was no fooling around."

"Okay, then." My heart is doing pitter-patters thinking about what those words mean. He hasn't wanted to do anything with someone from his hometown, but he wants me to teach him.

Me. Non-relationship, total hookup queen.

I push the thought away and shake my head.

You don't believe in love. This is simply sex and lust over your hot as hell roomie.

I haven't realized I brought the pen to my lips as I sit and day-dream yet again. When I look over at Brooks his gaze is heated, watching the pen as it traces along the bottom of my lips. I nibble on the tip nervously, thinking about how to approach the topic that I have zero other excuses to escape.

I watch Brooks' mouth move slowly as he goes to speak. "So... how does one make a sex bucket list."

"How about I start us out with some easy stuff, and then we go from there?"

"Sounds good to me."

"So, we've already established that you're terrible at sexting, so we'll work on that. How about next we start out with light touching and foreplay? Maybe try phone sex? Oral sex—me blowing you, you eating me out... High sex... that would be fun."

A blush creeps across his face, and he almost looks ashamed talking about it, but a part of him seems very interested in where this is going. I wonder if I should feel bad tarnishing his virgin self, but I quickly shake the thought away.

I can picture everything. Him running those big, calloused hands over my soft skin. Running fingers down my body—over my collarbones, breasts, ribs, and lower to where I really want him to go. I squirm in my seat, barely holding back a moan as I picture what could come of our agreement.

"Yes... all of that."

"Then I'm thinking we actually have sex. So you can feel what it's like, then we can go from there. There so many things we can do and experiment with... sex in the shower, masturbating in front of each other, using sex toys, public sex, anal sex, sixty-nine..."

"What is sixty-nine exactly?"

"It's when a guy goes down on a girl while she's blowing him."

"Oh, yeah. Definitely want to try that." His hand adjusts the front of his pants, and I know thinking about all this stuff is getting him horny. I'm having the same problem, but then again, I'm always turned on in his presence these days. Just the sight of all those muscles confined and bunched under a black tee shirt.

I wink. "I'm sure you do. Stay here, I'll be right back."

I get up, feeling his eyes on me as I walk to my bedroom and close the door. The only way to stop thinking too much into this is to just go ahead and do it. I've slept with plenty of guys. Brooks is just another guy. A little voice inside laughs at me.

I pull a black lace negligee from my drawer. Why not add in a naughty teacher outfit while I'm at it? Quickly stripping, I pull on the lace, put my hair into a messy bun, and add some glasses. One quick look in the mirror, and I head back to the living room.

My hand clasps the handle of my door as I take a big breath. Here goes nothing.

I creep down the hall quietly and watch Brooks lift the glass to his lips and swallow. His Adam's apple bobs up and down to get the liquid down.

Clearing my throat, he looks over and chokes. His eyes trail from my black polished toes, up my legs, over the curves of my hips, past my breasts, and then those dark chocolate eyes are on mine. He audibly swallows, and I can't help the elation that floods me over Brooks' explicit approval of my body.

"W-what are you doing?"

"You want to learn sex or not?"

"Yeah... but..."

"Take it or leave it." He stands as fast as his legs will let him and almost falls at the temptation to be near me.

"I'm in."

"Okay, good. Two rules: no kissing, and we're using your bed."

"Okay…"

I turn to walk toward his bedroom, but not before I look back over my shoulder at him still standing there. "You coming?" I run my finger down the wall as I walk, trying to be as seductive as possible and I can't help but feel like I'm about to defile the boy next door. Sex will change things between us. I know my feelings won't be involved, but I worry about him. I walk into his room and turn. "One more thing."

He gulps, eyes trailing my risqué outfit again. "Anything."

"Don't fall in love with me, Brooks."

"Okay."

"Good. Lesson one: Strip."

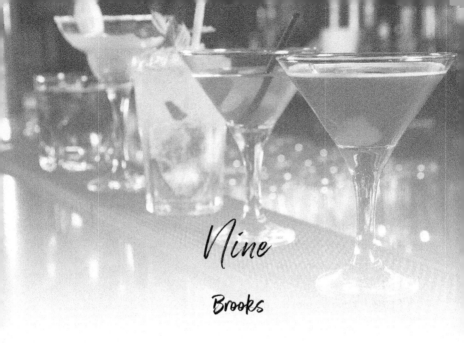

Nine

Brooks

"Strip." It's the only thing she says to me as I follow her into my room. My angelic rainbow-haired dream girl has turned into a naughty teacher in less than five minutes. Her hair is pulled up into an unkempt knot on her head. She's wearing glasses like a school teacher, and the sexy underclothes she has on make my dick jump for joy at what's hidden beneath them.

It's see-through, so I have a little idea, but I can't get ahead of myself, or everything's going to be over too quickly. I strip my clothes, shuffling out of my sweatpants and boxers, pulling the shirt over my head and I stand there bare assed, my length already thick between my thighs, waiting for her next instruction.

She tsks me, and I'm sure my face is laden with confusion. Hadn't she asked me to strip? I'd done so and quickly. "Put your clothes back on, Brooks."

"But you told me to take them off?"

"I said strip, not at the speed of light itself."

"But…"

"Give the ladies something to enjoy while you strip, Brooks. You see, stripping is like foreplay, and it shows how the sex will go. If you strip too fast, she's going to assume that you're just a pump and dump who's going to fuck her. If you strip slow, you're enticing her. You're showing her the dance. It should be appealing, erotic. Telling her exactly how you plan to ravish her, making love to her body over and over again."

I pick up my scattered clothing from the floor and start getting dressed again. Once dressed, I wait for instruction. "Okay, so start with your shirt." Grabbing the back of my shirt I start to lift it over my head. "Slower... make me want it, Brooks." I slow, the shirt raising slightly over the trail of hair leading below my waist, up my abs, slowly cresting my chest and then over my head as I toss it aside.

Ocean eyes trail up my body, finding my own and I have to swallow at the intensity in them. She's enjoying this. I give her my best smile and watch a shiver run down her arm. I'm not the only one affected.

"Pants next. Slowly." I follow her direction, starting to shed my sweatpants. I've gotten them halfway down my ass when I pause. "Stick your hand in and stroke yourself, like you're priming yourself just for me. Like you want me and have to touch yourself because you can't wait a second longer with all the lust pooling in your body for what we're about to do." My sweats tighten around me as I grow thicker, just hearing the dirty words spill from her mouth. She's making me crave her. It's exactly what she's doing. The sinful thoughts from time and time again crash into my brain and paint a beautiful picture of filthy sex.

"So hot, Brooks. Now pull them down." My dick springs free within my boxers as I pull my sweats down my thick thighs, bending as I push down and shuffle out of them. Looking up at her with a wicked grin as I did so. Her tongue darts, wetting her lips, and memories of my first blowjob flood my mind—her on her knees, mouth parted, begging to taste every bit of me.

"Here's the good part." She rubs her hands together, and a laugh slips from between her luscious lips. Her eyes linger on my boxers. She bites her bottom lip, and I hold back the groan I'm dying to let sneak out.

"Any special way I need to take off my boxers, or can I just take them off?"

"Nope, just let the beast free, Brooks. Let him out to play." I roughly slide my hands to each hip and shoved my boxers down, my dick springing free and wagging up and down. Appreciating the perusal Mia is giving him.

Mia walks across the room and slowly climbs her way up the bed, ever so slowly. Teasing the fuck out of me. Making sure that my full attention is on the luscious globes of her ass. My hands itch to reach out and touch her, but we're playing by her rules tonight and I don't want to risk any reason for her stopping. I'm in lust mode, and I want her. Badly.

"Come kiss me, Brooks."

"But you said no kissing?"

"I meant no lip kissing. Kiss me here." She points to the delicate line of her cheekbone, and I oblige. Hovering over a spot lower on her neck, my lips press there as well. I place more kisses to her neck and down her collarbone. Her skin seems to vibrate with excitement below me. My lips meet her chest through the lace she wears, and it's translucent enough that I can see the tips of her nipples.

I'm aching to touch her, wanting to slide my thumb across those full breasts I long to kiss.

"Touch me, Brooks. I need your hands on me. Make me feel like you want me. Like you're craving me so badly that you can't wait to do the naughtiest things to me." My hands find her lace-covered breasts and I massage them like it's second nature.

Her nipples peek below my hands as my thumb and forefinger

rub them slowly. The urge to feel her skin to skin overwhelms all my thoughts, but I won't without permission.

Continuing my ministrations, I allow my hand free reign to roam down her ribcage and over her stomach, stopping right above where I want to let me hand drift. Sliding down over her panty clad core, I feel the heat burning through it. My fingers slip lower, meeting with her wetness.

I was making her wet with just my touch and kissing? A soft moan escapes her lip. Gazing up her body, I find a blue lust-filled gaze looking back at me.

Pulling at the lace garment slowly, I wait for any sign of her to tell me no. When she doesn't, I continue my journey, exposing soft skin as I go. Her stomach is perfection. She doesn't have abs, and there's a slight layer of softness. I let the lace ride up over her chest, exposing dusty pink rose buds. They're perfect in size and my mouth waters at the thought of tasting them. She lifts up, helping me pull the lace over her head and tossing it away.

My eyes roam over her half-naked exposed body. Rainbow hair in pinks, blues, and purples fans out a bright contrast again my navy pillows. A few locks fall to her breasts, and I reach out to push it away, wanting to see all of her. Her gaze catches mine when I look at her. Fire burns brightly in her eyes. "Tell me what you want to do to me, Brooks. Talk to me."

"I'm not sure where to start, but I want to put my mouth here." My fingers linger down, swirling her peaked nipples.

"Then do it," she taunts me.

I let my mouth envelope one taut nipple, running my tongue over it gently, caressing it. A moan escapes her as she arches her back, giving me better access. She's enjoying what I'm doing, so I continue, only this time I reach up with my hand to tease and pinch her other nipple.

Leaning over, I lick my way up the path between her breasts, eliciting tiny goosebumps to litter her body. Peppering kisses down each rib and over her stomach. Pressing one small kiss above and below her navel and then continue. I crest the top of her panty line and wait for approval.

Finding her hips, I slip my fingers in the corners of her thong. "May I?"

"Don't ask, Brooks. Just do. If you do something wrong, I'll tell you. Let your feelings and desires guide you because me telling you what not to do won't be hot at all."

I nod once, slipping her panties down to expose a tiny strip of hair right above her mound.

I wondered if she was bare down here, but the strip is sexy, so I won't complain. It still blows my mind that she's giving me such up close access to her. Giving me permission to do as I please, and my dick wags at the idea. The desire to taste between her legs has been on my mind since the first time I moved in. I'd been dreaming about it for weeks, and now the time is here. I have no idea what I'm doing. Bending as I slide her panties off, I lean back soaking up the paradise between her legs.

Her feminine scent is sexy, and it only heightens how aroused I am, knowing that the glistening between her legs is because of my touch, my hands, my lips. Reaching up, I allow my fingers to slide over her folds, landing on the tiny bundle of nerves I've always heard other guys talk about.

They always say to pay special attention to it. My forefinger and thumb work it over, and Mia whimpers below me. "Yes, Brooks. There." I work it, circling it, and pinching it, enjoying every single pleasure noise thrumming from her mouth. My fingers slide back to her folds, and I allow myself to slip inside slightly. A groan falls from my lips at how soft and warm she feels wrapped around my fingers. Tighter than I thought she would be, although I had no idea what it was really like.

Being inside her is like nothing I've ever experienced before, a different type of ecstasy. More mewling sounds come from her lips, and she continues arching into me. Asking for me. Giving as much as she takes. Lowering my lips to her body, I take one long swipe from her folds to mound. I pull back, licking my lips. "You're sweet, Mia. So sweet." The taste of her on my tongue is like the sweetest honey.

My tongue breaches my lips, and a thrill zings along my spine as I watch her track the movement. She's so fucking perfect. So willing.

I start spelling out the alphabet over her clit, writing poetry with my mouth, and she scoots away, her hands pulling me away by the hair.

"What are you doing?"

"I was tonguing the alphabet against your... you know. I've read it feels good, so I wanted to try it."

"It's not working for me, Brooks. Does it feel natural to do it that way?"

"Not really."

"Okay, then you're doing it wrong." I feel my shoulders pull together in defeat, and I lose eye contact. She sighs, "Hey, look at me."

I look up again, and she winks. "You're in training. You can only get better from here."

I admit defeat. "Tell me what to do."

"How about I show you?" She rises up against my face and starts grinding her hips. I let my tongue slowly swipe against her seam, time and time again. Moving up, I suck her clit into my mouth and nip it lightly, teasing her.

She groans slightly, "Yes, good. That feels so much better." I continue, forgoing the alphabet and just following her body language with each stroke, kiss, and breathe against her core.

Another slow swipe of my tongue along her seam rips a scream from parted lips. I move up to circle her clit, tonguing her, pulling each moan and whimper from between her lips. A sweet song of pleasure, need, want. I let my eyes gaze her body, over her glorious breasts, and find her eyes closed, head back in the throes of pleasure. Mia's eyes find me and I'm glued to her as I lick once, twice. She clamps down on my face, and I glide over a spot inside her rougher than the rest with my finger. I slide against it once, and then again. And again.

"Brooks, YES!" She clenches against me again, and moisture starts to pour from within her. "I'm coming." Liquid heat washes over my fingers, covering me in her juices, and I lean in to lick her. My dick bobs below me, caged between my stomach and the bed. I feel like I'm going to explode with the slightest touch.

Her breath is heavy. She's panting, and I know I've done something right. I didn't even need much help to bring her this much pleasure. I look to her for signs of what she likes and doesn't like.

"Damn." One word whispers from her lips, a shadow of a grin parting them.

"Was it good?"

"Good, Brooks? Good? Once you got rid of that alphabet nonsense, it was epic. Like…. I've never had a man's mouth on me that made me want to climb you like a tree and let you fuck me so bad right here, right now."

My heart beats faster, just thinking about getting to put my dick where my fingers were just now. I'm going to volunteer as tribute. I will beg if I have to.

"Not today, Brooks. We can't do your bucket list all in one day… I would be dead afterward."

"I'm willing to try."

She chuckles, pointing to my erection. "I'm sure you are. Give me a minute. I promise I won't leave you hanging."

I watch her fine ass slowly glide to the edge of the bed and

Topsy Turvy kinda love

stand up. Lord help me. All thoughts of right and wrong flee from my mind at the first sight of her without clothing on. Heaven be damned. If I'm going to hell, at least I'd enjoy some sweet cotton candy first. Then the devil himself could gladly pack up my ass and deliver me there. Spiritual morals be damned.

"Switch me spots, Brooks. Lay down, dick up."

"Ma'am yes, ma'am." I fake salute her because the truth is I'd do anything to get those red lips wrapped around me right now. I feel possessed by my need for her, and I can't explain it. I need to get it through my brain that Mia will never belong to anyone, especially me, and she's just doing me a favor teaching me how to pleasure someone. But if she's really just teaching me how to pleasure, then why is she offering to suck my dick too?

I crawl up the bed and flop down, dick up, as requested. My length stands large and proud, perpendicular to the rest of my body, waiting for her next move. She moves over me, breasts swaying, and I swear to God my dick reaches out to her of its own volition, silently begging her to move faster. A small soft hand reaches over and runs up and down my length.

"Sweet mother of everything that's holy in life, Mia. Your hand wrapped around me feels like heaven." She smiles up at me briefly before leaning down to take me into her mouth. I won't last long. The sight of her angelic cotton candy hair bobbing up and down on my length, combined with the warmth surrounding me, I'd be a saint to not hold back. The groans and moans as she licks, sucks, and nibbles on me are definitely not saint-like. Neither are the impure images pounding my brain and making me want to bury myself so deep in her that tears form in her eyes from the desire and need pouring through us.

Where in the hell did that thought come from?

A spark of electricity runs up my spine, and my balls tighten against me. I'm so close. Light spots flutter in my eyes, and a

89

blinding explosion erupts through me. I feel my come shoot against her throat, and she swallows every last drop of it. I'm still shocked she swallows. I would think most girls would find that disgusting, but it's sexy as hell.

For the next couple of days, we move like zombies in the night, just coming or going from work. Crossing paths, but never really coming in contact. Topsy Turvy has been busy. Cornell is back in session after fall break. I can't believe it's October already, and the leaves have started to change. The cold will soon be moving its way in for another long winter. I don't mind the cold.

My eyes fall to the door as I hear the lock click and watch as Mia slips in. "Fuck a duck, it's cold out there."

I wrinkle an eyebrow. I've never heard that phrase before. "What does that mean? Why would you fuck a duck?" I ask.

"It's a phrase, Brooks. Kinda like shit on a stick or cold as balls?"

"Oh, interesting. So, you don't really mean fuck a duck? Because if everyone said that, then a lot of ducks would be getting fucked, and that's just weird."

"Oh, boy. No ducks were harmed in the making of that phrase. Feel better?" she says shaking her head and laughing. She removes the scarf covering her neck and removes her jacket. "Someday, I'll teach you my way with words, Brooks. Someday."

"I'm going to hold you to it." As soon as I say it, the oven dings. It's our first day off in two days. I know she's off too because of the calendar she leaves on the fridge. So I decided to run to the store and grab food, making us chicken parm for dinner. The smell of mozzarella cheese and basil permeates the air as I walk into the kitchen to grab it.

"Wait." Peering into the kitchen behind me she inhales deeply. "Do I smell dinner?"

"Yep, made some chicken parmesan."

"Where in the hell did you learn to cook?"

"Living with Wyatt. He was always with Kaylen, so I taught myself to cook. Fast food gets expensive when you're doing it every single day of the week, sometimes twice a day. Plus, I didn't want to lose my boyish figure and all that."

She smiles and it lights up the room. "You get more interesting by the day, Brooksy."

We sit in silence as we eat. Her delight over the food makes me happy. I've never actually cooked for anyone before so it's another first for me. It's a small gesture, me simply providing for my girl. "Mmm...This is really good."

"I'm glad you like it. It's my first time trying Chicken Parm."

"Another first... save some up for someone else too. Don't give me all of them." My response is a nod, but I'll never agree to that. Truth be told, I'm already growing feelings for her whether I want to or not. I've been in lust with her since the first day at Topsy Turvy, but that's my own secret, never to be shared with her.

"Right, you're just teaching me sex. Nothing more, nothing less." Lying between my teeth makes me feel dirty, but it's what she needs to hear in the moment.

"Exactly, speaking of. We're both off tonight. What do you want to do for the evening?"

"Why don't we get to know each other better and then maybe try sex?" I hate that my voice sounds hopeful, but I want to do this already. Have her naked and panting below me. I want to get to know her too. Isn't that the advice Willie gave me? Get to know her, woo her, and don't just go for the sex...

"Sounds good to me. Let me digest this delicious meal first, though. It's kinda like swimming after eating. You gotta wait thirty minutes, can't just dive right in." We finish our food, and I take our plates to the kitchen. As I'm washing them, Mia slips in and hangs out pouring us drinks. "Wine okay with you?"

"Yeah, sure. I'll take whatever—white or red."

She finishes pouring the second glass just as I sit the last plate in the drying rack. We make our way back to the living room, and I grab the remote and click through Netflix. Scrolling through the options and settling my feet on a pillow on her coffee table, I prepare to relax and chill for the next hour or so before my next sex lesson. Mia hands me a glass of wine and I take a gulp.

"Easy, handsome. For someone who doesn't drink a lot, you should probably take it slow." I nod, taking note that wine can obviously provide a good buzz. I won't tell her that I've never actually had wine other than the tiny glasses provided with communion at church, granted those were probably watered down.

She plops down on the empty spot beside me on the couch. "So, what were you thinking?" she asks while grabbing a throw and snuggling beneath it. She holds it up to me as if she's asking if I also want to be under it and I nod. Hell yes, I want to be snuggled under a blanket on the couch with her. But first.

"Hey, let me start up a fire. You're cold, and we can't have that, now can we?"

"You could just come over here and warm me up…" She winks at me, and I can't help but grin back at her.

"Oh, I plan to, Pixie."

Leaving the warmth of Mia and the throw, I make my way over to the fireplace. A couple weeks ago, I'd moved around the logs and gravel to dust them, preparing for the cold. Now all I have to do is hit a switch, and the fire lights up. It's a gas fireplace, not a real one, but it still gives a great ambiance to the room. Still makes it feel cozy and romantic, even though that's the complete opposite of what I should be going for with her. I walk back toward the couch, and she lifts the throw again, allowing me back into her bubble.

"What do you want to watch tonight, Mia?" Assuming we'll get into one of our favorite shows like normal.

She taps a finger to her lips, and I watch the slow movement. She's wavering. I can tell. "Well, I was thinking... Let's do something more fun, like play twenty-one questions. It's a great way to get to know each other. Plus, it lets you ask me any questions about sex before it actually happens."

"Okay... how do you play twenty-one questions?"

"Well, I like to play by my own rules. Basically, I'll ask you twenty-one questions, and you'll ask me the same. We'll trade off asking. Here's the part I switch up. If you don't feel like answering the question or don't want to, you can choose to take a drink of your wine instead."

"Okay, sure." She moves, her thigh brushing my own, and I press into her. She smiles at me, and something about that smile makes my heart pound faster.

Mia's bright blue eyes gleam. "I'll ask first, so you can get the hang of it. What's your favorite thing about this town?"

I blink at her. Okay, that is not what I thought she would ask first. "Honestly, it's just so different from where I grew up. There's always something new to do or see."

Mia looks over at me. "Alright, it's your turn. Ask me whatever."

"How about you? Why do you work in the bar? I look at the paintings spread throughout this place and they're good. Why aren't you doing that instead?"

"Believe it or not, it's hard to get a good job in the art business. You have to know someone to get anywhere. Now, I show off my paintings in some of the galleries around town, but I'd probably never be able to live off of it. They always say for those who don't teach, but I couldn't see myself ever teaching children anything. So,

Topsy Turvy it was. I worked there in college, and when I was done with college, I guess I just kinda stayed." I nod. It makes sense to me.

"Okay, my turn. What's so wrong with your family that you thought, picking up and moving to New York was the way to go?"

I take another gulp of my wine, not wanting to answer this question. I don't really want to go into the whole deal of it, but she's looking at me like she expects an answer. Mia lifts a brow, still waiting for me to say something, but I don't.

"Where is your family?" I volley back at her.

She gives me a glare and takes a long drink of her wine. "Touché." I watch her throat as it bobs with a sexy swallow. She catches me staring and winks. "You keep looking at me like that handsome, then I'm not going to be able to resist jumping you and riding you like a stallion." A chuckle erupts from somewhere inside me and I waggle my eyebrows like a fool.

"A stallion, huh?"

"Yep, rough, hard fucking that's going to make you come so hard you won't know what hit you..."

I gulp, resisting the moan that's trying to escape. "Damn."

"Okay, here's a good one. Would you rather someone always tell the truth or protect your feelings?"

She taps her chin with her finger. Pondering the question. "Depends, I guess. I find most people don't tell the truth, so would my feelings really get protected?

"You didn't answer the question. You simply questioned my question."

"I guess if I had to pick, I'd go with always tell the truth and hope the person telling it was being honest."

"How about this one... If you could find out how you were going to die, would you want to know?"

I cringe. "Geez, that's morbid. I guess unless I get to die in my sleep, then I just want to be taken by surprise and hope it's over quickly. I wouldn't want to suffer."

Mia smiles. "I think I agree with you on that one. Quick and painless is definitely the way to go." I watch as her cheeks get rosy and thoughts pound my brain. Is her skin as warm as her cheeks are rosy right now? Would she even let me touch her without it being part of my training?

"Here's an easy one… boxers or briefs?"

"Boxers." I don't even have to think about that one. I can't imagine wrapping my package in tight underwear. Boxers are constricting enough most days, but they also help cover up the raging boners Mia tends to give me too. "Okay, this is an essential question: tacos or pizza?"

I chuckle. "Definitely tacos."

"Oh good, same."

A grin spreads wide across her face. "Your turn."

I pull the blanket over and hold it up to cover my current situation, which prompts my next question. "Oral sex or real sex?"

"Depends on the guy, really. If he doesn't know how to use his tongue, real sex. If he's bad at sex regardless, I probably wouldn't be with him anyhow."

My dick instantly shrinks. What if she thinks I'm bad? Will the sex lessons stop? Maybe we shouldn't have sex tonight and continue just fooling around as she calls it.

She volleys back at me. "Have you ever had a real girlfriend?"

"Nope. Told you before, no one in the compound interested me. If you wanted to date them, odds are you'd be signing up for getting married later on. You don't just date without intention where I grew up."

"So, what is this compound you mention?"

"It's five thousand acres of land that a group of people live on, free from intrusion."

"Interesting."

I look her in the eye seriously for the next question. I don't want to ask it, but I need to know. I don't want to finally have her all to myself and then have her in someone else's bed the next night. We aren't in a relationship, but I won't share her. My fist bunches at the instant possessiveness of someone else having what is mine. Even though she's not really mine.

She quirks an eyebrow. "Your turn…"

I take a deep breath. "While you're giving me lessons, are you sleeping with anyone else? I know this isn't a relationship, but it would be weird to sleep with you and then know you're going to someone else the next night."

"Is that what you want?"

"Does it make me bad to not want to worry about what other guys have?"

She glares over at me… "Are you insinuating that I'm not being cautious with my sexual partners, Brooks?"

I throw my hands up in defense. "No, No, nothing like that. It's just I'd feel better if you were focusing on just me for the time being."

"Done. I've been tested recently, I'm clean, and I'm on birth control." I nod my head, accepting her answer even though it's not what I want to hear.

"Have you ever just slept in the same bed as a girl?"

I shake my head. "No."

She empties her wine glass and sets it on the coffee table. "You want another?" I say, nodding to the empty glass.

"Sure, that'd be great." I get up, moving toward the kitchen. Things have been sailing smoothly for most of the night, minus a couple of those questions. I feel like she's letting me in just a little bit by answering questions. Not fully, but I'll take it. She still won't talk about her family, and that's fine because I don't want to either. They've already taken up enough of my life; they don't need to follow me here too.

Ten

Mia

I'm glad for the brief reprieve in questions. Some of them I'm not entirely sure how to answer, like the was-I-sleeping-with anyone else question? I haven't slept with anyone since Brooks moved in. I thought it would be weird to bring random guys over and parade them in front of him, but he basically makes it sound like we're in a monogamous relationship. In a way, I get it. He doesn't want to worry about catching something, but openly saying it like I'd even allow myself to catch a disease really puts me off.

One part of me wants to tell him to suck it because I'll fuck who I want to, but the other part of me has learned to care about Brooks as a person, and I can't go against him like that.

I hear him rustling around in the kitchen, opening the fridge. A few seconds later, he reappears, wine bottle in hand. He passes me my glass and I hum happily. Any man who willingly refills my wine is a winner in my book. "Thanks for getting that." I swirl the wine in my glass and inhale the aroma. He laughs and drops back down into the spot he'd just vacated a few minutes ago.

Looking over at me, his smile is back, touching his eyes. "Where were we?"

I take a sip of my wine and pop my lips. "I think it's your turn."

Brooks waits like he's trying to think of the perfect question. He looks around the room once, twice, like he's nervous to ask. "Ask me." Two words are all I say.

"Condoms or bare?"

I choke, hacking up a lung on the sip of wine I just took and Brooks pats my back. Clearing my throat, I look over at him. "Well, I was not expecting that question. I prefer bare, but I don't trust most guys."

"What about with me?"

"I'm clean and on birth control. So, it's really up to you. You know my choice."

"Which feels better?" His face is serious.

"You really want me to answer that?"

"I'm assuming it's bare..."

"Think about it this way, Brooks. Do you want to feel the actual warmth of my V, or do you want to shove your dick into a hat that's way too tight and then feel like you're going to lose all feeling in it?"

"Bare it is. You know, I've never been with anyone else. No one's even touched me other than you, so I'm clean."

I try to adjust the way I'm sitting on the couch. My feet are cold, but I don't want to just shove my cold feet up against Brooks.

He must see me on the struggle bus. "Hey, you okay over there?"

"No, I'm trying to get my feet covered up. They're cold." I fake pout.

"Here, scooch over and put your feet on me under the blanket. I'll keep them warm."

"You sure?"

"Positive, pixie." His old nickname sneaks out between his lips. Heat steals across my cheeks, and I look down at my feet. Moving them to slide onto his lap under the blanket, I wiggle my toes. Big warm hands grab one and start massaging. I tense briefly but can't hold back how good it feels as he digs his fingers into my arch. I moan. It happens. Comes right out of my mouth and there it is. I'm getting pleasure out of having my foot rubbed. "Oh, yes."

The sound coming from my mouth again is all kinds of indecent, and I'm sure it's a straight hit to Brooks' dick, but I don't care. It feels good, and I want him to know it.

"Yes, keep going. Uh huh, right there.... yasssss," I purr. Brooks nonchalantly slips a pillow between his slowly growing dick and my feet. His fingers roll over my heel, up my arch, and between my toes, making sure he works every bit of them thoroughly. He keeps rubbing, and another groan slips from my lips. "You know you could do this for the rest of my life, and I'd be one happy lady." The words slip from my lips before I realize what I've just said in my foot massage euphoric state.

I catch Brooks' heated stare. I'm assuming it's based on the words I let carelessly slip from my mouth. We're suspended in this moment as time floats by.

Finally blinking myself out of my trance, I realize how untrue those words really are between us. I'm only helping him learn how to pleasure a woman so he can satisfy someone else. There will not be a rest of my life and Brooks.

My blue eyes stare up at his unending deep chocolate ones. He leans in toward me like he's swooping in to steal a kiss. Like he wants to lick the seam of my lips until I give in and allow him entry. He's so close that I can feel my breath against his jawline. My brain finally clues me in on what the plan is and reminds me of one tiny detail. I don't kiss, especially on the lips. I have a strict no kissing rule, and I plan to stick to it.

He leans in just an inch closer. "I can't," I whisper, and he jerks back. "I… I don't kiss, Brooks. I won't break my rule, even for you."

He nods once and then pulls away, losing eye contact, and for a moment I miss it. I miss the deep stare, the intense connection we share if only briefly and out of stupidity. I down the rest of the wine in my glass and grab for the bottle on the coffee table before realizing that what sounds good right now is actually a long slow hit of a joint. I leave the comfort and warmth of the couch to go in search of my stash.

"Where are you going?" I hear Brooks call out from behind me. "Wanna smoke something."

He says something else, but it sounds like a mumble so I don't pay it too much attention as I keep walking. I head into my room and grab my stash, quickly rolling up a joint.

A few minutes later, I'm back in the living room, cuddling back under the throw, wine in one hand, joint in the other.

"Much better." The look on Brooks' face is laced with concern, and I have to look away. I don't need his concern. I've been fine for years by myself, and just because we find ourselves in this close setting doesn't mean I'm going to throw all my beliefs out the window and jump into something with him. It's just the wine, the foot rub, and the closeness… that's all. My feelings are still very intact and properly buried. Thank you very much.

Now that I think about it, my movements are a little sluggish, and I can't tell you how many glasses I've actually had. The cotton in my brain is starting to clog up my good sense, leaving my instincts to the wayside. The alcohol always unlocks certain cravings within me which is why I don't drink to get drunk. It's why I usually limit myself to one or two drinks. Those little cravings whisper at me that maybe Brooks is different. *No.* I shake my head.

I eye him sitting on the couch, smiling at me. "Okay, Brooks, spill. Why is it you've never had sex? Plenty of people have the opportunity, but not everyone turns it down. I've seen you turn it down at the bar before so why?"

He drinks down the rest of the wine, clearly avoiding the subject. His eyes are glassy. "Ask me something else?"

"I guess my next question would be, how have you gone so long?"

"I'm good at controlling my urges."

"Does this have to do with the way you grew up?"

He nods once but doesn't go to speak up about anything else.

"Are you ever going to tell me about this mysterious town you grew up in?"

"Eventually. Are you?"

The alcohol has obviously loosened my tongue this evening. The next words coming out of my mouth shock me. It's as if my mouth takes on a form of its own and just starts talking while I sit back and listen.

"I have a complicated past. I grew up in a home where love was a dirty word. I saw it in its truest form. I lived with parents who fought constantly. A father who would talk down to my mother, who cheated on her multiple times. A mother who would turn to drugs when she couldn't cope with the world around her. Who would leave me to constantly fend for myself when I had no idea what the concept of fending for myself even meant? Who would bring home strange men when my father wasn't home and make obscene noises behind closed doors?"

The look of shock on his face doesn't go unnoticed. His eyes pass between my face and the joint between my fingers. And when he raises an eyebrow, I snap, "Weed isn't a drug. I'm talking about harder drugs. The ones that really mess you up. Leave you passed out so close to an overdose that you can't tell you're even alive anymore. There's no coming back from those after your brain is so screwed up."

"Hey, I'm not saying anything, Mia. I'm just listening," he defends himself. "So, your parents weren't in love?"

"Love doesn't exist, Brooks. It's a fairy tale people concocted to believe in something more than themselves."

"That's not true, Mia. Love exists."

"Okay then, tell me Mr. I-don't-talk-about-my-hometown. Did your parents love each other? Did they say I love you as they tucked you into bed every night while reading you a bedtime story?"

He turns away, looking anywhere but at me. "That's what I thought."

"Just because they didn't love, doesn't mean it's not possible. I choose to believe it does exist."

"You keep believing it, Brooks. Maybe someday it'll come true for you."

"You never know. One day someone could walk into your life and change your whole world."

I scoff, which probably isn't the right thing to do, but I don't see it ever happening. Life has a funny way of suggesting that love exists. And it certainly hasn't shown itself to me, so why would I believe the hype? Why would it wait until now to appear? Love, this figment of the imagination.

"So... let's get back to you never spending the night in the same bed with a woman. How do you feel about trying it tonight? I've been dying to try out that big ass bed you got hiding in there. Plus, another thing to tick off the bucket list!"

I stand up and figuratively brush off all the deep talk as if it hadn't happened. We have a list. A set of goals to get Brooks ready to date and be able to give a woman pleasure. *Stick to it.* I tell myself. Tonight was way too intimate.

"We'll be snuggle buddies tonight, but no funny business. Sleeping only. I've had a little too much alcohol to participate in full on sex." I start to walk toward his room and then pause. Looking back over my shoulder I realize he isn't following me, just staring. "Hey, you coming?"

Chocolate eyes meet mine, and I can see the ebb and flow of each thought. "What's wrong, big guy?" I walk over and rub his shoulder.

"Nothing at all," he mutters, but I know it's a lie. I can't get a read on him right now, and I hate it. I feel like I'm overthinking this, and I don't overthink things… He follows me into his bedroom.

"I forgot how big it was."

"That's what she said…" I hear Brooks joke from behind me.

"Okay, Mr. Smarty Pants." He gives me that typical Brooks smile, and I swear to God my panties are like bye y'all.

The rapid beat of my heart threatens to consume me. He walks toward me, placing a big, hot palm to the small of my back and I feel the energy that zips between us. He sweeps his arm toward the bed. "Shall we?"

"We shall." Where in the hell did Brooks come up with this smooth talk? I stare, confused, and he just grins at me. A whole night snuggling in the same bed with this man may just capsize every single thought I've been holding afloat.

Is it hot in here or just me? I feel an arm curl around me, grabbing me and pulling me tighter into him. A leg flops over mine, and I realize that it's not the covers on me anymore—notes of musk and sandalwood flood my senses.

I peep one eye open, finding myself face to face with one asleep Brooks. My eyes roam over his face. The sun peeking in through the window lights up every corner of his face, and I can't help but admire him. Eyebrows the same dark brown color as his hair. Strong jawline and a smattering of facial hair that makes him uber sexy. A smile crosses his face but then slips away before his eyebrows scrunch. Letting my eyes trail down, I realize that he doesn't have a shirt on, and those sexy as hell abs are on complete display for me to openly ogle.

I shut my eyes again and nuzzle in closer to him. Allowing myself a solitary moment while he's asleep to just enjoy the closeness without all the pressure of him being awake. It's the first time I haven't felt truly alone waking up, and for just a few minutes, I want to revel in it. Enjoy the feeling of a warm body against mine. Might as well take advantage of the opportunity that's unveiled itself to me.

Clearly, it doesn't matter how big the bed is because our bodies are unconsciously drawn together in this snuggle fest. I'm taking it back to the fact that he's warm, I'm warm... therefore, we just magnetically stuck to each other to supply heat. Two magnetically charged points finding each other.

I shouldn't stay here very long. That would definitely give the wrong idea. I'll give myself just a couple more minutes of snuggles, then I'll worm my way out of bed and start my morning. Just a couple more minutes. I say it to myself like I'll really stick to that idea.

Brooks shifts slightly, and all of a sudden, I'm prodded with the world's most impressive morning wood.

Well, hello there, big boy.

My thighs clench together as I think about what it's going to feel like once I finally get that bad boy inside of me. I squirm to get a better feel of it pressed against me. If only I could get him to move just slightly, then I could get myself right on top of him. *Oomph.* I just got stabbed again by his massive rod. I can't move. His leg is firmly holding me in place, but it doesn't mean my fingers can't roam...

But then reality hits me again. I'm not in teacher mode. I'm just in my-lady-bits-need-man-meat mode. *Don't do it, Mia.* I scold those lady bits like they have a brain.

Brooks moves and stretches beside me. Eight firm abs mesh up against the warmth of my stomach, and I almost moan at the feel of it but manage to keep my lips sealed. He stretches again but then freezes in place. Deep chocolate eyes open wide and gape at me. A smile crests his lips, exposing straight teeth, and I can't help the smile my lips automatically form.

"Morning, handsome." My voice is raspy like I've been screaming his name all night. Maybe in my dreams because he's been taking those over too these days.

He leans over and presses his lips to my forehead while his hand slides up the curve of my hip. "Good Morning, beautiful pixie." His voice is deep and gritty with morning breath, it scrapes along my soft skin and a shiver runs through me.

"I don't understand why you call me that…" I shake my head, hiding my eyes. I don't want him to see the chaos flaring within them. I should have gotten up and left this bed when he was still asleep. I clear my throat and attempt to move the conversation to something else.

"You have long wavy cotton candy colored hair; plus you're short and cute, therefore you're my pixie."

I peel myself away from his body and feel instantly cold.

Alone.

"Well, judging by the massive rod you've been poking with me all morning, I'd say you enjoyed your first time sleeping with a girl…"

"I've never slept so well in my life." His dark brown hair is disheveled in that effortless way that only guys can pull off.

I chuckle. "Your hair is priceless."

He runs his fingers through a couple strands, and I resist the urge to do the same. "Um, yeah. It always looks like that when I wake up."

I huff. "Of course it does. God, why do you have to give off this sexy and don't care look? You're killing me. All I want to do is jump on your massive cock and ride off into the sunset."

A rosy hue covers his face, and he makes a show of looking around. "I see zero people stopping you right now."

"Well, as much as I'd like to just go at it like rabbits. I need a couple minutes to freshen up. Plus, this morning breath thing... not working for me."

A small nod and I roll out of bed. I run to the bathroom, pee quickly, and brush the gross off my teeth from the previous night. Strolling into his bedroom, I don my teaching outfit as I like to call it. Pulling my hair into a messy bun, I put on my fake reading glasses and another piece of sexy lingerie.

Brooks is spread across the bed when I walk back in. Arms crossed behind his head, puffing his chest out. Cock standing tall and proud like it's ready for battle. Drool-worthy dimples coming out in full force, and damn, it's hot. He winks at me and strokes once up and down his boxer covered length.

"Obviously, someone was paying attention the other day."

"Well, I do tend to be a very good student." He winks again and heat pools at my core. I'm so horny for him. It's as if my body is drawn to him subconsciously. It craves his wants and desires or maybe just mirrors them back.

"Are you sure you can handle it? Sex..." My voice is husky with the desire to let him consume me. It's been a hot minute since I got laid, and I need it. My lady bits are screaming timber 'cause it's literally going down this time. Or... maybe up.

"I'm going to give it my best shot."

"Buckle in Brooks... it's going down. There's no rules, but one. No kissing. I'm sure you'll be imagining your first time for a while now. So you run this thing. Touch me how you want to. Tell me how you want me to touch you. I'm in the passenger's seat this morning."

Eleven

Brooks

Desire pours through me. I don't hesitate when she tells me there are no rules. I lean toward her like a man starved, craving something he's been missing for the last twenty-two years. *Her.*

She's told me no kissing, so her lips are out of bounds, but I have no problem running my fingers through that cotton candy colored hair like I've been dreaming about for weeks now. I grab a fistful and pull her closer to me so I can devour her.

My touch sends a spark running down her body, and I can't help the smirk that crosses my lips. "Beautiful," I whisper against her skin, causing a spread of goosebumps to pop up everywhere against her creamy soft skin. I drag my nose along her neck and kiss at the spot right behind her ear that I discovered last time I went exploring her body. I watch heat creep across her body, lighting her face and chest in rosy pink hues, letting me know what I'm doing is turning her on.

I press kisses and nips to her neck and collarbone like she's shown me. I come to a stop when I remember she's not naked. Not yet. This silly contraption she keeps wearing is keeping me from her sexy body, and I hate it. She sucks in a sharp breath, nails running down my back as I continue.

Fuck the rest of the afternoon if I can be this close to her. I would give anything up just to be here right now in this very moment. Looping my arms around her thin waist, I yank her closer to me, eliminating whatever space still lingers between us.

I reach down to the bottom of her outfit and lift up. She raises her hands as I pull it up and over her head. Running my hands down her curves, my dick is hard as steel, and I'm not entirely sure how I'm going to not come on sight. I grind up into her, and Mia hitches one leg around my hip, giving me better access to her bare center.

My fingers run down her sides, moving in tiny circles across her skin. I trail one finger down and rub her up and down her slit. She wiggles, attempting to get me where she wants me, and my dick reaches up to try and touch her, bypassing me as the middle man completely.

I want to kiss her so badly, but I won't cross the line she's drawn in the sand. I've been envisioning fantasies with her for as long as I've known her, and they will never compare to the real deal. Her moans and the way she's grinding against me is doing things to me. Intense things. Making me almost feral in my desire for her. I rock my hips up to her again, and she grinds down on me.

I can feel her heat through the thin fabric of my boxers, and it's driving me blindingly crazy. Running my hand down to her ass, I grab a handful. She feels like heaven, not the sinful deception I've always been told to believe came with lying with a woman. She's saving me from myself, salvation in a cotton candy haired pixie. She feels so good, too good.

"How's it feel, Mia?" I thrust up against her again, prodding her with my steel rod.

"Fuck yes, Brooks," she moans against my neck, running her

fingers up and through my hair. Depthless sapphire blue eyes burn into mine and then slide down my body. "God, your dick is huge." Her tiny palm cradles me, and it's almost too much.

I'm man enough to admit I think I've lost the feeling in my toes because the blood has been diverted to a more important location. If I don't stop us for a minute, I'm going to blow and it'll be over before I know it. I don't want to be that guy, the one who blows before he even gets the girl.

Her soft body melds into my larger one, cementing us in this sex, and sin filled moment.

My name whimpers through her lips, and it's what I've been dreaming about, only in real life, it's way more sexy. I don't need to hear it though; her pliable body bending to me is all the confirmation I need to know I'm doing something right.

I could split wood with my dick, and it's painful. How easy would it be to roll her under me and plunder her body like a caveman? To have her take away that ache that plagues my dick day in and day out when she's around me. I'm lost in consumption, bordering on needing white padded walls if I don't get her hand on me again soon.

Her hips swing sinfully over my crotch, and I curse out from the intensity. Her blunt nails claw down my back, and I want her to dig holes in me so I can remember this moment forever. I inhale her cotton candy and vanilla scent deep into my lungs, and I've become Pavlov's dog over it.

I want it all, everything and anything she's willing to offer me. I'm selfish. This intense craving for her makes me weak, but I'll gladly be weak for her. I'll sin for her. Fall to the depths of hell and be Hades' right-hand man just to get one more look, one more touch, and one more moment just like this one. Sell my soul to the devil for eternity without a blink.

"Need less clothes, Brooks. Need less pants," she croons over me, and I want to give her whatever she asks. I'm gone for this girl and the idea of pussy. I finally understand the term pussy whipped. I feel high. The blood loss to my brain is potent because all my filthiest desires creep just below the surface. Tingling at the base of my spine tells me this has to cool off for just a minute. I don't want to blow my load too soon.

"G-gotta... take a minute, Mia. Too good. Gonna blow if we don't stop."

Her hands slip from the biting grip she has on my back. She rests her forehead against mine, our chests rising and falling in a frantic rhythm, slowing slightly and sinking up. She crawls out of my lap, and I take the opportunity to hop up and shred my pants.

"Damn, Brooksy. That was hot."

"Yeah...if foreplay is that good. Let's see how hot the sex is..."

She looks over at me, our breaths finally normalizing, and winks. "You ready?"

"Am I ever... if it's anything like that... Hot damn. I'm ready to lose myself in your body. Do you have any idea how sexy as fuck you are?"

Seeing Mia strewn across my bed. Tousled, sexed hair spread below her. Pert nipples standing at attention, flat stomach, landing strip of hair above where I'll be in just a few short minutes, hopefully. I audibly gulp. "You're so hot." My words sound like that of a pubescent teen, but she's sent a short circuit to my brain with all this smooth skin.

I prowl up the bed toward her like a jaguar stalking his prey, my dick bouncing against my stomach. I lick my lips and find dark eyes following my every moment—her usual sapphire blues, darker than normal.

I grab the bottom of her foot and pepper small kisses up her ankle, calf, thigh, heading to the heaven between her legs. She squirms under my touch, and I inhale a scent that's only Mia. I moan into her satin skin, and the little break does nothing to calm down my raging boner. "You smell so fucking delicious."

My mouth explores higher, one single lick to her seam, and landing on her clit. I forgo the poetry with my mouth this time and move to the flow of her breathing and needs. I swirl my tongue around her pearl, and a whimper erupts from between her lips. She slips her fingers into my hair and pulls hard. I lift my gaze to her blue eyes. "I need you. No more teasing. Now." Her tone is wanton and demanding. She needs me, then I'll grant her whatever she wants. I will never for a minute, deny her. It's not possible.

My naked body covers hers and I prop myself up on an elbow, so I don't crush her. My blood is pumping like a race car going 200 miles an hour around a track. I fear this whole thing will be over before it all begins. I certainly hope not, but I'm not stopping now. Mia shivers under me, and I know she's just as ready.

I reach up and run one single finger down her body and rub her mound of nerves. She arches up into me, and our hips bump. My dick slides through her slickness, and I almost lose my mind. My heart feels like it just stops, and I wonder if maybe I truly have died and gone to heaven. Maybe I'm actually floating on top of myself watching down, dreaming all of this is happening. But it feels too lifelike. Too fucking real for it to be fake.

I curse, "Fuck, you're so wet, Mia." A groan escapes my lips as I lean over to suck on her earlobe.

She trembles below me and reaches around to grab my ass, bringing me closer to where she wants me. Her legs curl around my hips, locking us together. She clings to me, and I can feel every molecule crashing into her, much like it's crashing into me right now. I'm fucking alive for the first time in forever, and I wonder why I waited this long. But then, I remember. I've never wanted anyone else the way I want Mia Preston.

"I'm losing control," I whisper in her ear. She swivels her hips, and my tip traces over her entrance. The low groan that leaves my lips is indecent, but I can't help it. And I don't give a fuck. That's how she makes me feel. I can see her pulse hammering out a beat against her throat, echoing the need in my very soul. *Thump, thump, thump.*

"Lose it, Brooks. Fuck me. Own me. Give me every single inch of that massive rod you call a cock. Impale me on it and make me fucking need you like I need every single breath I'm fighting to take right now."

This close, I can see the sparkle in her endless pool of sapphire eyes. I drown in the sea wreck that's about to happen. The hypnotic thrashing of the waves, pounding me again and again as my heart beats a song of death, drowning. I'm lost in her ocean. Whatever the hell that means. I don't care.

When I slide into her, everything before this one perfect moment evaporates. I told myself before that one single moment in time could change the rest of my life and I thought I knew it then.

This.

This single solitary moment where our cells collide is better than any other solitary moment I've had in all my years on this earth. It's a full-body awakening, a prickling sensation coursing through every vein and nerve in my body and lighting me up from the inside out. She's snug and tight and fucking perfection.

Pleasure blooms across Mia's face, and I puff up knowing I'm causing all that pleasure and flushing.

"I swear you weren't this big the other day. Damn son, you're gonna break me in half."

"Never, you're made to take this dick. Anything else you want to comment on?" I thrust into her emphasizing that there should be less talking and more sexing.

"Fuck yes, Brooks. Break me on this dick," she pleads for it, with a tiny bit of demand.

Her body cradles mine perfectly, not fighting the intrusion at all. She's wet, and her arousal makes it easier for me, the glide effortless, the heat insane. In no time, I'm hitting a wall. I'm into the hilt, and I don't ever want to leave this pleasure land of heaven.

"Good God, Mia. If this is sinning, then send me to hell now. I'll gladly be a sinner for you." I chant it. As if I'm saying a prayer to the devil to keep her forever. Selling my soul off to the highest bidder at the price of her magical pussy.

"Nothing this fucking good is ever wrong, Brooks. I'll be your downfall if you want me to be."

I sink into her deeper, her body greedily clamping down around my own. I demand more with my cock, and she willingly gives. I would walk through hell and eternal damnation just for one more second exactly like this one.

Mia grips hard around my dick, and I lose it. A roar pummels its way through my lips.

"Fuck me harder, Brooks. I know you have it in you. Give me every fucking thing you've got." And I thought Mia's dirty talk was sexy before... her egging me on just makes me want to fulfill every request, every desire, every need. She wants to be consumed by me, then I'll help her give that word an all new meaning.

I pound faster into her—the headboard bangs into the wall with each thrust. I stare down at her dusty pink nipples and latch onto one. I suck hard on it, pulling it between my teeth, and she mewls out her pleasure. I want to ravish her. Possess her. I roll us over, so she's on top of me.

Her hips swivel, and somehow, I've managed to get even deeper inside her body. I want to crawl in and live there; that's how far in my dick is right now. Her fingers find my chest, and blunt nails dig their way down my skin. It's rough, and I wonder if she's trying to make me bleed. I'd be okay if she was. I want her to fucking brand me so that everyone knows I belong to Mia fucking

Preston. Scar me so that no one else exists beyond her. Because no one ever will.

My lust for her is incomparable to anything I've ever experienced. This is nirvana, plain, and simple. Not to be cheesy, but this sex is on fire like the Kings of Leon sing about in that one song.

"Does it always feel this fucking good?" I ask. She slides up my shaft, and I almost fall out before lowering herself back down onto my length. She does this slowly two more times before going all out and riding my dick like she's meant to do this with her body. I power up into her, our movements smooth as we move together.

"I've never had it this good."

She does one slow stroke again and that telltale tingle crawls up my spine. I know I'm going to come soon.

"I'm addicted already and it's only been once, Mia," I say.

"Uh huh. Me too. Good thing you've got an excellent teacher to experiment with."

"And what will we do next?"

"Whatever you want to…" Mia pants.

I nibble up her neck, feasting on her tender skin. I want to kiss her so badly. To overpower those bright red lips, but I stick to the line of where I can and can't kiss her. I won't cross it. She's riding me hard now, squeezing my dick like it's never been squeezed before, and I can't stand it any longer. My balls tighten against my body. I'm pistoning up into her faster and faster. I'm going to explode at any minute.

"I can't hold back much longer, Mia. Tell me what you need from me."

"Touch my clit." I'm glad for her instruction. I'm in this lusty haze, and she's the only thing telling me what to do next. Using circular motions, I put pressure on her clit and rub in tiny circles, finding purchase on her hard nub and adding pressure as her body responds to me.

"Yes, yes, yes, oh fuck yes. It feels so good. Yes, Brooks." She's panting and wheezing, high on me and the pleasure.

Her vise grip on my dick contracts like a fist, and I'm done for. Stars light behind my eyes, fireworks going off in my mind, and I roar out every single last bit of my control. I'm dizzy as uncut heroin filters through every vein and blood vessel in my body. I free fall, Mia dragging my come from my dick so hard I see nothing but black. I feel Mia spasm around me, and I know we're going to be dead after this round. She lays on my chest as we ride out our orgasms together. Erratic heartbeats pound out like a clock keeping time.

"I'm sorry I didn't last longer."

"You were perfect, Brooks. I have a few tips, but no need to worry about those right now."

Both of us are consumed in what just happened between us. Because that isn't just heated sex and lust... there's a bond that formed. The look on her face tells me everything I need to know. She felt it too, and if I know anything about Mia, she's going to pull away. It's what she tends to do when stuff gets too deep. I need to let her. It's clear she's been hurt, and she pushes people away, but I'm not going anywhere. Even if I have to let her believe it's just sex between us.

"Damn," she whispers above me.

"Yeah. Fuck. We can do that anytime you want to. Dick at your service. Sign me up on the dotted line. I'm done for... finished."

She laughs. "I have a feeling I'm really going to enjoy this bucket list we've created, and after that, I've thought of a few more things to add to it."

"Oh yeah, care to share..."

"We'll just have to wait and find out, won't we?"

"Tease," I growl out. Her mouth is so close to mine when she lays on my chest that all I'd have to do is move a few inches, and I'd be able to claim it as my own.

Mia's cheeks turn a bright shade of red and she sighs. I scoot us up the bed, so my back is resting against the headboard, and I can look at her. I haven't pulled out yet, and I don't really want to either. She hasn't complained.

"So, it was good?"

"God, yes, Brooks. It was probably the best sex I've had in my life." A smile grows across my cheeks, and I feel ten feet tall. "Don't let it get to your head though."

"Oh, and why would that be?"

"Because then, you're gonna wanna do it all the time."

"And the problem with that is…"

She laughs, and my dick jerks inside her. "Ready to go again?"

"Yeah, the end came way too soon, I've been holding that in for way too long. Let's just say you feel way better in person than in my dreams."

"So you have been having sex dreams about me?"

I quirk a brow. "Never denied I wasn't…"

"Naughty Brooks."

"Only for you, Teacher."

"I like it when you call me teacher."

"Oh yeah…Teacher." My voice is grizzly with lust pouring back in. I buck forward, and she laughs.

"You know what the good news is? You'll only get better with practice."

I lean up, nipping her hardened nipple. "Well, we should probably get another round of studying in while we're at it."

She wrinkles her eyebrows at me. "Only if I can use my ruler when you get out of hand."

"Do I get to spank you if you're out of line?"

"Only if you ask me nicely."

"Fuck, yes."

"Let's try a new position this time… gotta check off more bucket list items and all."

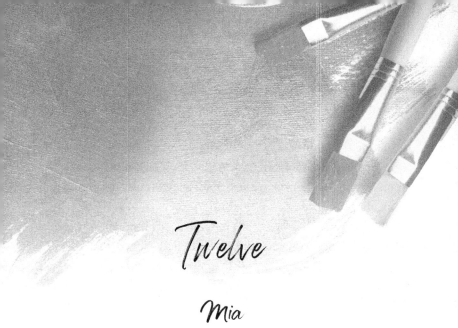

Twelve

Mia

We spend the rest of the day trying all sorts of positions and techniques. Marking one thing after the next on our wish list. For a recently dethroned virgin, he has some insane sex moves. Granted, at the beginning I was a little worried he'd explode as soon as I slid down him. He seemed to pick things up after a few minutes, though, literally and figuratively.

He has sex like he moves, all smooth and swagger. He's gotten bolder, learning to bring out his flirty, sexy side. Maybe he really has been thinking about this for weeks and months. I smile, thinking about how many orgasms I've had in the midst of a day. Once we got over that alphabet mishap. God, now that was horrible. I'm not even sure where he got that, but he's been banned from doing it ever again.

He's even different during sex. It's almost like he has a controlling alpha side where he gets all growly, versus the normal polite and fun Brooks. And the sex... The most intense I've ever experienced. It isn't just physical with him. My emotions are all out of whack on a rollercoaster careening down a snow-covered mountain with failed brakes.

Now that the fog has faded, I need to sort my feelings about all of this, but I don't want to. Not yet. Thinking about it will be admitting that it may be something more. It's not. It's only sex between us because these aren't feelings. It's a lack of oxygen to the brain over all the hot sex we've been having. Brain deprivation due to big dick overload.

Every time I move, I'm reminded of the delicious soreness from our sexcapades yesterday. It hasn't been that good in years for me. That's also the first time I haven't gotten stoned out of my mind right beforehand. So maybe being sober is the reason all these thoughts are competing for space in my brain. Overwhelming me.

My growling stomach reminds me that we forgot to eat dinner last night, and I need to replenish myself, but first, I need a shower. As much as I don't want to wash Brooks' scent from my body, I need to get my mind on straight and remember why I'm doing this with him. It's also why I dragged myself from his bed late last night instead of staying in it for two nights in a row. I'm teaching him sex for someone else. For someone that isn't me. Straightforward and simple. No attachments, no feelings... So why do I feel so weird about it now?

I get up and head toward the bathroom, needing to freshen up. I crank the shower too hot, letting steam fill the bathroom. Stepping under the spray, I let everything sink in.

Brooks.

The look he gives me that's filled with so much hope for us. A look that tells me he thinks I'm possible of love. Shaking my head, I abandon that notion. It isn't possible. I'm too scarred against love to ever believe. It's only taken 25 years to figure out that I'm broken.

The way he looks to me for instruction and asks if I'm okay every step of the way. He lets me lead and never once makes me feel pressured or tells me what to do. He's becoming a strong force in my life. One I refuse to lean on. People don't stick around. People want what they want from you, and then they throw you away like a discarded dish towel that's been used one too many times.

Brooks is getting to me, and for the first time, I realize that my heart isn't really made of steel. There's tiny fragments on the surface that can turn into deep fractures if I'm not careful. A tear slips down my face from all the emotions pounding me. But what if Brooks is different? What if...maybe... for once, I'm not really alone.

Dude, she totally fell for it. I did all the normal boyfriend things. Told her she was pretty, told her I loved her. You should have seen her face. She straight up believed me.

Chad laughed with his friends, unaware that I had heard every word. It hurt. Like a dagger to the chest. A confession I shouldn't have heard shattered the very way I thought about love and relationships. I'd given him my virginity just to find out that I was another notch on his bedpost. Yet another man in my life that I couldn't depend on to do the right thing.

I'd say he broke me, but I won't give him that much credit.

That was the day I swore to myself that I'd never let a man get anywhere close to taking my heart. So I put it under lock and key. When I confronted him about it a couple days later, he adamantly denied all of it, but I knew the truth. He tried to kiss me after he realized I didn't believe him, backpedaling fast to tell me he was just shooting the shit with the guys. *A little too late,* I'd thought.

Words can't be taken back. I choose to believe actions always speak louder. So I'd adopted this persona. I'd dyed my strawberry blonde hair into cotton candy colors and started wearing gothic clothing. I spent most of my time holed up painting and smoking, trying to drown out the feelings with some THC. I noticed that people who look differently tended to be ignored and left alone and that's exactly what I'd wanted.

I was fine with that life until Brooks walked into Topsy Turvy a little over a year ago and changed every thought. I guess at this point, I need to decide if giving Brooks a chance is worth the eventual downfall of my soul when it doesn't work out.

A knock on the bathroom door has me wiping my eyes quickly. I didn't realize how long I've been in here. Long enough to wash my hair, had I remembered. I hadn't even washed anything yet. "Knock, knock my sexy pixie." He pulls back the shower curtain and smiles that panty melting grin. "Hand check."

I raise my hands and can't help but laugh.

"Good. Just wanted to make sure you weren't getting frisky in here without me."

"Nope, just taking a shower." His eyes roam my face, and I see a hint of concern before that brilliant smile comes back. Only it isn't as big this time. He knows something's wrong, but I also know he'd never force me to talk about it. Brooks is a good man like that.

"You need some help getting clean?"

"Pretty sure you're the reason I'm here in the first place... because I was so very dirty last night." I wink at him and he groans.

"God, you're so beautiful, and last night was... hot. When can we have a repeat? I think I could learn a few more things..."

"Well, luckily, there are still some things left on that sex bucket list of yours..."

He waggles his eyebrows at me. "Uh huh." One look down confirms that he's ready for another round right here and now. The front of his pants are tented. Following the path, my eyes lead to, he chuckles and shrugs.

I raise my hand up and wave it.

He smirks that devilish charm my way. "What are you doing?"

"Raising the white flag. I surrender. My lady bits need some recovery time before we do any of that again. I think you almost split my V with your monster D last night."

He winks, that dimpled grin crossing his face. "You loved it."

I fake pout. "Did not."

"Did so."

"Good Lord, Brooks, are you five?"

"Nope, just trying to get a laugh out of you. It worked. Victory is mine! Whenever you're done here, I'll have breakfast ready for you."

My stomach growls at the suggestion of food. "Ugh. You're going to make me fat with all this cooking."

"Good thing we have our exercise plan all mapped out then, right?" He winks and I can't help but shake my head. This guy.

"Right," I say dryly.

"Okay, then. I'll go make food. Don't take too long or I'll have to come in and do another hand check. Maybe offer to help with your lady bits." My words coming back at me from his lips have me laughing again. How does he always, always know what to say?

Brooks leaves me in peace to finish showering. I do so quickly, not wanting to miss out on breakfast. I'm becoming a dependent little food whore on his offerings. I've never had someone that made food for me, but I can't say I don't like it. As I put on black leggings and an oversized gray sweater, the smell of bacon and eggs assaults my nostrils. My mouth waters at the anticipation of a homemade breakfast.

I finish putting my hair into a messy bun and head out to the kitchen. Sitting down at the table, I think about how real it feels. Eating at the table with another person instead of just shoving a Pop-Tart down my face while I paint and smoke. It's nice. The closeness. The feel of normalcy. Although, I'm not sure I've ever been normal...

Plates are already set out on the table along with silverware. Brooks brings over the steaming hot skillet and I can't help but ogle every bit of him. He hasn't put a shirt on, and I watch his muscles as they bunch with each movement. My eyes trail further down, stopping at the Adonis belt and dragging down that very happy path to down under. "I've got bacon or sausage first?"

"Mmm... bacon. God's gift to people. I swear I could eat bacon for the rest of my life and die a happy lady." I bite into it. The crunch is that level of perfection you get when you fry bacon precisely how it's meant to be because non-crispy bacon is the worst. I moan, my eyes rolling back into my head.

"Mia," he warns.

"Yes, Brooksy?"

"Don't make those noises unless you want to deal with the consequences."

"Can you please explain all the consequences to me now? They sound like fun." Elbows on the table, I put my chin on my hands and flutter my eyelashes like a girly girl. He shakes his head, places one sausage and three pieces of bacon on his plate and goes back to the kitchen.

He peeks out from the kitchen with that killer world stopping smile that brings me to my knees. "How do you prefer your eggs?"

"Um... I'm partial to sunny side up, but I won't complain over scrambled either. I'm pretty easy that way."

He winks with a chuckle. "Wouldn't have pegged you for easy at all."

"Don't make me murder you before I get my tea."

"Oh, tea, right. The kettle isn't done yet, but it's on the stove."

"Thanks, Brooks. Really, I mean it." It's easier to say things like that when he isn't actually in the same room as me.

He speaks to me from the kitchen as he continues cooking, "Well, I did need some extra tutoring last night, so it's the least I could do. Feeding you." I hear the fridge open, what I assume to be eggs being whisked, and then the sizzle of the hot pan as they're added to it. We are being so domestic, so couple goals…

"Do you work today?" I ask, trying to keep the conversation going so I don't get in my own head.

"Nope, off today and tomorrow. Same as you."

"Any plans?"

"Netflix and chilling, I think that's what the kids call it these days."

"You know what that means, right?"

"Yeah, something to do with sex, but I was thinking about actually binging something fun. Maybe just hanging out with you. I feel like we know nothing about each other."

"Alright, Brooks. That sounds nice." I won't mention that my heart's pounding so hard trying to escape my chest at the mere thought of letting him into my life and explaining just a tiny bit more of my past.

I'm losing feeling in my fingers and toes over coming clean. Spilling my life story seems like a mountain I'm not willing to climb yet, but I want to give it a try though. We are roommates, after all. Friends talk and share things. Maybe I can too. *Maybe.*

He finally finishes cooking and brings the rest of the food to the table. Eggs, bacon, sausage, toast, and fruit. He's made a feast.

"So, what about you?" I ask him. I spilled some of the crap in my life last night and now I want to hear about him.

"What do you want to know?"

"Where you grew up, what school you went to, what your hobbies were…"

"We called it the compound. A bunch of religious nuts living under one roof, not interacting with the outside world because our leaders believed that by not doing it, we were pure. They chose who we would marry. Some men were offered more than one wife if they were true believers. Any children brought up in the fold were told to think and act a certain way. Outsiders were an abomination. Our schooling was based on religion and the one true way to God. We were raised on fear. Fear of speaking out against the leaders or believing something other than what we were supposed to. Everyone on that compound has a job too. You work for the leaders in some way, supporting everyone else. Farming, practicing law, doctors, we had it all."

"It makes a lot of sense. The way you interact. How you first acted toward people when you first showed up at Topsy Turvy. You were literally learning how life outside those walls worked."

"Was I that weird?"

"Honestly, you were pretty strange. I accepted it because weird is my thing, and you started to grow on me." I pause quickly before my next thought hits. "Wait, so you didn't get to do all the normal kid things growing up? Sneaking out late at night, throwing parties, any of it?"

"Nope, my parents were fairly strict. Don't get me wrong, I snuck out and hung with friends every once in a while. Some of the guys would grab their parents' liquor stashes and we'd sneak out into the fields late at night and drink. Always had to be in bed by the time your parents woke up in the morning. Else your hide got tanned. My parents had my whole life planned out for me, but I wanted more."

"What do you mean by more?"

He rakes his fingers through his dark brown hair. "I didnt want to be told how to live my life and who to marry. I wanted to find someone, fall in love, and have kids. I didn't want to be forced to be a husband to more than one woman. My town was like its own mini cult. You did what you were told. Marrying who you were told. It wasn't just a religion there, it was a lifestyle. You followed the teachings. You played by the rules, or you dealt with the religious justice mafia. That's what they called themselves."

He sighs. "Making furniture was a fun side job, but that's about the only part of my previous life I enjoyed. I wanted to see other places. Live a little."

I shove another spoonful of eggs into my face like a fat kid eating cake. It's fascinating hearing about this way of life. I thought I was rebellious, they'd surely throw me in purgatory for my life choices. "And moving here… was it worth it?"

"Sure was. If I hadn't, I wouldn't have met you, and we wouldn't be here now. So yeah, definitely worth it."

Cue the swooning and dopey grin. I can't help it. He's making me cave, and damn it, I really want to.

Shut it down, Mia. Stop the swoon. Stop the swoon NOW!

"Do you ever want to go back?"

"Nope. Nothing left for me there. Truth is, I was always an outsider. As soon as I left, it felt like a weight lifted off my chest. Couldn't tell them I was leaving, or the justice mafia would make it difficult, so that didn't happen. I snuck out one night with just a duffle bag knowing I'd never be welcome again. For once, something made sense, leaving the compound behind."

"So, you'll never see your family again?"

"Probably not. They didn't seem to see me even when I was standing right in front of them. You were expected to be seen and not heard. To obey no matter what you thought. I was never a child. I was an instrument to be used. To be cultivated into the perfect believer and the second, I questioned something I was smacked down for voicing it."

Sadness consumes me, and I blink away the quickly forming tears. My heart hurts for him. I can see the pain behind his eyes as he talks about his family and what he's left behind. I believe he truly is happy, but at the same time, I can tell it bothers him. I don't feel emotions. I've spent so much time shutting them from my life that I appear to be losing my damn mind. I've cried more times in the last day than over the last three years of my life.

"I'm sorry for what you've been through, Brooks. I guess you could say my childhood was similar. They never cared about me a day in my life. It says a lot about your parents when they flat out tell you they didn't want you. Going day to day wondering if you'll get fed or if you'll have a roof over your head. My parents only cared about money and what it could buy them. My father spent the money he did have cheating on my mother with every other Betty in town."

A weight sits on my chest talking about it. The memories hurt. The feelings swarm me.

"I've always been an afterthought. Shoved around, forgotten. I can't even remember a day when my parents were ever happy together. A day when they weren't threatening each other with bodily harm or my mother going into her room to dose herself with her new brand of illegal medication for the week..." A shiver tears up my back thinking about every time my mother had gotten so high. The things she said...

"Well, I don't know your parents, but it sounds like they're a couple of idiots. I want you, Mia. You are wanted very much, so don't keep thinking for a day that you aren't. You're... important to me."

I muster up a smile as he stares at me with those soulful chocolate-colored eyes. "You like me as more than a friend and roommate, as more than just a teacher, don't you, Brooks?"

"What was your first guess?"

"Besides the dragon in your pants... No one has ever willingly treated me like something more than a doormat. Most people only want something from me. I mean, I guess you want sex lessons from me, but something about you is different. You're the first person who's made me feel like I'm worth anything at all. Like I'm a human being. Someone you want to be around. It's like you care for me." He chuckles, but it's not hardy. Before I can pull away, he reaches up and rubs his calloused thumb against my cheekbone, making me look up and get lost in those dark brown eyes.

"Why don't you really believe in love, Mia? Why don't you kiss people? Why hide away under your brightly colored hair and gothic clothing facade? Who was it that wrecked your whole entire world? Let you down? Crushed your spirit? Your parents were clearly idiots, but someone did this to you. Someone did this to you, and I want to crush them for you."

I shake my head, and a tear slips out. He leans over to wipe it up as it falls, and I can't take these emotions. My pasts lock is breaking open without the key. My heart's going to shatter itself into every single corner of this room—fragments upon fragments of heart littering the floor like broken glass from a windowpane.

"You don't have to tell me today, but boy, do you have a knack for shutting down."

We eat the rest of our breakfast in silence. My mind whirls with everything that's been said and not said between us in such a short period of time.

It's been a couple of hours since we've eaten breakfast, and we're snuggled on the couch watching a Star Wars marathon. We started with Episode IV: A New Hope. I don't want to tell Brooks, but I keep getting lost and can't seem to follow along. He is distracting.

He'll laugh at something or cringe when a bad part comes up, and I find it interesting, just watching him. His eyes sparkle when he laughs, and when he looks over at me and winks, I could die right here. I've successfully told Brooks more about myself in a whole two days than I have to anyone else in years and I can't understand my propensity for such word vomit. I've never been a sharer, but now my brain decides to dispense all of my past like a PEZ dispenser. One sugary morsel at a time. It's like he's brainwashed me into sharing all my demons.

I let my gaze linger on Brooks for just a little while before he finds me staring at him and smiles. "You like what you see?"

"Something like that... Hey, you want to try something?"

"What'd you have in mind?"

"Getting high and painting."

He nods. "I'm down to try it."

"Okay, I'll be right back." I hop up and run to my room to grab my jar, papers, and grinder before returning to the living room. Cleaning off the coffee table, I pull out a few buds and start to break them down before dropping them into my grinder. Fully ground, I dump it out onto the coffee table and scoop it into the paper. Rolling up the ends, I lick the seam to hold it together, making sure the ends are tight. I use the lighter real quick to heat up the place I just licked, so it's not wet.

Raising the lighter to the end of the joint, the fire ignites the paper to a slow burn. Lifting it to my lips I puff a couple of times, exhaling in between. Now that it's going, I pass it over to Brooks like a good host would do.

He takes a puff on it, but doesn't truly inhale.

"No, no, no... you have to inhale it. It doesn't count if you don't."

I watch as he puts it between his lips again and breathes in way too deep. An instant intense cough breaks free from his chest, and I grab the joint from his fingers. He can't seem to stop coughing and hacking up a lung. He'll be good with that one hit, being his first time and all. "Hey, it's okay. Just breathe." I hand him a drink to try and help with the coughing, and he willingly accepts it.

"Jeez, that was intense," he says, hand pressed to his chest like he's still fighting to breathe in the air his lungs are probably crying out for right now.

I hit the joint a few more times, letting my head rest against the back of the couch. We end up sitting staring at each other for the next twenty minutes. "I feel like I'm floating and my head feels like it's not even attached."

"Welcome to the high life, my friend."

"It's weird, but I feel so relaxed and a little…"

I raise my eyebrow. "A little what?"

He leans over and whispers "Horny," and I can't help the giggles that follow.

"Hey, what's so funny?"

"I don't know, but I just can't stop laughing. I don't even know why it's funny." Brooks starts laughing too and we can't stop… two fools laughing at nothing in particular. "Hey, let's go paint something…"

"Okay, what do you want to paint?"

"You… on the floor."

His brow furrows in confusion. "Why me on the floor?"

I roll my shoulders in a shrug. "Because it'll be fun, why not?"

"I'm not sure." I pull him up as I stand and walk toward my paints on my art table. His hand dwarfs mine, and it's a little rough. His eyes catch mine and I can't help the grin that slips across my face. Leaning over, I gently place the sheet on the floor to avoid any paint splatter.

"Okay, you lay right here." I watch as Brooks lowers his fine self to the floor, muscles flexing in all the right places as he does so. "Why are you going so slowly?"

"It feels like I'm moving way too fast." I chuckle again. Stoner Brooks is fun. He finally gets in position. "Okay, what now?"

"Let me grab paint. Stay right there."

Grabbing blue paint, I start slowly pouring it over him. "Stay still. I'm going to make your shape on the floor." He does as I say, and I pour more paint over him. Reaching down, I smear it over his arms and his face. He grabs me and pulls me down on him.

"It's not fair for you to be the only one painting. I want to paint you too, pixie." He smears paint across my cheeks and down my chest. "There. Much better." I straddle him, and he pulls me against him. He looks up at me, those deep brown eyes searching mine for more, for anything. They glide over my lips sinfully, and my tongue peeks out to say hello. He swallows, and I can tell he's holding back. He wants to kiss me, and it's killing me, but I want the same. We can't go down that road, not yet.

I start to slide back and force over the very prominent prize in his pants and he moans. "Mia…"

"Yes, Brooksy? Next lesson… high sex."

"Hell, yes."

Euphoria is great being high alone, but sex while high makes everything heightened. The pleasure, the feel of everything. Him, me, in a twirl of paint and lust. Another amazing lesson in the books.

Another hit. Another stroke. Another color. Blue for Brooks. The bristles of my brush caressing the canvas with color. One more line. Black fading out as it runs off the paintbrush. I pull back, needing to refill my brush with paint and realize that I've run out of black on my pallet. I'm forced to use blue.

Like my life.

Forced to think about Brooks in such close proximity. I peer over the top of my easel as I speak of the devil in an angel disguise. Musk and sandalwood assault my senses as I notice the towel-clad man heading into my kitchen. Freshly showered, still dripping, and mouthwatering. Suddenly I want to do a little more than painting. Well, a different kind of art. I want our bodies to do a little mixing without the mess. Painting the walls with our shadows is more like it, but the sun isn't out and bright today. A thought for later.

A grin steals across his cheeks, and I can't help but reply with my own smile. His hair glistens in the sunlight. Another hit on my joint to make the feelings go away. To numb myself. He crosses the room to kiss me on the forehead, his new morning ritual, and the gruff stubble covering his jaw almost gives me something akin to a rug burn, but I relish in the feel of it. I want it to mark me.

To tell the world that he's mine. But that's not true, because he'll never be mine if I only give him my body. He wants my broken heart too. It's like he wants to put it back together piece by piece and I hate that it's working. "Morning, my beautiful Pixie." *Insert dopey grin here.*

"Hey, Brooksy." He smiles at the nickname that's slowly become what I call him.

"You working on my painting again this morning?"

"Yeah, I ran out of black paint."

"You ever think about using something other than black for everything? Like adding a pop of color?"

"Why do you think I'm using blue?"

He shakes his head. "That's not what I mean. I'm saying, why not try lighter colors in general?"

"I've always used black. It's comfortable for me."

"Would you paint outside the lines if I asked you to?" His eyes fill with hope. It's a loaded question. *Would I paint outside the lines with him? Would I give myself willingly, hoping that I didn't end up broken even more in the end?*

Every day it gets harder to understand why I'm telling myself no, yet a little voice inside still whispers. *Look what happened to your parents. Look what happened with Chad…* Fear keeps me standing in place, never moving forward.

I'm safe here.

With Brooks, I'm in danger. In danger of losing my heart.

"I made you coffee. It's in the kitchen." I'm glad for the brief reprieve to his question.

"This is why you're the best roomie."

"I know."

He turns to walk away, and I watch his ass muscles scrunch under his towel. Even his ass is sexy, and now I want to jump him again. "Hey, Brooks, when do you go into work today?"

"Two hours. Why, what'd you have in mind?" The tent in his towel suggests he knows exactly what I'm talking about, but sometimes you just have to spell these things out.

I waggle my eyebrows. "Wanna knock something else off that wish list of yours?"

His upper body shakes with laughter. "You know I'm down for anything."

A chuckle pierces my lips. "Using my phrases now, are you?"

He shrugs. "Seemed appropriate."

Brooks is getting to me. I'm a lady enough to admit it. He's been making me waver in my thoughts all morning, thinking about surrendering and letting go. Giving in to all the desires I've been having. Like the dreams, I've had about kissing him for weeks. I don't kiss. It's one of my main rules, but aren't rules meant to be broken? I sure as hell break them all the time, so what's one little rule. If he's a saint then I'm a demon. I'm heading to hell anyway might as well enjoy the ride. Lip locks and all.

Plus, I can't stop thinking about my desire to kiss him last night. The way his eyes begged me relentlessly to give it and let go. To live a little.

I glance at Brooks mouth and lick my bottom lip. "A taste of a little something different. Maybe a little bit of rule-breaking."

He lowers his face down to mine, and his hands reach up to cradle my face.

"And just what kind of rule-breaking did you have in mind, my sexy Pixie?"

I shudder, my need for him coursing through every vein in my body as the distance between us gets erased inch by inch. My defenses are breaking down and it's all because of this tall hunk of a man standing in front of me waiting for me to give him permission. Waiting for me to just say yes. I'm more than ready to give in to anything he wants right now just to have his hands on me. I don't deserve him or the kisses he may give me, but right now I'm too selfish to care.

"Kiss me," I murmur.

Thirteen

Brooks

I find myself moving before the word me comes from her lips. I've been waiting for this moment. Biding my time for when she'll finally give in and let me break her one single rule. I know what this means to her. She's giving me a little bit of herself and I won't waste my opportunity. I don't hesitate. I won't give her the chance to take away this moment. I comb my fingers through her brightly colored hair and grab a fistful. My hold on her is tight but not painful, keeping just enough pressure so she can't pull away from me. Like I said before, no take-backs.

Lightning zaps up my body, and it feels like lightning bugs are trying to escape from the prison of a mason jar.

"You're so fucking gorgeous," I whisper softly against her cheek as I drag my nose along her skin. Mia sucks in a breath, and I know she's ready. She's not pulling back; it's almost like she's waiting for it. Anticipating my next move. Sending out a frequency only I can hear.

Stupid heart trying to beat out of my chest. I can hear it in my ears. I once asked myself if I could live without a heartbeat, and the answer is no because the heartbeat is her. She's becoming my everything. One touch and I'm gone for her, completely wrapped around her finger so tightly. And I'd fight anyone who tries to take that away. I've never felt more complete than when I'm with her.

I drop my mouth over hers and press softly, waiting for her to pull back. To tell me to stop. To tell me that she's changed her mind. But she doesn't; she leans into me. Giving me all the permission I need to beg for more with my lips. Looping my arm around her waist, I yank her closer to me. My towel drops, and it's hanging off my fully erect mast.

Her eyes never leave mine, and I get so lost in that unending shiny sapphire color for just a second. My large hand grasps the small of her back, and I tuck her into me tighter, needing every square inch of her body pressed up against mine; the only thing between us now is my pulsing dick. My fingers drift under her short top, and I rub circles on the soft skin below me. I run them up her back and realize that she isn't even wearing a bra.

I growl at the possessiveness I feel about my woman not wearing a bra for me. *Fuck, it's hot.* Mia's tongue darts out and licks my bottom lip, and a moan erupts from my mouth. She's so damn sexy, and I can't figure out why in the hell she thinks no one wants her. I sure as fuck do. I open for her, matching each tease of her tongue with one of my own. She tastes like mine. Our tongues battle it out, like lost lovers who've reunited after years apart, finding love after losing it time and time again. Weaving our story with the tips of tongues and heated breath.

We're still in the living room, and I want her in bed under me so I can ravish every bit of her more. I'm drowning in this ocean of one simple kiss, and I never want to come up for air. So be it if that means the death of me. At least I'll die with her fucking kiss on my lips.

Tiny palms sweep up my back until I feel her fingers running through my hair, nails digging slightly into my scalp. There's a pinch of pain, but I don't mind it. I grind into her, and she rides my thigh like she can't hold back any longer. My mouth consumes every single one of the pleasure noises coming from hers. I reach down and pull her up, lifting her up and pulling her tighter against my thigh as she covers my leg with her excitement. I walk us to my bedroom, our lips never parting.

Mia sucks on my lip, and I'm momentarily distracted from my previous idea of stripping her naked. I delve into her mouth, ravenous for more. Laying her down onto the bed, I crawl up it with her, still kissing her. Every single one of the fantasies I had about kissing her falls absolutely fucking flat to this intense moment we're having. Her perfect red lips are feather soft, and the moans coming from them are driving my arousal off the charts. My need for her is spiraling into a lusty haze and coiling into a demand for her body wrapped around me. I'm closer to the edge, and dear Lord, I hope she's coming with me. I rock into her, my naked cock against her wet core.

My fingers find the edges of her oversized tee shirt and lift at the hem, pulling it up over her: no panties and no bra, double score. My eyes roam over every inch of her. There's something different about her this time.

She's in a regular tee shirt, and she hasn't donned her normal teaching apparel. At the risk of sounding hopeful, I hope this means she's giving me a chance. The unsaid words in this kiss sure give me that impression. The floodgates are open, and I'm pouring myself heart and soul into whatever this thing is that I'm choosing not to label just yet. This is more than just open sex and lust. It's affection, whether she chooses to believe in it or not. I'll believe in it enough for both of us. Every tempting touch shoots my desire for her higher.

I haul her into me, pulling her leg to wrap around my hip while I grind my dick into her. She feels so fucking good. My little pixie. She gasps into my mouth at one especially hard thrust against her, and I hear the soft murmurs of pleading and begging abandoning her lips.

"You want me, Mia?" I ask, hoping yet again that she doesn't pull away from the intensity. Her tiny body is molding to mine perfectly, just like the first time, and I relish it, barriers be damned.

"Yes, need you Brooks. Need you now." Her breathy pants are enough to make me burst.

"Thank fuck." I'm so abso-fucking-lutely hard for her, painfully so. She runs her blunt nails down my back attempting to scratch me into submission of whatever she wants me to do, and I fully oblige. I rub her swollen pussy lips and slip inside her warmth. She moans as I enter her tight little core. The pulse pounding within me is shouting that this is a deeper connection, and I hope she feels it too.

I start out thrusting slowly. Fully aware that if I go in guns blazing then I'll be going out in a blaze of embarrassment. I calm myself. For a minute, I sit and just feel the pleasure of being inside her. Being this close to my girl. I pull back from her lips and admire the puffy red that has become of them since I start devouring her.

The timer on my phone goes off, and I curse at it. It's a blatant reminder that I have to go to work in an hour. I'm pissed that I can't spend the afternoon making sure my woman is naked and as sated as possible. I'm also worried that as soon as I walk out the front door, she's going to run. This is a lot for her. I'll make up for lost time now.

"Brooks, don't stop. Need you right now. Fuck me." She reaches up and pulls my face down to hers, letting her lips brush against mine. Hells yes. Back in the moment with Mia, I start thrusting into her harder. She squirms below me, her legs wrapping around me to hold me tighter with each thrust. My tongue is moving in and out of her mouth, making love to her like my dick is doing to her lady parts. And I am. I'm making love to her. I won't say it out loud, but I know what this is. I've never questioned it.

"Let's try something new," she whispers to me, and I nod.

"Anything you want. Let's do it."

I slide from her warmth and I shrink slightly at the instant cold. She flips over and presents her ass to me, looking over her shoulder with a small smile. "Doggie style."

I've never tried it before, obviously, so I'm game. I slip back into her, hitting lower than I was before, and it's fucking heaven. Everything about being inside Mia is worth every bit of hell the leaders from back home used to preach about. I'm lusty as fuck right now. She moans as I slide into the hilt, and we start going at it again.

No longer humans, but feral-filled animals in a rut. My balls smack her clit as I thrust in and out of her. She hums and whimpers her delight every time my dick rubs over her special spot inside. She feels good. Too good, and before long that all too familiar tingle starts to creep up my body. I reach around below her and find her tiny nub of nerves and rub it in circles.

Her walls start to clamp down on my dick, and I know she's close. "Yes, Brooks. Fuck me. Fuck me harder." I do as she wishes, pounding into her like my life depends upon it, and it's my last day on earth. More moans escape her mouth, and her orgasm crashes into me so hard that it brings on my own. I see stars behind my eyes, and for a moment, everything goes black before the world is back. I lean down and kiss her back, whispering praise of how good her body feels around me.

We both collapse, but I'm held up by my elbows so I don't crush her. I pull out and roll beside her, one arm wrapped around her, pulling her closer. I don't want to give her any room to run. Zero. She lays her head on my chest, and we lay quietly as we come down from the high. Her soft breaths puffing against the nakedness of my chest. Erratic heartbeats coming together to form one beat. A bond. A closeness that I can't help but get enough of.

The damn alarm on my phone blares, letting me know that I now have thirty minutes to shower and get ready to go to work at the bar. It's the last thing I want to do. Leaving her alone with her thoughts. I know it probably isn't the best idea, but I don't have a choice. I've never been one to call off work. Haven't called off a day since I started and don't intend to start. "Ugh. I don't want to go to work now."

"Then don't go. Play hooky with me today. Stay. Stay with me." Those words tear through me. I figure she'd want me to go so she could sit and analyze every single moment and work it out in her mind. The fact that she wants me to stay changes things. It's as if she's finally ready to accept that maybe there's something between us more than just sex. I'll take whatever I can get. But that's crazy, right? Could mind-blowing sex really win her over so easily? I don't see it.

"Okay, I'll be back." I slip out from where she lay cradled against me. Picking up my phone, I duck into the kitchen and call Eddie. Bouncing my knee nervously up and down as I lean against the sink, I wait for him to answer. One ring. Two rings. Three rings.

"Hey, it's Eddie."

"Eddie, it's Brooks. Sorry about the short notice, man, but I'm not gonna be able to make it into work today."

His voice sounds unamused, almost angry when he responds. "Seriously, you're scheduled to be here in twenty minutes."

"I know. It's short notice, and I'm a total dick for calling in, but it's my first time."

"Alright, alright. I'll call Zara and see if she can come in on short notice and cover."

"Thanks, man. I really appreciate it."

"Hope whatever you're doing is worth it."

"It is." I know that for sure. She'll always, always be worth it. Now, I just have to convince her.

I stand in the doorway and watch her shoulders shake slightly. She's facing away from me on the bed, and I know the telltale signs of crying better than most people. I'd seen it often growing up. Walking over to the bed, I sit down and slip under the sheets, wrapping my arm over her hip and pulling her closer. She shudders against me, and I hold on tighter, pressing kisses to the back of her hair and down her shoulder.

"Hey, baby. Shhh… what's going on?" I let my fingers trace over her bare hip bone trying to soothe her. To let her feel the comfort in my presence.

She shakes her head right before her eyes find mine. The light streaming into the room kisses her tears as each one slips free, unbeholden to gravity. "I don't know how to shut them out."

"Shut who out?"

"The emotions," she whispers, another sniffle escaping her.

"What emotions? Tell me what's going on up here." Moving a stray strand of hair from her face I lean over her, tap her forehead lightly, and kiss her cheek. My heart breaks to see the torment within the deep blue eyes I've learned to love.

"I have feelings and I can't shut them out."

"Feelings, Mia? This is what all of the waterworks are for, my Pixie girl?"

She nods against me. Rolling over, she curls into my chest and I feel the warm tears falling from her eyes. "Hey, hey. It's okay. I feel them too, Mia. Do you want to talk about them?"

"No." One word spoken so softly in a whisper that I almost miss it.

"Okay, we don't have to."

"Thank you. Can you please just hold me for a little while?" This is the first time she's let me in, and I'm lured into the magic of it. Into the allure of being needed.

"Of course. Anything for you, my beautiful girl." I don't know how long we stayed there wrapped in each other's embrace, sharing one sip of air after the next. Our heartbeats marry into the perfect union after a while and start to beat as one.

"You deserve better than me. I'm a sack of emotional baggage who's not good enough for you."

I don't respond because I won't grant her a comment to her pathetic excuse at pushing me away. I'm not giving up on her. Not now, not ever.

I'm a hopeless romantic, so help me, and I want her to believe in it too—love and everything that comes with it.

The only thing standing in my way of showing her is Mia. She needs to want this, or it won't work. I won't handle her with kid gloves, but she needs to know I'm serious without scaring the shit out of her by moving too fast.

Her breathing slows soon, and I know she's drifted off to sleep in my arms. The feelings aren't overwhelming her, at least for a little while. I like the feel of her in my arms where she's protected and loved. I watch her sleep. She has a small snore, and it's adorably perfect, just like her.

Her flaws are abundant, I can see them, but we all have scars. Some of us just hide them better, and I have a feeling that Mia has been hiding hers deeply for a few years now. She's told me bits and pieces of her life, but I crave knowing more about her. Knowing what makes her feel alive. I want to know everything down to the simplest detail. If she opens up, maybe then she'll trust me to know every truth and hold it like the most precious thing.

I don't remember falling asleep, but her soft breathing has obviously put me to sleep too. She stirs slightly, and I watch as sapphire blue eyes open in front of me. The beginnings of a smile tracing those pert lips. "Hi."

"Hey you." She stretches, and I enjoy a face full of Mia boobs. And there goes my dick. *At ease soldier.*

"Well, hello big fellow." A tiny palm cups my shaft, and I'm ready to go in an instant.

"Mmm... someone's happy to see me."

"Always, Mia. You make me crazy for you." I chuckle as her body presses against mine, causing all sorts of inappropriate thoughts to build in my mind. I shove them away. We've just had the most passionate sex, she cried and then fell asleep. I want to gauge where we stand before doing anything more sexual with her. It's more than sex now, and I refuse to give her an out by fucking the daylights out of her no matter how much my dick protests.

"Let's get dressed. I want to take you somewhere."

"Where to?" She quirks an eyebrow at me.

"It's a surprise."

"Okay..."

"Come on. It'll be fun," I say, pulling her hand to follow me as I get out of bed.

"I need a shower. I smell like sex."

I wink at her. "You smell amazing." She does. Her cotton candy vanilla mixes with my own smell and the possessive part of me likes that she smells of me.

She groans as she gets out of bed. Her cotton candy hair drapes down her back as she stands. It's wavy like I imagine a mermaid's hair would be in the water.

Her pert little ass. Curvy hips. Slim waist.

The bold black gothic tattoo that covers her right thigh, identical to the painting that hangs in our living room. Beautiful shoulder blades. I'm openly ogling her sexy self and when she peeks over her shoulder catches me, she bites her lip, and the urge to haul her back into bed and do anything she asks hits me. I refrain. I've been planning this for a while now and today's the perfect day. "You realize that it's really dumb to leave a naked woman in your bed to get up and make her go places?"

"I promise you'll like this place."

"Worth losing out on all the hot sex we could be having instead?"

"I hope so."

I watch Mia as she pulls on her typical outfit. Black leggings that slip up her legs and hug every single one of her delicious curves. I want to be those leggings. Overly jealous of them, to be honest, because I want to cocoon her body that closely. To hug her slim legs, her sexy hips. She slips on an oversized sweater that hangs off her shoulder.

"No bra?" I lift an eyebrow, surprised.

"Problem with that?"

"Yes, I don't want anyone other than me knowing that you don't have a bra on under there. It's going to drive me crazy just thinking about the fact that they're free, and I can't touch them whenever I want to." I grind my teeth at the thought of another man noticing she isn't wearing a bra.

"Self-control, Brooks."

"It went out the window a while ago, Mia. I blame you. You make me lose control."

"Oh, is that so?"

I growl at her seductively. "You know it is." She walks over to me, pressing her soft lips to mine, giving me the sweetest of kisses, and I want so much more. The truth is I've lost control. She's taken me heart and soul, any semblance of normality hanging by the tiniest thread.

"Uh, uh, uh, Brooks. You said no naked sex today. That means we have to get going, you ready?"

"But..."

"Come on, Brooksy. Let's see this place you have picked out." I grit my teeth and will the boner that'd risen down yet again over her teasing.

I quickly grab my sweatpants, a long-sleeved shirt, and my jacket. Mia stands in front of me staring. She looks to my crotch, then back at me and points. "No boxers?"

I point right back at her. "No bra."

"That's not fair, Brooks. Do you have any idea how much women are going to ogle your boxerless package? You're basically dangling yourself out there in dude lingerie with those sweatpants."

"About as much as other men will ogle your braless breasts."

She crosses her arms and huffs. "Fine."

"Do you have any idea how hot this bossy side of you is?"

"Oh yeah, you have a bossy side, Brooks?"

"I can be quite demanding when I want to be..."

"Later." At that, she winks and opens the front door, disappearing.

I follow her out, locking the door behind me, and race down the stairs. She stands waiting at her black Miata.

"Let me drive," I say, walking around to the passenger's side.

She quirks an eyebrow. "Do you even have a license?"

I puff out my chest, proud of myself. "Yep, I was very proficient in tractor driving." She snorts. "I'm serious."

"Me too, but tractor driving?"

"Hey, don't judge, tractor racing was a big deal at our compound fair every year. I will have you know that I got first place more than once."

"Oh my God, you really are serious!" She bends over laughing. A full belly laugh, and I can't help but join her.

"To answer your question though, yes, I can drive a car. The tractor thing isn't a joke, though. I can drive a mean farm tractor. You're looking at a three-time champion."

"I am sure you can, Brooks. Maybe one day you can show me your mad skills so that I can have all sorts of lusty fantasies about it. That's a new one for me. Doing it over a tractor. Another thing for the bucket list."

"You'd think my tractor was sexy." She stares at me for a minute, a smile curling the red corners of her lips, before laughter bursts from within.

"You can drive if... you never, ever use that phrase again. Okay?" She tosses me her keys walking around the car. I jog around her, and she looks at me like an alien.

"Aren't you driving?"

"I am, but I'm also opening the door for a pretty lady first."

"This isn't a date. You know that, right?"

"Date or no date, Mia. I'm opening your damn door. Now accept it and get in the car, please." I smile at her.

"Mmmm... do I detect the bossy coming out, Brooksy?"

"You haven't seen bossy yet, Mia."

She slips into the car seat and starts buckling her seatbelt. Looking over at me, she winks. "I'm looking forward to it."

The car is filled with music on the way to our destination. I gaze in Mia's direction to witness her jamming along to whatever song is streaming through the speakers, bumping the doors. It's dark and gritty. The simplicity of driving together feels so normal, so comfortable. So...couple-like.

"What song is this?" I ask.

"Oh my God! You've never heard of Billie Ellish. Gah... this is one of my favorite songs by her! She's just so good." She pumps her fist in the air, dancing in her seat and singing along.

"What's it called?"

"Bad Guy."

"Interesting…"

She lightly smacks my arm. "Don't tell me you hate it."

"Never said that… it's just interesting…"

"Uh huh…"

A few seconds later, I'm pulling up in front of Rising Tides Art Gallery and slow to a stop. Mia looks at the window, then looks back at me. "Why are we here?"

"Wait and see." I smile at her. Every fiber in me hopes this isn't a bad decision on my part. I've gone back and forth on the decision, but even if she hates me for it, someone else needs to see her art. To enjoy it like I do. I've done my research, and if you can get in here, you've made it.

"Okay…" I turn off the car, pulling the keys from the ignition and get out, walking around the front of the car to open her door for her.

Lending her my hand as she steps up onto the curb, her sparkling pools of unending eyes find mine. It's clear she knows exactly where we are and that in itself holds promise for me. Walking to the front door of the gallery, I yet again hold it for her.

"Thank you," she says with a smile before stepping inside.

"I love this place. I've always dreamed of showing off my artwork here. Only the best of the best gets picked."

"You want to walk around?"

"Of course. I haven't been here in a while." We walk through every exhibit looking at every single piece that lines the walls. Some are dark, others light and bright. Every painting or sculpture is a contrast to the one beside it, almost like they planned it out this way.

I find myself looking sideways at some of the pieces. Some are confusing, and you have to wonder what they were thinking when they created it. They're odd, and most I don't understand, but I watch Mia as she spends time analyzing each. The look of pensive admiration crosses her face as we stop at one.

Sometimes she chews her bottom lip like she really wants to get inside what's going on. I imagine her crawling into the brain of the artist and examining each neuron used in creating such masterpieces.

As if she can tell where each brushstroke comes from and goes to. To me, they all look like lines on a canvas. But to Mia, they are fantastic pieces of a story. Each with a past and a purpose. Each artist tells a tale of their life. Stories of hope, love, pain, the past, the future, and everything in between. She's in her element and to be able to watch her doing something she loves is nothing short of the perfect afternoon. She tells me little things about each piece as we pass it. Most are artists from the New York area. Her passion for art is endless. I wonder if it's the thing she loves most in this world, even if she claims to not believe in love.

"Brooks," a man says my name from behind us, and I turn to see him walking our way, his arm outstretched to shake my hand. I watch as Mia's mouth drops open in shock.

She leans over before he reaches us and whispers softly, "You know him?" I nod at her and turn back to Mr. Leonard. "Geoffrey."

"I'm so glad you could finally come in." He turns to Mia. "And you must be the impressive Mia Preston I've been hearing about..." Her mouth opens and closes twice, only breath escaping, unable to form words. "I've heard and seen some pretty incredible things about you, Miss Preston."

"W-What... how..." Her eyes lace with confusion as she looks back and forth between us, trying to figure out the game plan.

"Brooks here showed me some pictures of your work, and I'd like to extend an offer to show your work here at the gallery for a month-long show. How would you feel about that?"

She nods excitedly. "Um. I would love to show my work here, but I'm confused. It normally takes months to get a show here, and there's an application and..."

"Well, of course, I'd like to take a look at your pieces in person. Pictures, I'm sure, don't do them justice. I'd like to extend the offer on a preliminary basis if you can bring them in."

"You know, I've been dreaming about showing my work here since I started college. Never in a million years did I ever imagine it becoming a reality. So, I guess all I have to say is thank you for the chance."

"Don't thank me. Your boyfriend practically begged me to offer you a spot, and I can definitely see why. You've got an incredible gift, Mia. I don't say that lightly. I've turned many artists away from showing their work in this gallery."

"Boyfriend..." The smile that's been covering her face leaves at the mere mention of me being anything other than just her friend and fuck buddy. It hurts, painfully hard. Of course, she won't see me as anything more. Mia doesn't do boyfriends. She doesn't believe in love. She'd told me all along, and my damn hopeful heart had hoped that maybe I was the one that'd make a difference. I can't blame her. At least she's honest about it.

"He's not my boyfriend... he's my..."

"Roommate." I supply the words, afraid of what she'll say next.

"Oh, I was under the impression." He looks between us. "My apologies."

"No worries."

"So... you're still interested in doing a show with us?" he says, looking at Mia.

"If it's okay with you, I'd like to have a couple days to think it over." Well, at least she's going to think about it. I didn't think it would be a big deal.

"Sure, Mia. You take a couple days and let me know. Sooner rather than later would be best, though." He winks.

They talk for a few more minutes before she turns to leave

through the same doors we'd walked through just half an hour ago. She whirls at me once we reach the car. "You had no right."

"What are you talking about, Mia?"

"You had no right to show someone else my paintings. Those are mine." She points to her chest. "Personal. That came from me— my thoughts, opinions, feelings. Now you've gone and shown it to someone else. How could you?"

"They're fucking good, Mia. I know it. Geoffrey knows it now. You know it, even when you choose not to believe it. Besides, you show them off at other galleries, what makes this one any different?"

"Don't tell me what to believe."

"Heaven forbid I try to do something nice for you."

"I don't need nice, Brooks. You aren't my boyfriend. You're my roommate. So what, I kissed you. I broke my own rules. Get over it."

"Why are you being such a bitch right now, Mia? You don't mean that."

"Maybe I do, Brooks. Maybe I've always been one. Remove those rose-colored glasses, and we'll find out, won't we."

"I don't understand."

"No, clearly, you don't. I just can't be around you right now. I need some… space."

"Fine. You want space, done. I'll just go into work like I planned to anyhow. Maybe Eddie will give me a few extra hours so you can have all the time you want to figure it out."

I storm off from the gallery, leaving her there staring after me. Or maybe she isn't, I don't give a flying fuck. She isn't ready to accept something real, and she's lashing out because of how she's feeling inside. Every border wall she's placed around her heart is masking her real feelings and instead of accepting it, she's going to fight it. So be it. If I have to fight her to get through to her, I will. Even if it kills me. Even if she hates me afterward.

Luckily, Topsy Turvy isn't too far down the road from the gallery, so I walk there. A cold breeze blows around my shoulders and a chill creeps down my spine. Pulling open the door, I'm hit with the all too familiar bar smell. Eddie's eyes are wide as he watches me walk behind the bar.

He furrows his eyebrows. "Thought you called off today?"

I shrug it off like it doesn't matter. "Thought it was worth it, I was wrong. Here now. Keep me as long as you want."

He nods. "Alright, well Zara's here. Guess I'll tell her she can head out."

"Thanks, man." He doesn't ask anymore questions.

Setting up my station, I start working, getting lost in the endless movements of bartending. One shot, two beers, one fuzzy navel. I chide myself for wondering if Mia got home okay and if she's ever going to let me in. Focus on the drinks and the customers.

"Well, you're a sight for sore eyes, boy." I watch as Willie meanders up to the bar and takes a seat in front of me.

"Sure I am right now."

"Something happen with your lady friend?"

"Yeah, guess you could say that."

"You wanna tell me what you did?"

My eyes widen. "What I did?"

He quirks an eyebrow. "Yep, normally the guy does something to mess it all up, so out with it. What'd ya do?"

"I got her a gallery showing at Rising Tides Art Gallery up the road. Don't know what's so wrong with doing something nice for her."

"Huh, didn't know your lady painted..."

I smile. "Sure does, she's great at it too. Which is why I thought she'd like to get into Rising Tides. I found a flyer in the kitchen with the gallery name on it."

He points at me. "See, there's your first problem son, thinking.

Second problem, you took something of hers and shared it with some-one else without telling her about it or asking if it was okay. I imagine her artwork is personal to her. It's something she created. Maybe it's not meant to be shared with the world. Maybe she paints for her."

"But she shares it with other galleries. I don't see the difference. Plus, she said she would think about it."

"Course she did. She'd be too smart to turn it down."

I sigh. "Then I don't get it..."

He makes a weird noise of agreement. "She's a woman. Look, don't you go trying to understand them, because I have news for you. You'll never ever figure it out. Sure, after a while, you'll be able to read her tells. But it's what makes them such an interesting creature. Keeps ya guessing."

My shoulders lift in a huff, and I blow out a long breath. "Yeah, well, it's annoying. One minute she's hot, the next she's cold and closed off. Anyhow, what can I get ya?"

"My usual, please."

"Whiskey, it is."

I allow my eyes to drift over the patrons seated at the bar. My eyes make another pass when someone familiar catches my eye. No... it can't be. My eyes find him again, and it's not just a figment of my imagination. He's a dead man walking. One I thought I'd never see again. My feet travel toward him without being told, but they move slowly as if he'll disappear if I walk too fast.

"Matt?" My voice seems unsure, but how can I be? It's been years since I've seen him. I'd know him anywhere, though. Why is he here of all places? At Topsy Turvy.

His eyes find me, widening. It's unexpected. "Brooks?"

My mouth drops open. I thought I was going crazy seeing things. "You're actually here. I was told... I never believed the stories, but dude, you dropped off the face of the earth without a trace. They said you were... dead."

151

He shakes his head, and I walk around the bar to hug my old friend. "I bet they did. Spiritually dead is the same as dead to those brainwashers."

"But how…"

He shrugs like it's not a big deal. "Simple, I ran in the middle of the night. I couldn't exactly say goodbye and take the chance that someone would come after me." I nod my head, understanding completely.

"Why here?" I'm confused.

"There are others here from the compound. We all ran at the same time. I couldn't stand there and let the leaders run my life anymore. I wouldn't marry who they wanted me to, I couldn't do that life. They wanted to strap me down to two wives, and you know how I feel about that kind of thing."

Wait, did he say there are others? "Who else?"

"Thomas and Samantha."

I can't help the thousands of questions currently pounding my brain. I've thought he was gone for years, and now he's here right in front of me. Living and breathing. "What do you do for work? Where do you live? Man, I thought you were dead for years, and now you're here out of nowhere."

"I own an adult club called Pelle. I changed my name too, so no one could find me. I go by Donatello Knight these days."

"Ok… Donatello… What's an adult club?"

"Oh, come on, Brooks. I know you don't live that far under a rock."

"Hold up… you own a sex club?"

"That's exactly what I mean."

"Damn, that's a 365 flip from life in the compound, isn't it?"

"Told you. I wasn't cut out for compound life. You should come some time. Let's just say it's a night you won't soon forget."

"Um…"

"Tell you what, I'll leave your name with my doorman, and if you show up, cool. If not, also cool."

"But why are you here at Topsy Turvy?"

"Oh, right." He points to Zara. "I can't get her out of my head. Sexy little thing shows up at my club a couple of nights a week, and she's like a drug I can't quit. Has a taste for domination, and I enjoy letting her live out every fantasy. I'd say she's my new flavor of the month, but there's something more than that going on. Something about her…. I just can't put my finger on it."

"You like her."

He takes a drink of his gin and tonic and swallows. "Something like that. It's just that I've never met anyone like her. Zara doesn't back down from a challenge, and she doesn't always let me get what I want. She pushes back, and I live on it."

"I get it. Seems to me I'm having my own challenges these days."

The door to the bar opens, and a whiff of cotton candy blows my way. My gothic, combat boot wearing pixie is here. My eyes lock on her endless blues as she walks through the front door. Wearing the same clothes from earlier. Her small body doesn't even take up half of the door frame, and she looks like absolute perfection.

He turns to follow my gaze before clearing his throat. "Yeah, there must be something in the water. The girls here are quite different from the ones back home, and I'll be the last to complain. We can chat later."

Maybe I am wearing rose-colored glasses, but damn them, because she's perfect for me, even though her actions cut deep. I'd done something nice for her, and she'd blown up in my face. The worst part is that I'm willing to let her hurt me again and again if it means eventually I'll get through to her.

But I still firmly believe that I didn't deserve to be treated that way, so I don't smile at her. Not this time. Ignoring her, I walk back and attend to the guy at the end of the bar and a few college girls that dropped by to drink.

Sophie walks up behind me at the bar and winks when I turn around, but it falls flat. She's a pretty blonde, but she does nothing for me. I want to flirt back so badly, but my cruel, stupid hurt won't let me. It keeps whispering that even flirting is cheating and although I know it's true, I hate it. We aren't even together, so why does it matter?

I want to be mad at her. To hurt her the way she hurt me. It's idiotic. To blame her for being so closed off, for not letting me in, but the truth is I can't. *Stupid, stupid heart.*

She makes her way to the bar and sits down. Walking toward her, I pretend to be oblivious to the little tick in my heart every time we're in the same room together. "Hey, Brooks." Her voice is smooth like honey—the voice of an angel in devil clothes.

"What can I get you?" I keep my voice monotone as if she's just another customer.

"I want to talk."

"What's changed from the gallery?"

"Don't be cruel, Brooks."

My heart does that damn tick again. "Don't be cruel? Really, Mia? I did something nice for you. Something really nice, and you treated me like I was the fucking scum of the earth for doing so."

"So, what? You decided to come here and flirt with fucking Sophia, Brooks? You thought that was the best decision?" Sophia huffs and leaves the bar with a mumbled bitch under her breath.

"For the record, she was flirting with me. Did you see me once flirt back? No. You didn't. Because my stupid fucking heart wants only you. Every time you're near me, it rapid fires. When you're not around, I can't stop thinking about you. I want to do nice things for you. Be with you. So, sue me. Why is that so wrong?"

I run my hand through my hair roughly. "I know the word

boyfriend is too much for you, but Mia, that cuts really fucking hard when you dismiss me like I am not a part of your world. I've been inside you. We've made love, whether you choose to believe it or not and I refuse to accept that there's nothing between us. Refuse to because I know there is and if you choose not to accept that, then so be it, but I'm tired of hiding my feelings when I'm around you. I won't hurt myself anymore."

"Brooks…"

"I don't know what you want from me, Mia."

"We never said we were dating Brooks. We were fucking. I made it clear. You weren't supposed to go and fall in love with me. I made you promise not to break that rule. There was always an end game with us."

"Well, that's my fault because it looks like that's what happened. I broke my own damn rule."

"I'm sorry."

"Just… Give me a fucking chance to prove to you that I'm not that idiot. The one that broke your heart. The one that got you so fucked up that you lost all hope in men. I am not him, and I guarantee you I will never treat you the way he did. I just want one chance, Mia. One single chance. It's going to be up to you, though. None of this wishy-washy shit. So when you decide, better make damn sure you stick to it because there are no take-backs."

"Okay. I get it."

I nod. My heart is on the line, and the cards lay in her hands. She'll decide where this goes from here on out. She slips behind the bar and starts getting her station set up.

"What are you doing?"

"Getting set up. I work tonight."

Great.

Fourteen

Brooks

It's been three hours since we talked. Now, she's clearly avoiding me. Every time I try to talk to her about earlier, she walks away or magically finds another customer to help. I've watched her laugh and flirt with every single guy here tonight, and I know she knows I've been watching because her eyes always trail back to me.

Mia's head tips back in a laugh as she brings a table their food. It's not busy tonight, but sometimes she runs food. Like she's running food to the man I've thought was dead for years. I still can't truly wrap my head around the fact that he's been on the outside this whole time. A part of me is mad that he didn't take me when he left, but that was years before I realized I wanted out. He'd been one of my few friends on the inside, and I always wondered what happened to him.

Some of the guys she's been delivering drinks to are getting a little wasted and handsy. I've been keeping my eyes on them every time she meanders past. One of the guys at the high top across the way keeps staring at her with a look that I know all too well. I've found myself giving her that same look time and time again. She evades his arm for the first time but isn't as lucky the second time. He reaches for her again, successfully looping his arm around her waist.

I hear his words as they slur from his mouth. "Come on, sweets, let me touch you. We could have such a good time together."

My blood boils. Only it's more anger than jealousy. Although, the little green monster sits just below the surface.

She smiles and tries to step away from him but his grip gets tighter. Rage lights my veins on fire as I watch her face go from a smile to something else. There's a fucking line that you just don't cross when it comes to women, and he's coming bouldering across it in flying colors. I saw too much violence against women back home. I won't stand for it here too. I drop my glass on the bar top, not even waiting for it to shatter before I hop over the bar, my fists balled in anger.

She escapes his arm right as I get to the table. Mia looks over at me with wide eyes, not sure what to do next. She moves farther away from him.

"Brooks, don't."

I pull her behind me and stare down the idiot that dares lay a hand on a woman, mine. She's mine now and forever. I don't care if she sees my angry caveman or not. Woman or not, if she says no, you back down.

"Apologize to the lady," I say, staring down at Captain grabby hands.

He holds up his hands. "Look, man, we were just having a little fun. Didn't mean any trouble."

"Didn't look that way to me. Looked like you were touching her without her permission, and last time I checked that's not okay. It's never, ever okay." Mia touches my arm, but I jerk away.

A brief turn tells me that Matt- eh, Donatello—is here for backup if I need it. It's a small show of solidarity. It gives me peace knowing he's got my back. He nods at me, standing behind Mia.

"It's fine, Brooks. It happens." She reaches out to touch me, trying to soothe the anger writhing within.

"No, Mia, it's not. It's never okay to be disrespected. " I go in for a kiss before she can stop me. My lips press against hers roughly, and she gasps at the force of it. "You are mine," I whisper gruffly.

A soft "Oh" falls from her lips at my command. Then my lips are back on hers, kissing furiously. Both of us grabbing for each other trying to pull ourselves into each other more. She melts into me.

"Damn, Brooks. Get a damn room." I see a grin split across Donatello's face.

I shake my head, looking back at Mia's gorgeous face and cotton candy hair. "We're leaving."

"But… I'm not done with my…" She points back to the bar.

"Doesn't matter. Not important. We have issues to discuss and makeup sex to be had."

"How do you know about makeup sex, Brooks?"

"I've been researching just for you."

"Lead the way, handsome. I'm down for whatever you want."

I want to pick her up like a caveman, swat her ass, and leave the building but there's a couple of things I need to do first. Like, make sure Zara can keep covering for me. Luckily, when Eddie told her to go home earlier, she decided to just stay. I probably have Donatello to thank for that. He's been chatting her up all shift.

I walk over to the bar but don't even have to ask when I see her.

"Go get your girl," she whisper-shouts, looking to Mia over my shoulder and winks. I nod once, not taking another second to think it over. I grab Mia by the hand and rush to the door like I'm walking on hot coals. Eddie shakes his head and tries to seem angry, but at the last minute, a smirk tears across his face as we pass, Zara catcalls in the background at us.

We run the whole way to the apartment since it's only two blocks from the bar, her car completely forgotten. Bounding up the stairs with Mia on my heels I quickly unlock the door, fling it open, and turn around to grab her, dragging her inside with me. I'm being a whole lot reckless. The door bangs against the wall behind us, and I know there's no way there isn't a hole. I'll repair it later. I don't have time right now. I've gone full caveman, but I don't care. I need to be inside her like it was yesterday.

Kicking the door shut, I back her against the wall. "You think it's okay to flirt with other guys all evening? You think I'll just sit by and not watch as you twirl that cotton candy hair and laugh just a little too loud at jokes that aren't funny? Are you trying to make me jealous, Mia?"

"Why? You jealous, Brooks? Does it make you royally pissed to see someone put his hands on me, knowing that I only want yours? Does it make you jealous knowing that while you stood and flirted with Sophie, I sat and wished it was me? I hate these fucking feelings I'm having. I hate that they exist, but the sad truth I've been pushing away is that I do. I have so many fucking feelings for you. You aren't my boyfriend, so I don't need you to stick up for me."

"You may not want to label us, Mia, and that's fine. You don't wanna give whatever is going on between us a title, that's fine too. I'm completely okay with going at your pace, but I will tell you this now. You. Are. Mine. So, you tell yourself whatever makes you comfortable because I'm not going anywhere. No matter how unsteady your feelings are toward me. I'm in this for you."

She smiles. "So you were jealous?"

"Hell yes, I was jealous. I'm a greedy bastard, Mia. I want all of it. Every single scrap, or morsel you'll give me because my heart is a fucked up asshole and only wants you. So if you need something, you come to me. You want to be fucked, you ask. You want attention, you get it from me. You want me to make love to you so hard we can't breathe afterward, also me. Welcome to the rest of your life, sweetheart. I'm going to be the air you breathe, every dream you've ever had, and the worst nightmare to anyone who dares to lay a finger on you again. You got it?"

"So, you're going to make love to me now? Have us some nice romantic makeup sex?"

"No, I'm going to fuck you. I'm going to do to you what I've been dreaming about and researching. I want to hear my name tremble from your lips as you come. So you remember that you belong to me. So you remember that every time my dick thrusts inside you it's me doing it. So you remember that you're fucking mine. Every time you walk afterward, you're going to remember what it feels like to have my dick inside you. Then maybe you won't be tempted to look for it elsewhere. Ever again because my sweet, sweet Pixie—there's no getting rid of me now."

"Damn... is this bossy Brooksy? Cause this is hella hot."

"Good, now strip. You wanted bossy, you wanted to push me, to make me jealous? Now you get to see what happens when you accomplish all three."

Mia whips her oversized sweatshirt over her head and flings it to the side, leaving her naked except for her leggings. My eyes trail over her body from head to toe, taking in just how sexy she is when she's flushed. Rose red paints her cheeks in need, and she bites her lip in anticipation of what is to come. I don't wait for her to take off her leggings.

"I may need help with these," she says, holding out her leggings.

"Gladly." My strength is so raw, so pure right now as I rip them from her body. A gasp escapes her lips, and I can't help but love the fact that she's completely okay with my manly man behavior. It's not tender; it's rough and desperate. Needy for her attention, all of it.

"You make every other woman on this earth dull in comparison to you. You're fucking gorgeous, and I can't even believe that you're here with me." I slid my hand up along her spine and bury it in the fullness of her hair, cradling the back of her head as I look into her eyes.

"I've never wanted anyone else as much as I want you, Brooks. It's a crazy feeling. I've shut people out for so long that it became second nature. You... you came in here and basically demanded my heart beat for you, and the motherfucker listened."

I point to my room. "Need you on the bed. Can't guarantee I'll be gentle either."

"Good. I hear gentle is totally overrated anyhow. I need you to boss me around. Use me, Brooksy."

"Don't call me Brooksy. Not when I'm being manly."

She laughs. "Duly noted."

I strip as quickly as I can, discarding shoes, pants, and shirt as I stalk her into my bedroom. She backs up until the backs of her knees hit the bed and she's forced to sit down. Her head's the same level as my dick when I approach her seated position.

But she isn't going to suck me. Not yet at least. I need her, but she needs to be ready for me first. I pull her up against me hard so she can feel what she's doing to me. She holds my gaze as I slip my fingers down her side, teasing in circles as I go. She's tense with desire. Down her side, over her hips and around to the front. My hand slips between her thighs, while my fingertips graze up the inside until I feel her wet heat greeting me like it always does.

"Oh, Mia." I tsk. "Wet for me already? What, can't talk when my hands are on you?"

She gasps, thrusting her hips forward toward me as I slip my finger between her folds and rub against the pearl of nerves at the top.

"Does my Mia like it when I talk to her dirty? When I tell her what I'm feeling? When I tell her that it's so fucking sexy that she's already wet and ready to take my dick."

"Mmmm... I like... I like..."

"Words, Mia. Say the words," I moan at her, my voice deep and raspy.

"I like bossy Brooks."

"Good." I run my fingers over her wet opening again and again. She reaches out and grasps my shoulders, arching into me, begging me for more with her body and I won't disappoint. I lean down to her as if I'm going to kiss her, but refrain. I simply stand there, sharing her air, breath for breath. She parts her lips when she feels my breath on them as if she's begging for off-limits kisses. I pause momentarily, my eyes soaking up every square inch of the expression on her face, memorizing it.

"You like that, my dirty little Pixie. You like it when I part these wet lips with my fingers and thrust into you?" My words come out at the same time I shove inside her. I capture her moan with my lips, letting it sear me to a third-degree burn. How is she always so fucking tight? God, it's heaven.

Her fingers grip my shoulders tighter as her hips move to ride the fingers I have buried within her. Harder and harder, she moves over me. I move my hand to her clit like I know she craves, and she erupts, letting out a cry, my name on her lips.

Her wetness covers my hand as she comes. I slowly slip my fingers from her core as I lean down to bite one breast and then the other. Raising up again slightly, I hold her gaze as I bring my fingers to my lips and lick them dry, one at a time. Her moan at the sight of me tasting her on my fingers, almost has me losing control. The taste of her alone is the best treat. Sweet like her cotton candy hair.

I turn her around to face the bed pulling her hips back until she's almost folded over into a ninety-degree angle. Perfect. My mouth water at the sight of her glorious ass bare in front of me. I lean down for just a little taste. "Ouch," she squeaks at me. "What'd ya do that for?"

I shrug my shoulders. "Wanted to. I own this body right now. If I want to bite it, so you know what it feels like to have my teeth on you, I will."

Mia

Every single one of my fantasies is coming true. Every time Zara talked about her session with Donatello, I'd wondered what it would feel like to be dominated that way. Brooks is not a dominant by far, but he's definitely bossier than I thought he would be, and it turns me the hell on. My eyes slide shut, waiting for the next thing he'll do to me.

I stand waiting for the blunt end of his cock to shove through my entrance and push me to ecstasy, but it doesn't come. Instead, I feel the end of his tongue circle my clit, driving me insane. When he fingered me and then licked his fingers afterward, I was gone.

Talk about insanely hot. I rock back against him as he demands everything from me, ringing yet another orgasm from my body. I'm spiraling in a matter of minutes since the last time. His teeth graze over my clit, and I almost lose it.

The man is getting good at this stuff, and it's so damn sexy. The fact that he's researched what will turn on a girl does something to me. And not just for any girl, he'd researched for me, because he hasn't been with anyone else. We're together almost all the time.

Another lick of my seam tears a scream from my mouth. His tongue's working me like a man starved. One more swipe, and then I lose his heat. Until the head of his cock finds my entrance and dives deep with one long stroke. I whimper, and he groans as he enters me.

I love the way he stretches me out. He stands still until he's fully seated, and I've adjusted to his large size. Dude has a huge cock, and it feels gloriously delightful between my thighs. His balls rest against my clit, and each time he thrusts into me, they smack me. He's literally spanking my bundle of nerves with his balls, but I want him to do the real thing. I peek over my shoulder and lick my lips. Brooks looks over from the view of his cock thrusting into me, and I wink. "I want you to spank me, Brooks."

"You dirty girl. Wanting me to spank her sexy little ass?"

"Do it."

"Fuck…" he whispers, then he answers my request. He smacks me once against one cheek and then a little harder against the other. "You like that, baby?"

"Mmhmm. Do it again." And he does as requested.

Raising up against him, my ass burns from his last spank, I wrap an arm around the back of his neck. My back to his front. His warm breath assaults the back of my neck as he groans. His hands leave my hips and trail up my sides, wrapping big palms around my breasts and squeezing while he hammers in and out of me.

"I love your boobs, Mia."

"Mmmm." I love the way he squeezes them. It's like he holds back all his power, afraid he'll hurt me, and I love him for it. That thought terrifies me. *Love.* There's no way I'm in love with Brooks Jansen, right?

The scary thing is… it didn't freak me out as much as it did the first time I thought about it. This time it feels real. Like it isn't something I should be terrified of any longer. I'm starting to trust that Brooks won't let me down like everyone else in my life has before him.

I want to kiss him so badly, but I'm not about to ask him to stop so we can change positions. He's hitting just the right spots. Why mess up a good thing?

The familiar light-headed, lost in a daze feeling rushes over me, and the urge to let go pushes at me. "Please, Brooks, Please" I beg, hoping that he'll grant me mercy and give me one more orgasm to match the other two he'd already given me tonight. His fingers slide down and find my clit, circling and circling it. A few more swipes and I shatter completely, calling out his name as if he's my only salvation. Now, there's an idea.

He presses his forehead to my neck and shatters with me. "I love you, Mia Preston," he whispers it and then freezes, almost shocked that he'd uttered it aloud. "There is no one else. It has only ever been you."

"Wait, what about the other girl? The one you were learning to pleasure?"

He shakes his head. "There is no other girl."

"No?"

"Only you." He turns me around, kissing my forehead. "You don't have to say it back, Mia. But now you know."

My voice is shaky as I respond, "If it helps, I do really like you. I'm just not there yet."

"I know, and it's completely fine. I have all the time in the world to make your heart beat for me, my little Pixie girl. You shoot up a flare when you're ready, and I'll be here to see it."

Fifteen

Mia

Brooks left me earlier this morning to go into work and help get things set up at the bar. I'd gotten up with him while he showered. We had a quickie after he got back from his run, and then he'd left with a kiss to the forehead.

I'm starting to like this domesticated person I've become. I crawl back into bed and try to fall asleep, hoping that this queasy feeling will go away. When I wake again, it rears its ugly head in vengeance. I've spent the last couple of days trying to figure out what I've eaten that's caused such a horrid stomach bug.

Zara will be showing up soon, and I need to get up and look presentable at the least. I debate calling her multiple times today and telling her not to show up, but I know I've pushed her off too much lately, and I can't keep doing it. She's my bish, and I love her ass, even if she does annoy the piss out of me.

A weird ass knock sounds on the door, and there's only one person I know that knocks like she does. Walking over to the door, I unlock and open it. "Bout damn time, woman. I've been standing out here waiting forever."

"Jesus, Zara. You just knocked, chill the hell out."

"Okay, captain cranky. What's wrong with you?"

"I think I'm dying and the only thing that sounds good right now is baked lays with chocolate sauce."

Zara lifts a brow at me. "That's an odd request…"

"Who the hell knows, but it's basically all I've wanted lately. Can't stop thinking about them. Basically craving them as much as Brooks' dick these days."

Zara tilts her head. "You're a little snappy today… you doing okay? Maybe you should smoke one out. Help those jitters you've got pouring through your body."

"That's the other thing! I have zero desire to light up right now, and every time I think about it…" I shake my head and gag. "Yeah. Nope."

"Interesting. Any other issues?"

"Good Lord, I feel like I could sleep for a week uninterrupted and still not want to wake up."

"Do you mind if I light one?"

I wave her off. "Nah, go ahead."

The smell of citrus and weed lines my nose. That gagging sensation comes raging back, and I slap my hand over my mouth and run to the bathroom. Just in time to lose the very little contents left in my stomach after puking earlier today. Saliva pools in my mouth, and I know I'm not done yet. I heave again. Zara follows me into the bathroom and holds my hair, rubbing my back. It's embarrassing, but it's nice to have someone there.

She hands me a napkin to wipe my face and a glass of water. "How long has this been going on?"

"The last week. I think I picked up a nasty ass stomach virus somewhere, and I just can't shake it." I take a few small sips from the glass. "Mmm… that helps."

Zara pats me on the back lightly. "You think you're done, or you want to hang out here for a while?"

"I think I'm alright." She helps me up, and we head back to the living room. I flop down in Brooks's ugly recliner and inhale deeply. His scent lingers from the last time he sat here, and it gives me some comfort. Isn't it funny how little things are so important once you take the time to realize the significance of them. "So, what do you think you ate?"

"Brooks cooked steak the other night, but I watched him check the temperature when he was done cooking. It was perfectly cooked. It's the only meat I've eaten lately."

"Other than Brooks' cock for dessert, am I right?" She lifts both hands and high-fives herself. Good. Lord.

I shake my head and laugh, then cringe when my stomach threatens to rumble again. Ugh. This is the worst. I hate puking.

A look of concern crosses her face and then disappears again.

"Wait? What are you not saying…"

"It's just, girl when was your last period."

"I dunno. Why are you worried about it? This is just an… oh…"

She purses her lips. "Is it possible?"

"Are you asking what I think you're asking?"

"Well, you have a lot of the signs, Mia. Can you remember when the last one was?"

I don't want to believe this. "But I'm on the patch."

"I hate to break it to you, but birth control isn't always one hundred percent effective. When was the last time you swapped out your patch?"

"Last month. Aren't those things monthly? Like the shot, right?"

"Mia… I think you have to change those every week…"

I let my eyes count along the tiny dots on the ceiling. *Shit. It's been over a month.*

Better yet, we didn't use a condom once because I told him I was protected.

Oh. My. God.

My head falls to my hands, and I shake it. *How was I so stupid?*

"Fuck..." I drag the k out at the end.

"What?" Zara blurts out. "What is it?"

"I'm an idiot. I was so preoccupied with teaching Brooks sex that I couldn't even remember to change my damn patch."

"Well, before we jump to conclusions. Let's take a test or six."

I nod quickly. "Yes, good idea. I still don't understand how this happened..."

"Hunny, it's very easy to explain. The P goes in the V, and a little swimmer meets a little egg and bada bing bada boom, a baby, happens."

I give her a light shove. "No, no, no. I know that, doofus. I mean how. We haven't even been sleeping together that long..."

"Hunny, you've been fucking like rabbits. It only takes one time to get knocked up."

"Ugh," I groan again.

We both quickly grab our stuff to head out, but before we do, she leans over and hugs me. "Hey, don't freak out yet, Mia. You don't know if you're pregnant, and even if you are, you've got me."

"I'm not sure about any of this," I mumble in a haze. What happens now? What if I really am pregnant? What will Brooks think?

Oh God, I need to tell Brooks... No, I need to know for sure first. My feet take me down the stairs to the ground level, and we walk to Zara's car. She shoves me into the passenger seat and then jumps in to drive.

I groan, leaning against the window while thousands of thoughts plague my brain like pinpricks. *What am I going to do?* I wipe away a few tears that have formed. Suddenly, my crazy emotions start to make sense too. I'm such an idiot.

The ride to the convenience store is utterly silent. It wears on me. The fact that I may have a tiny human growing inside me freaks me the hell out, but I also feel somewhat attached to the idea.

A tiny Brooks and I. A little life. We may or may not have a little peanut on the way. Another tear slips down my cheek, and I wipe it away. I want to break down, shut the world out, and cry myself to sleep, but I can't do that right now.

She pulls up to the curb outside the store, and we get out. My heart is in my chest as we make our way to the aisle that houses pregnancy tests. I've been in this aisle before, but it's not the same. Before it was for condoms, now I'm looking at pregnancy things. Had I been in this aisle a couple of months ago, then maybe I wouldn't now be looking at the pregnancy tests. I internally slap myself. *Knock it the hell off, Mia.*

"How in the hell do you choose? There are like six different choices."

She shrugs and starts pulling them from the shelves into the basket. "Easy. Get one of each. Then you'll know for sure."

"I don't have that much pee, Zar."

"Well, grab some bottled waters on the way out. That'll help the flow. Ha, ha. Get it, flow."

"Not helping…" I mumble. In my haste to get to the store, I completely forgot my wallet. Tears form at the corners of my eyes, and I feel like I'm on the verge of a complete breakdown.

"Oh, good Lord, what now?" Zara looks over at me.

"I forgot my wallet at home."

"No worries. I got you. What are best friends for, right?"

"Thanks, Zar." I smile at her, but it feels fake. I don't know what to think right now. Being pregnant is a huge kink in all of the plans I'd made.

Ha, the girl who doesn't even believe in love gets knocked up. Doesn't it figure?

She pays for the six tests and mouths off to the older checkout lady when she looks at us like prostitutes. This is why we're friends.

Zara looks over at me when we get back in the car. "I can see a million things running through your mind. Look, it's going to be okay."

"It's fucking karma, isn't it, Zar? The girl who doesn't even believe in love is more than likely knocked up. How am I going to do this? How am I going to tell Brooks?"

"I think he's going to be just fine with it, sweets. Like put a ring on your finger and buy you that house on the corner of suburbia with a white picket fence in love with you. I can tell these things."

"And how can you tell that exactly? I'm pretty sure we have the same feelings on love."

"Just because I don't believe it, doesn't mean I'm blind. He's completely gone for you."

"He likes the hot sex we have, that's all."

"You keep telling yourself that if it's how you sleep at night."

"I'm in an emotional crisis over here, and you're telling me how to sleep at night?"

"What did you expect, Mia? We've never been the ooo and ahhh type. You're my bish, you know that, but this is even out of my league. Empathy isn't my strong suit."

We get back to the apartment, and I have an overwhelming feeling of dread pooling in my gut. What if it's really just a stomach flu? Would I really be disappointed? I walk into the bathroom, and Zara follows. "You wanna watch me pee, Zar?"

"No, I'm just providing emotional support shit and all that."

"Thanks." My eyes get misty, and she laughs at me. "Hey, don't laugh."

"If you aren't pregnant, there's something seriously wrong with you…"

I pee in front of my audience of one on six different sticks. "The box says two to three minutes until we know for sure, Mia."

I nod, wanting to scream and cry. I chew my nails down to the nubs, my nerves all jacked up like I shot straight heroin into my veins. *But that would be bad for the baby,* my mind whispers.

The two minute time I set on my phone dings, I look at Zara, and she smiles. "Deep breath, girl."

I'm frozen to the toilet seat. "I can't."

"Okay, I'll look." She takes a moment to look at each stick in front of her, and my heartbeat pounds more with each second that passes. "Well, the jury has decided that you're definitely growing a bun in there." She holds up all six sticks, and sure enough, every single one has a pregnant, two pink lines, or plus signs. My heart sinks. *It's true.*

"Looks like I'm pregnant."

"It's definitely Brooks' right, Mia?"

"Yeah, he's the only one I've been sleeping with. We agreed to be mutually exclusive while we were fucking."

"Well, looks like you're going to be a little bit more exclusive now... you're going to be a mom, Mia."

My heart quakes at the thought. "I'm scared shitless, Zar. I don't know how to do this. You know my childhood. My mother was a piece of shit. What if I end up just like her?" Tears slip down my cheeks, and I can't hide the fear that escapes with each droplet.

She wraps me in a tight hug. "You are better than your mother, Mia. So much better, and I know that you're going to be a great mom."

I notice a tear slide down her face and pull back. "Hold up, is that an emotion, Zara? Do I see a tear shed for me?"

"Get over it. I'm trying to be an emotional support or whatever shit you call it. Now, do you want a hug or not?" I nod my head, resting it on her shoulder as she hugs me. I have no idea where we go from here or what will happen when I finally grow balls and tell Brooks he's going to be a dad.

"Seriously, though, how are you feeling other than scared shitless?"

"I think this is...shocked. Yeah, I think I'm just shocked. I never thought I would be in this position. For years, I've played it safe. Brooks comes crashing in, and all of a sudden I can't tell up from down, left from right, on from off. I don't really know what to think."

"If you want, I can stay here until Brooks gets home? I'll leave once he's here. I just don't want to leave you alone right now."

I nod, stifling a tear. "You're my best bish, and I love your face."

"I love your face too. Now, what was it that you wanted earlier?"

"Wavy lays chips and chocolate sauce?"

"That sounds horrible. Do you have some?"

"Yep, sure do. Chips in the pantry and chocolate sauce is in the fridge."

"Okay, let's go sit on the couch." She tucks me under a blanket on the couch and puffs up the pillow behind me. I can't think straight right now, so I appreciate her thinking for me. I sit there numb, not sure of anything other than the fact that I am for sure pregnant. Running my hands over my still skinny stomach, I wonder when I'll see the baby bump everyone talks about. I hear Zara rustling around in the kitchen, and she appears in front of me minutes later. My weird ass craving in her hands.

"You're my favorite person right now."

"I know I am. Now scoot your fat ass over, I'm sitting on the couch too." I huff, trying my best to pretend to pout over giving up my space but then I just accept it.

My phone dings, and I see Brooks' name pop up on the screen. A smile tugs at the corner of my lips, and I wonder what he's sending me this time. He's been genuinely trying to figure out this sexting thing, and even though it's still horrible, I appreciate the effort he's putting into it.

Brooks: *How's my sexy little pixie doing this afternoon, missing me?*
Me: *You could say that.*

Brooks: *You going to get wet for me later tonight? I want to lick your cotton candy pussy until you swear allegiance to the empire.*

Me: *Oh God, Brooks. Did you really just Star Wars theme sext me?*

Brooks: *Um... *shrugging shoulders emoji**

I can't help but laugh out loud. In the midst of my anxiety, he still manages to take my mind off of it only for just a few seconds. I show it to Zara, and she laughs along with me. "I thought you said he was a boss in bed?"

"Oh, he is. He's just absolutely horrible at sexting, no matter how many times we try."

"Well, I guess it's good he's better in person. I mean, obviously, he must be doing something right, or he's just got mega swimmers. Either way, you're the evidence of his amazing skills in bed. Less than two months, and you've got a bun in the oven."

I throw a pillow at her, shaking my head. "Have you lost your mind?"

"Nope, just wanted to see you smile again. It's been a hard day. Might as well have a little fun with it. Have you figured out how you're going to break the news?"

"I figured I would get a big banner and hang it on the front door so I can really freak him out before he can start processing it when he comes in?"

"That's a horrible idea..."

"I know... I just. I don't want him to think I trapped him into this when I'm the one who told him that I didn't want to label us."

"I don't think he'll think that at all."

"How do you know? You've never even talked to him."

"Not true, sometimes he asks me to hand him a glass or bottle of alcohol at the bar. Occasionally, I'll say something off the wall and mildly inappropriate just to freak him out or give him that cute little blush he gets when he's embarrassed."

A laugh escapes me. "You're a dork. Do you know that?"

"I resent that. I am not a whale penis."

"That is not what a dork is... is it?"

"Look it up, I swear to God, it's a whale dick."

I pull up Google on my phone and type in whale dick called dork. Sure enough, the results pull up, and she's right. I start reading it word for word. "The blue whale's penis, or dork, is the largest that ever existed. The average size for an adult male is 5m (15ft). The testicles weigh 10kg (22lbs)."

"Holy shit. 15 feet long, and it's balls weigh 22lbs! 22lbs! Jesus."

"Told you! Just think about swimming around with that shit. Like, look here, ladies. Look at my enormous whale dick. I don't know about you, but I'd let that shit all hang out like... Look. At. My. Dick, y'all!" The hand gestures match how she's talking, and I'm laughing so hard tears are streaming down my face.

"Isn't that stuff internal on whales? I've never seen a whale swimming around at the aquarium with balls hanging out, and I think you'd notice 22lbs of them!"

"Oh, so maybe he has a blowhole for his dick. Like... peek a boo. Now you see dick, now you don't?"

I'm rolling with laughter, bent over on the couch, holding my stomach.

"And I thought Brooks had a massive dick."

Zara perks up. "Let's take a minute and talk about it, shall we?"

I shake my head. "No...we aren't discussing his dick."

"Then why'd you bring it up, freaking party pooper man. At least tell me how big we're talking here like...average man size five inches... or eight inches... or like huge at nine inches?

"Huge."

She fans her face dramatically. "Damn, you probably got knocked up just looking at the damn thing. One look, and it's like oops, definitely pregnant."

"You're a trip today."

"I aim to please ma'am." She salutes me, and I can't help but grin. "Hey, speaking of shocking news. Did Brooks tell you?"

"Did Brooks tell me what?" I look at her with concern. What am I missing?

"Brooks and Donatello used to be friends. They came from the same compound."

My eyes widen. "Interesting. I noticed them talking at the bar the other day, but I wasn't close enough to hear the conversation."

"It's funny how small this world really is, some days, but apparently that compound turns all the men into sex fiends when they leave." She laughs, and I can't help but shake my head. Brooks is definitely into all the sex. Not that I mind it. "Don said that his name used to be Matt Singleton and that he had to change it when he escaped. What kind of a place did these guys come from? It's just so weird. I can't even imagine how Brooks feels, finding out that one of his friends has been alive this whole time after being told he was dead…"

Is finding this out in addition to my news too much? Anticipation of what Brooks will say creeps back into my cerebral cortex. Similar to a kettle brewing before it whistles. Anxiety snakes its way into every part of my body. I should be worried about why Brooks didn't tell me something so monumental like finding someone he thought was gone, but it's the farthest thing from my mind.

I'm going to be a mom. I've never dreamed of being a mom; hell, I decided my sophomore year of college that boys would only ever be play toys for the rest of my life. Look where that got me…

I wish I'd had a mother that loved me. I wish she had sheltered me from watching her get addicted to drugs and making bad choices.

I have no one to talk to. No one that can give advice to calm me down and tell me that everything's going to be okay even though it managed to fall apart brilliantly in the course of just an hour. Zara's older than me by five years, and although we goof off and act like idiots most of the time, she's the closest thing I have to a big sister. I have Macy too, but she's off living with her dog rescue sex god. Too busy to be bothered with my nonsense. And she doesn't need to deal with my issues either.

Me: *When are you going to be home tonight?*
Brooks: *Same time as always. You need anything on my way home? I can stop. I don't mind.*

Swoon! Why is he always so nice, I just don't understand?

Me: *No, I'll see you when you get here.*
Brooks: *Miss you.*
Me: *Miss you too.*

He'd taken to texting me randomly and telling me he misses me. The first couple of times, I tell him it isn't possible that he misses me because he's only been gone a few hours, and he responds that he'll always miss me when I'm not with him because I'm home for him. He hasn't pushed me again or mentioned anything about wanting more or to label us, and I'm happy with that. He's slowly letting me come to terms on my own without feeling pressured. I don't do well under pressure—case in point.

After setting the phone down, I lay back and prop up my feet.

"Was that Brooks?" Zara looks over at my phone.

"Yep, just checking to see when he was going to be done tonight."

"And…"

"Same time as always." Looking at the clock, I mentally count down the minutes and seconds I have until he gets here. Fifty-five minutes stand between me and the biggest conversation I will ever have in my life. When I asked Brooks to move in with me, I never realized it would change the rest of my life, literally.

Thirty minutes later, and my skin is coated with sweat. My hands are clammy, and I'm pacing the room. Zara keeps telling me to sit down, but I can't. I have to walk, do something because my nerves feel like a spark plug waiting to be lit. Tiny pin pricks that sting just enough to be irritating. Things will either go well tonight, or they will go horribly wrong. Given my past and everything bad that's ever happened, I'm thinking the odds aren't in my favor for a good outcome.

Admitting that I don't have feelings and hoping that Brooks is happy is dirty because it's a blatant lie. I want him to be happy because I care. I just hope that when the time comes, he doesn't leave me shattered on the floor, split open with gaping wounds.

For once I want someone in my corner. Someone willing to fight for me. Who will set off flares just to remind me that he needs me as much as I need him.

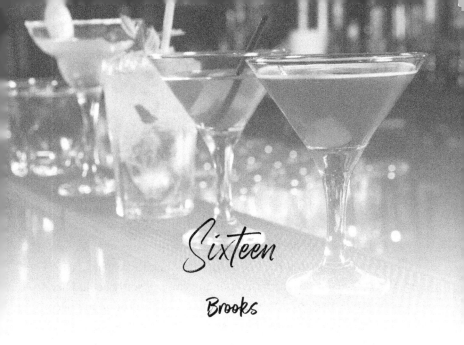

Sixteen

Brooks

Anxiety swarms through my veins like angry bees. As I stand outside, I calm my breathing. A sense of foreboding overwhelms me.

Mia's never texted me to ask when I was coming home before, so I'm not sure what I'm about to walk into. Cement sits in my gut, and worry ebbs and flows in my mind. Is she going to kick me out? Stop having sex with me? I still need time... time to convince her of how good we are together.

Opening the door slightly, I catch sight of Mia, and it has my nerves standing up at attention. Mia is pacing and cracking her knuckles, an anxious habit I've seen her doing previously.

Obviously, something has her worked up, and I want to run to her and fix everything with a big ass hug. I don't know the reason for the waterworks streaming down her face. Her makeup is smudged and trailing tracks down her cheeks. She's the cutest little raccoon ever.

My heart beats as if it may just rip from my chest to get to her. "Mia, what's wrong? What happened? You're freaking me out right now." She runs for me, and I brace myself to catch her as she launches herself into my waiting arms. I pull her close and inhale her cotton candy scent. My lips press a gentle kiss on her forehead. She's not warm... so she's not sick. I can mark that off the list. I see Zara getting her stuff together in the living room, and she gives me a warm smile. Mia leaves me momentarily to say goodbye to Zara, and I don't miss when she whispers, "You're right, one look does it."

I'm confused by her comment, but I don't question it. Zara is odd, to say the least, but she's good for Mia. She's there when I can't be. She lets herself out the front door and closes it softly behind her.

Mia strolls back over to me, looping her arms around my neck and kissing me with white-hot passion unlike anything she's given me before... as if she's pouring her heart and soul into this kiss. That's gotta be a good thing, right? Maybe this means she isn't kicking my ass to the curb.

She pulls back to look at me. "How was your night?"

An odd question, but I'll bite. Something's clearly bugging her, so I'll let her tell me in her own time. "It was kind of dull. I have something to tell you."

She looks unsure but nods. "Okay?"

"You know Donatello, right? He's been hanging out with Zara?"

"Yes..."

"We used to be friends at the compound. He was almost 14 years older than me, but he was kind. I thought for years that he was dead because that's what we'd been told..."

She smiles at me. "Why didn't you tell me sooner? Zara just spilled the beans."

"It was just recently that I found out. I guess you could say I've been trying to process it all."

She nods. "I guess that's understandable." Her bottom lip worries, and I can tell she's about to tell me what's going on, so I shut up and wait. "Brooks, I need to tell you something. Will you come sit with me on the couch?" She grabs my hand, leading me into the living room, and we both take a seat. She clasps my hands in hers and leans in close. This isn't helping my nerves at all.

Fingers and toes metaphorically crossed that she doesn't tell me she's dying or some shit like that. I can't handle it. My mind blanks to the worst possible things.

Mia sits back on the couch and takes a deep breath. She's clearly been crying, and my heart breaks for the fear in her eyes. Fear from what she's going to tell me? "We're having a baby," she whispers almost too softly for me to hear, but I do.

My world comes to a slamming halt. Am I still breathing? My heart is beating. I must be breathing, but did she just say. "W-what?" I stammer.

"I'm pregnant, Brooks. It's yours."

I blow out a breath and run a hand through my hair. "But how did this happen?"

"Well, your P went in my V and..."

"No, I know how reproduction works, Mia. It's just... I thought..."

"I know. My doctor switched me to the birth control patch, and I never changed it. You're supposed to change it every week, and it's been a hell of a lot longer. I'm so sorry, Brooks." She chokes up on her words, and I see another tear slip down her cheek. I can see the fear of everything that's happened, and the last thing I want to do is blow up at her. I'm freaking the hell out, but I need to be strong for her. Her blue eyes are alive with fear, the unknown. She's probably afraid I'll run.

So many questions tangle inside my brain, my thoughts are shot to hell. I'm completely in shock. I always wanted kids one day, but I thought I'd be more settled than I am now, but I love Mia. I know that for sure. So I'll do whatever she wants to keep my girl and our child.

"Hey, this is not your fault. It takes two to make a baby. You didn't get yourself knocked up, pretty sure I helped with that part."

"I know, but I still feel like this all got so screwed up."

I want to demand that we get married, that she let me make an honest woman of her. All of my church lessons pound my brain, saying she can't be an unwed mother, but Mia hasn't even told me she loves me yet. So marriage is out of the question. I know she'll explode if I even suggest it. She looks over my face, trying to get a read on me.

Endless blue tear-filled eyes find mine. "What are you thinking, Brooks?"

"Everything in my gut is screaming, let's get married tomorrow, but I won't ask. You don't love me, and you're not ready, so it would be pointless to even suggest such a thing."

Mia removes her hands from my grip, and time slams to a halt. She slowly inches away from me on the couch. I know in an instant I'd fucked up. That wasn't the right thing to say, but it's true. She wouldn't say yes to me. "What, so I'm not even worthy of a simple wedding proposal because I went and got myself knocked up? Is that what you're saying?"

"Shit, no. That came out all sorts of wrong, Mia. I love you. I would marry you in an instant. When I marry you, I want you to know that it's not because I knocked you up. Marrying me is not dependent on having a child together. I want you forever. Always. So when I ask you to marry me, Mia, you're going to know I'm all in. Talking about forever."

"Well, isn't that romantic. You're right, Brooks, I wouldn't have said yes, but at least I would've had the chance to voice my opinion on it before you just shut it down without even asking me first. You made the decision for me."

I furrow my eyebrows. "You can't even tell me you love me, Mia. You don't want us to be labeled. Any time the word boyfriend is mentioned, you lash out. What are we doing, Mia? Am I just your fuck toy when I'm convenient? You're close to me in the apartment, but outside of it, I'm just a roommate. Shred that inner badass and let me in a little. You either want this, or you don't. I won't be your fucking secret, Mia. I won't let you do that to me."

She shoves off the couch and stands up, pointing at me, a tear slipping down her cheek again. "I don't believe in love. You know that."

I scoff, "It's not love that holds you back. No. It's the fear that you're going to let someone in and give them your heart and they're going to destroy it. Well, you don't have to worry about that with me, Mia. You want to know why? Because here's the fucking truth, if your heart gets destroyed mine will be shredded on the floor right beside yours."

Her shoulders shake with quiet tears. "I'm freaking out, Brooks."

"And you think I'm not? I'm terrified."

"I'm not ready to be a mother."

"Look at me, Mia. I'm not ready to be a father, but we're in this now. We will figure this out together. Nothing about us has been normal. We went from friends to roommates to a sex bucket list. We've both spent so much time running that now we have a reason to stay. A reason other than the fact that I want this with you. Plus, I think you'll be a great mom."

"Great mother, but not wife material?"

I swallow the bile creeping up my throat. "Just stop, okay? Don't twist my words. I'm just saying we aren't ready for that step yet. I want to make you happy, and I thought by not asking I was keeping us from going here, to fighting. I don't want to fight, Mia. I don't want us to have regrets either. A forced marriage may make you hate me, and I'm not willing to take the chance."

I get up and walk over to where she's standing, but she steps back her hands on her flat stomach. Reality hits hard when I realize that she's now growing our child. "Can I hold you, please? I need to feel you in my arms."

"I don't know, Brooks. My heart and head are such a mess right now. Maybe…maybe we need some time apart to think about all of this stuff…"

A bucket of cold water is dumped over my head. I don't understand what I did wrong yet again. I keep fucking things up every time I open my mouth. I watch as she walks toward her room.

I sigh, running a hand through my hair. "I'm here when you want to talk, Mia. I'm not going anywhere. I'll give you space, but please don't shut me out from our child. I want to be there for both of you. All I want is the chance to make you happy and be there for you and our child. Please."

She nods her head before closing the door to her room. I wait long enough for the door to click, signaling she's in for the night before doubling over.

What the hell had I done? My hands slip through my hair, pulling on the ends. The pain burns, but it keeps me grounded. I want to do what is right, and it'd come out every bit wrong. My heart feels like it's slowly ripping apart at the seams, and for once, I'm not sure I know the outcome of our situation.

She's having my child.

I want to be there for them. Go to doctor appointments. Get her every food item she craves. Hold her hair while she pukes. Every sacrifice her body makes just so she can give me my own flesh and blood. A child that I can raise with the woman I love. I won't let her push me away. It doesn't matter how freaked I am about becoming a parent. I'm still going to get my girl. It may just be a little bit harder now. I don't care how long it takes.

Seventeen

Mia

The drive to the chalet has flown by. The snow's coming down lightly, and I still can't believe that winter's here already. I've heard so many pregnant women say that the time to get pregnant is during the winter versus the summer because it's always so hot. Huh, one thing to be happy about…

I stomp the snow off my shoes and ring the doorbell. Looking through the window, it looks like everything I pictured it would the first time Macy described it. She invited me up this week when I texted her after the fight with Brooks. Her in-laws are at their weekday home in the city, and I need her advice. Zara's great, but there's only so much she can give me, given that she isn't in a relationship.

My eyes are probably red from crying the last day. My nose is running, and I have the sniffles. I've been avoiding Brooks. I know his schedule, so it's easy to be gone when he's at the apartment. I should be so happy.

Finding out I'm pregnant is supposed to be one of the happiest days of a woman's life, and here I am, freezing my ass off, running away from all my problems. The door opens, and I'm greeted with her smile. My eyes get misty, and the emotions are on a roll again. Thank you, pregnancy hormones.

"Aww, sweet girl. Come in, come in." Furiously wiping my eyes, I try to hide the tears, but it's no use. "Let them out, Mia. It's okay to not be strong all the time."

They just keep coming. "Is Trevor here too?" I don't want him to see me like this right now. Trevor's nice, but I need Macy. No men. Men are confusing and frustrating.

"Nope, just you and me, girl." I walk past her into the foyer.

Her eyes trail over me, taking in my appearance. "Looks like we need some ice cream, and…"

"Do you have any dill pickles?"

She winks. "Got it, grab a seat in the living room, and I'll be right in, babe. Want anything to drink?"

"I guess just some juice or water. I can't drink now that I'm all sorts of knocked up. That's gonna be an adjustment."

"Alrighty, be in soon."

I hear her moving around in the kitchen and look at my surroundings to pass the time. I'm trying not to think about Brooks, but every single thought leads back to him.

Does he miss me?

What is he doing?

I left him a note this morning saying that I'm going to see Macy. I don't want him to worry about us too much.

Damn, it's crazy how right she is about this place. It feels exactly like an upscale version of a log cabin. These ceilings are huge, and there's leather and fur everywhere. I walk over to the photos and see the family pictures from over the years. Young Trevor, to images of him with his parents and Macy at their wedding. I smile because Sadie, their rescue dog, is also in the picture. I wonder how she's doing.

At the end of the photos on the table sits a stonework fireplace, and I plant myself in front of it, holding my hands out to warm them from the cold.

She walks up behind me, and I look over at her. "You weren't lying. This place is extra for sure. I mean look at all this stuff. Did we walk into a hunting/ski lodge? What's up with the antler and diamond chandelier?"

Her laugh shocks me. "Yeah, it's a little much. It's not how I'd design it, but they like it, and I can come whenever I want, so I can't really complain."

"Cheers to that."

"Let's sit down. So, tell me what happened. You and Brooks got into a fight after you told him you were pregnant?

"He told me he wouldn't ask me to marry him because I wasn't in love with him."

"Well, are you in love with him?"

"I don't know, Macy. I think so, but I don't know. My feelings are out of control. These emotions hurt. My heads messed up. Add in what I'm assuming are pregnancy hormones, and I have no luck piecing two thoughts together."

"Tell me this. If he walked out the door and never came back how would you feel?"

"It'd feel like my heart was being physically ripped from my body while I was still breathing." My admission is not what I expected.

"Honey, I hate to break it to you, but that sounds an awful lot like love to me."

"But I don't believe in love."

"I think you do. Somewhere in there is a girl who believes in love. You did once. You told me so. What Chad did to you in college, sweetie, was horrible, and your father is a bad example of a man too. Are you going to punish Brooks for Chad's actions or your fathers? Because it doesn't seem like he has anything in common with either. Has Brooks ever given you an indication that he wasn't being completely honest about his feelings for you?"

"No, but still, Macy. It scares me. He told me that night that we weren't ready for that step in our lives. How does he know we're ready to be parents? Because that's happening whether we're ready or not."

"Mia, if he knows anything about you like I do, then I get why he didn't. I wouldn't have asked you either. He knew it would scare you shitless. He knew you would run, and what are you doing right now? Running. Proving his point. Give that man a little bit of credit. He knows a lot more about you than he lets on. From everything I've heard, I'd say that man is in love with you and just wants to be there for you. He didn't want a marriage with you based on the fact that he got you knocked up. He sounds honest to me."

I sigh. "But I don't know how to let him in."

"Let him earn your trust. Give him little details about you. Form a relationship, a bond. I know how much you like sex, Mia, but there's more to a relationship than that. Do you even know his favorite color? Where did he go to school? Where was he born? What's his favorite food? These are all questions you find out as you build a relationship. Rome wasn't built in a day, and neither are relationships. They take work and commitment. You have to decide if you're in it for the long run or not."

"His favorite color is blue. He came from a compound in the middle of nowhere. I know those things. It's just we're going to always be connected by this little one now, and I don't want there to be drama over it."

She reaches over and rubs my arm as I shove another scoop of ice cream into my face like a fat kid. "Then don't let there be drama. I think honestly, you're blowing it a little out of proportion. Have you thought about it from his perspective?"

I stare at her like she's speaking a foreign language. "Wait, you agree with him?"

She puts her hands up in defense. "No, hear me out. I'm just saying that maybe it's time to give him some slack. Stop acting like he's going to fuck you over like every other man in your life did and give the guy a chance to prove himself. Maybe he needs a do-over. Obviously, he knows you aren't ready for commitment, but you said so yourself that he asked to be there for the both of you. Regardless, you need to take a chill pill. All this stress is not good for the baby."

I rub my hand over my belly. I still can't believe it, but she's right. It's no longer just about me. It's me and the little nugget now.

"Maybe you're right. It's entirely possible that I was a little out of line with how I handled things, but it's a lot to take in. Plus, he's my main dick and I'm a horny little freak these days. It's all I think about—ice cream, dill pickles, and Brooks' dick. It's seriously becoming a problem."

"I'm fairly positive he could help you with that problem if you let him."

A tear slides down my cheek. "I guess I just don't know what to think or how to feel about all of it. I'm confused, and I can't tell if it's the pregnancy talking or true feelings I have."

"Sweetie, it's okay to be confused. I'm sure he'll be making it up to you for a while. Saying he wasn't going to propose probably wasn't the best knee jerk reaction, and I'm sure at this point, he knows it. I bet he'll try and fix this between you two. It seems like he really cares for you."

"Yeah... I'm sorry I'm such a basket case. I'm just so messed up."

"Mia, it's expected. You found out you were pregnant, what, two days ago? I think you have a right to be all out of sorts."

"Yeah."

"So, tell me what else is new? Get your mind off it."

"Brooks got me into the Rising Tides Art Gallery for a showing."

"Wow, that's amazing. Are you going to do it?"

"I don't know…"

"You need to do this, Mia. Do it for yourself. Don't do it for him. You've kept those paintings locked up for too long and you deserve it."

"But…"

"No. No ifs, ands, or buts. Your art deserves to be seen."

"But it is seen. I show it at other galleries."

"But those galleries aren't Rising Tides. You've been talking about exhibiting there for years, Mia. Years… So you're doing it. If I have to come and drag your butt there myself."

"Okay, then."

"Good. Glad we had that talk. I'd suggest waiting until after the pregnancy if they'll let you."

"Good point. You know, I've really missed you, Mace. Maybe next time, it won't take me getting knocked up and into a fight with Brooks to get you to hang out with me. I mean, I know I don't have Trevor dick, but still…"

"I've missed you too, girl."

I laugh as my conversation with Zara comes back into my head. "Speaking of which, did you know that a blue whale penis is called a dork?"

"No, I didn't, but I'm sure you're going to tell me all about it." And I do just that. We spend the rest of the day and evening catching up and laughing. We have a light dinner and call it a night. I've missed Macy.

For years we've been attached at the hip, and then she'd fallen in love and gotten married, leaving me. I don't blame her. After Trevor got his head out of his ass, he'd become everything she needed in a man, and I'm so happy for them.

Thinking about them makes my mind drift back to Brooks. I wonder how his day's going. I miss him. I can admit it to myself.

My heart hurts being apart from him. It makes sense after my talk with Macy about why he did what he did, but that doesn't make it any better. I guess I just need to lay my heart out on the line and hope he doesn't jigsaw it apart. Although he'd hurt my feelings, I don't feel any burning desire to walk away from him. In fact, walking away from him would be like a dagger straight to the heart at this point.

I cry myself to sleep that night. For once, I just let all my thoughts and emotions flow freely.

My stomach woke me up again, bright and early this morning. I hate the puking, but I'm finally starting to come to terms with it. The porcelain goddess and I will become the best of friends by the time this is all over.

I've taken a shower to make myself feel a little better. Ran a comb through my hair, put on leggings and another oversized sweater.

The smell of breakfast wafts into my room. Sugary sweet bakery smells. I finish getting ready, wondering who's cooking breakfast. My feet lead me to the kitchen, and I come across an older lady standing in front of the stove. She turns and smiles when she hears me come in, motioning for me to sit at the table—a few seconds later, Macy bounds in too.

"Morning, Mia."

"Morning, Mace."

"How'd you sleep last night?"

"Ehh, it was tough getting my brain to shut off. I just kinda laid there for a while and stared at the ceiling."

"Well, I have just the thing that may help you relax today."

"Oh yeah?"

"Mmmhmm. Roberta is going to cook us up some breakfast, and then Trevor hired a couple masseuses and nail technicians from the ski resort to come over and give us massages, pedis, and manis. Girls days in. How does that sound?"

"Heavenly. You got a good one, Macy."

"I sure did. Sometimes, he's a royal pain in my ass, but I wouldn't trade him in for the world."

Roberta, or Bertha, as Macy calls her finishes up breakfast and brings it to the table where we've planted ourselves. "Anything else you ladies need?" she asks politely.

Macy smiles at her. "Thank you, Bertha. I really appreciate you coming out on an off day to make us food."

"Oh, I don't mind at all. I'm going to head out now. Sounds like you two have a fun afternoon planned." We watch her finish cleaning up and then leave us alone.

"Did we really need a cook for breakfast?"

She shrugs her shoulders and laughs. "Trevor insisted. How could I resist?"

I proceed to make a vulgar thrusting motion. "I'm sure he did."

"Oh, good Lord, woman. Do you ever not think about sex?"

"Currently, no. It's all about the dick…"

"Alrighty then. So we've got a couple hours until they show up, what did you want to do? I could show you around the lodge, and we could watch people learning to ski. It's always funny when they fall on their ass time and time again."

"Ugh, I don't really feel like doing anything, to be honest. How about we throw on some *Gilmore Girls* and catch up with Rory and Lorelai."

"From the beginning?"

"Yes, to Stars Hollow we go!" I throw my fist into the air, and we both laugh. Finishing up the rest of our breakfast, we make our way to the media room so we can watch it on the big screen. Plopping down on the couch, we put our feet up, click on Netflix, and proceed to sing along with the opening credit song.

Macy sighs. "Oh, Dean…"

"Ehh… I was more of a team Jess girl, myself."

She rolls her eyes. "Of course you were!"

"Come on…the dark hair, the bad boy attitude, the swagger… I had a lady boner over him for sure."

"It's not like Dean was a goodie two shoes either…"

"Still. Team Jess."

"Nope. Definitely Dean."

"Let's just say we agree to disagree." We both nod.

The ladies from the spa show up right on time at two o'clock. They set up quickly in the living room, and we're in the middle of our massages.

"Oh," I moan. "That feels amazing." I sound like a hooker having a fake orgasm, but damn, it does feel good. I have been dealing with a lot of stress lately and this is just what I needed.

We move on to pedis, and I chose attitude black for my color, while Macy goes for lavender.

"Hey, you said his favorite color is blue, right?"

"Yeah?" I say, looking back at her.

"Maybe paint your ring finger blue, just for Brooks then. A pop of color and something to let him know you were thinking about him."

I lean back in the leather chair and groan as the nail tech digs her fingers into my arch and squeezes. Is it weird that I actually like foot rubs? I blame Brooks. He's got me hooked on them, and now I can't live without them.

Susan isn't doing as good of a job as Brooks does, but he's not here. Gah, will I ever stop thinking about him today?

Probably not, my brain whispers.

Macy's eyes find mine with a concerned look. "You're thinking about him, aren't you?"

I shrug. "How can I not? I miss him, and it's only been a couple days since I've seen him, avoiding him and all."

"Oh, girl. He's stolen that heart right from under you. You got it bad for him."

I take a deep breath and sigh. "Something like that...I just wish I knew what he was thinking, ya know? I thought some part of him would be happy because he told me he loves me, but then we got in that huge fight, and I have no idea how he feels about me and the little nugget."

"I'm sure he's happy, babe. He loves you, and that little nugget is a part of both of you. How could he not?"

"I guess. I just..."

"I know, your brain is going on overdrive. Just let it pan out like it's going to. You guys will figure it out. That little nugget is going to change things, but I guarantee it won't change the way he feels about you. You're going to have to be brave. This badass vibe you have is cool, I love her, but sometimes it's okay to let people know that there's a real person in there with feelings and love."

Eighteen

Brooks

I rub the sponge against the glass a little harder, quietly letting out a string of elicit words.

"You scrub that glass out anymore, you're going to kill it." I look up to find Willie eyeing me from the other side of the bar top.

"You can't kill a glass, Willie."

He grunts his agreement. "Nope, but I got your attention, didn't I?"

"Guess so."

"Uh, oh. What'd you do this time?"

I put both hands on the bar top and blow out the breath I've been holding. "Ugh. Yep, I opened my mouth and stuck my fucking foot right in it."

"Been there, done that, son."

"I highly doubt it. It was... bad. She didn't even tell me good-bye. She left me a note with no mention of when she'd be back or if she'd be back. I fucked up really good."

I've been replaying every single line of our conversation on continuous repeat for the last two days, and every time I try to get home early or get her to talk to me, she disappears.

I should've kept my mouth shut. Hell, maybe I should've asked her to marry me just so I wouldn't be in this situation. Now she seems to think that I don't want her, which is an absolute lie. I should've wrapped her in my arms and told her how lucky I am that she's carrying my child. That she means more to me than anything I've ever wanted, but I didn't, and now she's gone.

"I'm sure she'll be back, kid."

"Oh, you don't know that."

"I have a feeling about these things. So, ya gonna tell me what happened or not?"

I question whether it's really a good idea to share all the shit that happened, but it's eating me up. I need to talk to someone, and my family isn't a viable option. They basically disowned me when I left, never looking back. I could try talking to Donatello, but I don't want to drop all my problems on the guy that just walked back into my life. Willie's always been here for me. "She's having my kid."

Willie hoots. "You knocked her up? Damn, son, that was quick. Definite way to get her to stick around. You sure took rocking the boat to a new level. Congrats."

I nod slowly. "Didn't plan on it. Just sorta happened."

"I'm sure you're probably not the first guy who stuck his foot in his mouth after his woman told him she was pregnant with his child. How do ya feel about it?"

"I love her. I'm so happy, but I didn't even tell her how I felt. I just went on and told her that I wouldn't ask her to marry me because that wasn't a reason to get married," I admit.

"Ouch… I imagine that wasn't a great idea."

I clear my throat, emotion clogging my throat. "Exactly. I messed up, Willie. I'm going to be a father, and I have zero idea where I stand with my baby mama. She owns my heart and soul, has since the first time I laid eyes on her in this bar. She is everything to me."

"You got it bad. You think about trying to call her or send her a text?"

"No, I was trying to give her some space, and it sucks. For the first time in my life I finally felt complete, whole. Like she'd closed up the part of my heart that was still cut open, but now she's gone."

"Well, this ain't the end. Last thing you need her to think is that you don't care. Just because she said she needs space doesn't mean you stop fighting for her. You fight like hell. You don't run."

"Yeah, maybe that's a good idea. It's just... I wanna raise the baby with her. Hell, if I knew she'd say yes to a marriage proposal I'd have already been down on one knee, ring in hand, but she's still closed off from me. I want her to be happy, but after that night, I'm not even sure if she's going to keep me. You want another? Your glass is empty."

He chuckles. "You know, I do."

I reach over, grabbing the whiskey, ice, and another glass. "Here you go, friend. It's on me, say it's for good advice."

"You know you could grab her some flowers and do something nice for her. She got any big events coming up or things happening that you can make her feel special over?"

"The gallery that's showing her artwork is doing a big opening night for her event, but I don't know when it's scheduled."

"There ya go. Pretty sure you could do some snooping and find out when it is. I happen to know she's friends with Zara. I'm also sure you can come up with a little something to celebrate with her. Can't have champagne on account of the kid and all that, but flowers and sparkling juice may be nice, Brooks."

"So you do know my name?"

"Of course, I do."

"Why do you always call me son?"

"Cause you remind me of my own son."

My eyebrow raises. "I didn't know you had kids…"

"Now you do, but I don't need to get into all that. You need to talk it out more?" His admission shocks me. Hell, maybe he does understand a thing or two about women and what I'm going through.

"Nah, I think I'm good. I appreciate you listening to me."

"Anytime, now I'm gonna head on over and harass Charlie. It ain't fun if I can't get a rise out of him at least once a day. Good luck with your girl. Remember, listening is helpful. Take little clues from her on how to act. She'll tell you what she wants from you, ya just gotta know what to look for… You've got this. I think you'll be just fine." I shake my head and chuckle as he walks away. A few minutes later, I hear hoop and hollering from where Charlie and Willie sit in the back corner of the bar.

The next couple of hours go smoothly. A bachelorette party came in for a little while, but it's mostly college kids coming in to shoot pool or play darts. I mess around with some new drink ideas.

It's up to us to keep up with drink changes, and I've been trying to make something specific for Topsy Turvy. I'm thinking something green that would happily turn your world upside down with just one sip like Green Chartreuse or Absinthe, but those aren't exactly shit college liquor. Maybe something cotton candy pink, something that reminds me of the spicy little pixie I can't stop wanting to call mine. The urge to go home and see if Mia's there hits me like a ton of bricks because I miss her. Being without her is like not being able to breathe underwater.

My heart beats faster with each step I take toward our apartment. The wind is bitter cold tonight, and snow is still falling in crystalline shaped diamonds from the sky. Not enough to lay, but enough to make you freeze being out in it for just a little bit of time.

I can see my breath with each puff out. I pull my knit hat further down over my ears and my scarf just a little tighter. Anxiety spreads its wings wide inside me, not knowing if she's even home yet. There's been zero communication about when she's coming home, and it worries me. I fling open the door to our apartment building and take the stairs two at a time. Quickly unlocking our front door, I fling it open, hitting the wall, but I'm not sure what I expect. At some point I'll need to stop slamming open the door. That's what I do know.

Her bag isn't hanging off the chair like it normally does. There's no cotton candy and vanilla scent permeating the air.

She isn't home.

My heart sinks.

Our apartment just isn't the same without her. There's no smell of marijuana mixing with the smell of paint as she creates patterns and shapes on the canvas. Her loud, obnoxious laugh is gone as well. It's lonely. For once, there's no purple, pink, and blue hair in my shower drain, reminding me I live with a cotton candy haired pixie. I refuse to believe that she isn't coming back. I have to keep hope alive.

I miss laying with her in bed, being inside her. I've become the lovesick guy after only a couple of days. I miss how she chides me at my lack of knowledge about sexual innuendos.

I grab a cold beer from the fridge and plop myself down in my recliner. A smirk crosses my face at the look she gives me every time I sit in this chair. The one she hates so much, but I always catch her in.

Maybe texting her isn't such a bad idea.

Me: *Hey. I miss you.*

Mia: *Miss you too.*

Me: *I don't want to rush you. I know you wanted space, but I wish you were here. I miss wrapping my arms around you and giving you one of my bear hugs.*

Mia: *I miss that too.*

No indication of when she's coming home, but I still have hope. I have to.

Me: *What are you wearing?*

Mia: *Brooks…*

Me: *Come on. I'll start out. I'm wearing your bright red lacy thong and thinking of you. Ya know, this color is actually very ravishing on me if I do say so myself. And the way it cups my balls. Makes my package look nice…*

Mia: *Oh, my God. Please tell me you aren't wearing my underwear right now.*

Me: *I'm not really, that would be super uncomfortable, plus having something in my ass crack all day, I'll pass. They look sexy as hell on you though.*

Mia: *I'm still mad at you.*

Me: *I know you are. Come home, pixie girl. I want to apologize to you over and over again.*

Mia: *Does that include dick? If not, I'm not interested.*

Me: *He's ready and available, waiting just for you, baby.*

Mia: *Thanks for making me smile, Brooks.*

Me: *Please come home, Mia. We can talk this out. I don't want to do it over text.*

Mia: *I'll be home tomorrow. I expect flowers, groveling, and your dick with a big ass bow on it.*

Me: *Anything for you. I'll be ready and waiting. I can't wait to see you.*

Mia: *Me too, Brooks.*

I wake up the following morning after tossing and turning all night and race to Mia's room. I'm not entirely sure what I was expecting. Her bed still sits neatly made and my smile disappears. I know I need to chill out before seeing her again. She might freak out if I come on too strong.

I decide on a workout and run. It'll do me good to get my thoughts in order before I see her. For the next hour, I let my lungs have it, until they start screaming at me to stop from all the cold air.

Exhaustion pulls in my limbs, and my running clothes are drenched in discarded fear and sweat. I've got a plan, now I just have to execute it.

Getting home, I quickly take a shower. Throwing on Mia's favorite pair of grey sweatpants and a tee-shirt, I make some breakfast quickly and sit down on the couch to wait.

Hopefully, she'll arrive soon. Ten minutes later, I hear the lock on the door click.

It's now or never.

Mia

The spa day yesterday was exactly what I needed. A day to just relax and try to chase my overwhelming fears and panic away. It hadn't done that specifically, but it had given me a chance to get my thoughts in order.

The drive home gives me more time to think. I think I've finally figured it out. It's almost like Brooks brainwashed me into having feelings, but somewhere along the line, I started to believe in them too. Who knew that all this love he threw at me would make me believe in it after all.

Bertha made me a muffin for the road and then made a puss face at me when I asked for a coffee. Apparently, coffee is off-limits too, unless I want decaf. What is the purpose of decaf coffee? Instead, she gave me some juice.

I hated saying goodbye to Macy, and she was sad to see me go, but it was time. She understands my desire to go home and deal with everything.

The time has come to stop hiding from my life. Brooks and I have a baby on the way, and we need to get our shit together. No matter how today pans out, I need to be prepared to walk away if he says he doesn't want to do this anymore.

This baby deserves everything I can give it. It needs to know it's loved. I never want this child to go through what I did, wondering if you're more than just a mere existence that's never been wanted.

I put the car into park outside the apartment and stop to breathe in the chilled air. It's a shock to my lungs, but I cling to the initial zap. Rubbing my hand over my still flat stomach, I whisper, "Okay, nugget, let's hope this goes well."

The stairs seem daunting, and my heart beats harder with each step. Taking another deep breath, I notice that my hands are shaking.

The events of three nights ago rain on my parade, and I feel nauseous about all of it.

What if he doesn't want us? A little voice in my brain whispers.

He's not Chad, I remind myself. Taking the stairs, this time seems to be the longest journey of my life. When my feet come to a halt in front of our door, I can't bring myself to just open it.

A sob works its way up my throat, and I start to panic thinking maybe I'm worked up and Brooks isn't even staying here anymore.

Maybe he got smart and moved out. I wouldn't blame him. I would've given up on myself a while ago.

But why would he have asked me to come home if that was the case? I'm still hurt and frustrated over our last talk, but I tamper it down. We need to talk, and I'm going to hope that when I walk through the door he'll be sitting waiting for me.

The door opens before I have a chance to grab the knob, and there stands Brooks looking like sex on a stick. A smile crosses his face, but never reaches his eyes. I can see that he hasn't been sleeping either. His eyes are bloodshot and dark shadows hang in bags below them.

His look is weary and worried, and I can see myself mirroring the same exact look. My shoulders sag with the unknown weighing them down. I have no idea what he's thinking. He motions me inside and then has me wrapped in his arms seconds later. "Thank you for coming home to me."

"Thank you for giving me some space to figure my shit out, but I'm still mad at you. You hurt me, Brooks."

"I know. We need to talk." I nod and just stand there in his warm embrace. I've missed him. His strength. His smell. The way his body wraps around mine when he hugs me. That huge boner between us.

"Brooks..."

"I know I can't help it. He has a mind of his own. I plead the fifth."

"Well, you have a lot of making up to do, and I expect the good dick."

"When do I not give you good dick, Mia?"

"Touché, but first. We need to talk about us."

He looks down at me pointedly. "Okay, let's start with how long you've been standing outside our front door?"

I startle and look up at him. "Not that long. I was composing myself."

"Why did you have to compose yourself?"

My shoulders rise with a deep inhale. "Because I just ran, Brooks, like I always do when shit gets hard. Like I've been doing since I was a teenager. I start getting emotions, they rampage out of control, and when I can't shut them down, I bounce. I didn't want to say anything else I couldn't take back."

"Let me apologize first, Mia. I think everything got completely out of line that night. Things were said that shouldn't have been said. Emotions were flying high."

"Truth, I was thinking that maybe you were gone. Maybe you'd had time to think about it last night and decided that I wasn't worth all my drama. That you could find another girl to settle down with and have a real relationship. This heart," I said, pointing at my chest. "Doesn't work like everyone else's does. It gets scared. It shuts down and hides."

"It's not a weakness to admit that this scares you, Mia. I think you're brave for being honest about it. Hell, it scares me too, but I have faith in us. I think we'll make great parents."

"You go straight to talking about the baby again, Brooks. What about us?"

"I want this, Mia. I want you. I want you like I've never wanted anything in my whole entire life. Leaving the compound and moving here was the best damn decision I've ever made, and the fact that you're carrying my child. I'm so fucking lucky, Mia. You've made me a father and that's something I can never ever thank you enough for…This baby is half you and half me. It's going to be perfect, and I will never take either of you for granted. I'm also terrified that I'll be a shit dad and that I'll do something that will hurt you or make you want to run. I had a shit role model, so I'll figure it out. But I know I can't lose you. It would break me."

"But what if I can't do this? What if I do the wrong thing or say the wrong thing?"

"You can do this, I believe in you."

"How do you know?"

"Because you are a badass pixie, Mia Preston, and I will be right here beside you the whole entire time. I'm not leaving you."

I pull back and cross my arms. "What about the marriage thing? You seemed pretty sure that you didn't want to ask me."

"Mia, I know you aren't ready for that. In hindsight, I shouldn't have even brought it up. I would love for you to be my wife someday, but I'm not rushing it. I want us to have a real relationship, to be in love. Not to get married and rush things just because we're having a baby. I was freaking out. You had just told me you were having my baby. Can I get a free pass just this once?"

"I guess."

"I need to know where you stand on all this, Mia."

"What do you want to know? I'm freaked out, wondering if I can even be a mom. If I'll even be good at it. I had a shit example growing up."

"You're going to be great, and what we don't know, we'll learn. I need to know how you feel about me, Mia. I can't stand not knowing. Where do we stand?"

I take a long, deep breath. I want to give him the words that have been pounding my brain for the last two days. "I love you," I whisper it.

He smiles at me and leans in. "What was that? I'm sorry you kind of whispered it."

"I love you, Brooks."

"You sure, cause I'm not allowing any take-backs on that one."

"I'm sure. We got pedicures yesterday, and the only thing I could think about the whole time was that I wished it was you rubbing my feet. I wished it was you that I was hanging out with. My heart feels lost in a fog when you aren't here with me. It physically hurt, not knowing where we stood. I never want to feel like that again. I don't want to lose you either, Brooks."

He reaches over and picks me up in a hug—kissing my face. "I." Kiss. "Love." Kiss. "You." Kiss. "So." Kiss. "Much. I'm going to mess up and do stupid shit, but that will never, ever change how I feel about you. Our love may be kinda topsy turvy, but it's ours, and no one else will ever have one exactly like ours. We may not be your typical fairytale love. We definitely started out backward, but we won't have regrets. You can trust me, Mia."

"Yes, I want you, Brooks. I want you to hold my hand proudly as you walk down the street. If you feel like walking up to me in the middle of Topsy Turvy and kissing the hell outta me because you feel like it, then I want you to. I want to be brave, to be bold with our love. This whole situation is totally out of the blue and unexpected, but the truth is I don't want to do it with anyone else. These next nine months may be hell for you. I've heard pregnant ladies are the worst sometimes. I'm going to have cravings. I'm going to need dick, and I'm going to need you to step up and handle it. I want a partner in this. I'm growing our child, that's a miracle. I thought I didn't believe in love. I thought it was a figment of the imagination, but you've shown me that it's so much more than that."

"Wait, can we back up to the you needing dick part of that speech?"

I slap him lightly on the shoulder. "Think with your head, Brooks, not your dick right now."

He fake pouts. "But he was super happy at the prospect of being needed."

"I'm sure he is, and I've been hella horny, so I'm going to need some tonight, so be ready."

"Always ready for you babe, always and forever. You're mine, and so is that little girl or boy you're carrying, damnit."

I lick my lips, and his eyes watch every second of the moment. I want so badly to jump his bones, but I feel like that would make me seem desperate. No, I need to keep composed for at least another hour. It's a respectable amount of time to wait. And about all, I could handle. But first...

"Hey, Brooks. I need to apologize to you."

He furrows his brows. "What for?"

I step into him, hugging him to me tightly. "I rushed into thinking the worst and jumped to conclusions. You've never given me any doubt that you love me. You've loved me to death. I should have taken a minute to think about things instead of just spouting off. It's just... I know I'm not easy to love, but you seem to do it so easily."

"Oh Mia. You don't have to apologize."

"I do. We both have something to learn from this whole situation, and I think if I tell you a little about my past then you may understand why I act the way I do."

"Okay." He's quiet, waiting for me to speak.

"My sophomore year of college, I was dating a guy named Chad. He said all the right things, called himself my boyfriend. The night he told me he loved me, I gave him my virginity. The next day I overheard a conversation between him and his friends..." I take a deep breath, and a single tear slips down my cheek.

"He explained to them that I was just another virgin on his bedpost. That I'd fallen for every single word that he'd said. They'd laughed about it. About me. Like I was nothing more than just another lay. Like I wasn't even a human being with feelings." I peek up at Brooks and notice his jaw's tight in anger. He pulls me in closer, trying to comfort me. His hands clench in fists at the small of my back.

"When I confronted him about it a couple days later, he told me I was crazy that he was just shooting the shit with the guys. When he realized that I didn't believe his lies, he tried to backpedal and tell me that it wasn't true that he really did love me. It was the day I decided that love wasn't worth it if it hurt that bad. I thought he really liked me. I fell for every single one of his tricks, and I felt betrayed. Needless to say, several guys walked away from me when they wanted more than I would give them. I just couldn't let them in, and they hated me for it."

"My sweet, beautiful girl. You deserve so much more than any of those jerks could give you, and if I could punch Chad in the face, I would."

"I think he's part of the reason I lashed out. All of my fears with him came back when you said you didn't want to marry me. My first thought was, oh God, he doesn't want me either. It's college all over again. I know you're different, Brooks, but my past wouldn't let me see through the fog of it."

He presses harder into me, eliminating all the space previously between us. "Now, I understand why you acted out like you did. Dealing with that would be hard for anyone and I'm sorry that you had to go through it. I don't blame you for running, I just hope you don't plan on doing it again because I won't let you."

I puff out a breath of air. "I don't. I promise next time I'll fight for us. I won't run. Not again. I've missed you so much these last couple of days that any more time apart may just kill me. It was pure torture not being in your arms these last couple of nights. I slept like shit."

"I love you, Mia."

I sniffle. "I was so worried that you wouldn't want me. That was the only thing I kept thinking about the whole way here. That's what made me hesitate. I didn't want to know that you were done with me. With us. I didn't want to see the empty spaces where your stuff used to lie just yet."

"You don't ever have to worry about that, Mia. You're not getting away again. I'll pull you back from the brink every time."

"I love you, Brooks."

"Say it again, Pixie."

"I. Love. You. Brooks Jansen."

He leans down to my flat stomach and talks to our child. "I love you too, little one. I don't know if you can hear me yet or not, but know you're loved. Your parents may not have all their sh-crap together, but we'll do our best by you." He lifts my sweatshirt slightly and presses a small kiss to my stomach, and my heart literally skips a beat, and guess what? I didn't die! It does exist! There, I said what I said!

I reach up and cup his jaw. "I can't believe we're having a baby."

He leans down, brushing his nose against mine. "I'm so happy."

"Really?"

"Of course, how could I not be?"

I lift up, pressing my lips against his lightly, testing the waters. He kisses me back with a fevered passion, and I can't help but get lost in his lips. He licks the seam of my lips and I open immediately, loving the feel of his tongue wrapping against mine like two lost souls reminding one another of what they once were to one another. Each kiss burns into me, memory after memory. He grabs my ass, lifting me up, and I wrap my legs around his waist. It's been two long ass days without him, and I'm grinding up against him like a cat in heat.

I pull away from him. "Brooks, I'm feeling dirty. I think I need a shower. How would you feel about checking off another on our sex bucket list?"

He whispers into my mouth, "Won't last that long. Need you now." He walks over, pulling the blanket and pillows down from the couch, laying me on top of it on the floor. He leans over me, starting to kiss me, pulling one side of my leggings down and off and then ripping the hem of my thong at the hip. I start to huff when he cuts me off. "I'll buy you a new one, don't complain."

"No complaining here, it's hot when you go all growly alpha on me."

He makes quick work of grabbing his pants and shoving them

down just far enough to get his massively hard cock out. He slips past my entrance with one thrust, not even making sure I'm ready, but I am. Always ready and wanton for him. Consumed with a need that only he can fulfill. There's a tiny tinge of pain, and then pleasure fills my core.

He kisses my lips, nibbling on his journey down my neck. Pulling my sweatshirt up halfway, I lean up so he can slip it over my head. His lips go back to my chest and continue on their way, pulling one breast into his mouth while his hand works the other.

It's a sensation overload and everything I need at that moment. He slips his hands down my sides and over my stomach, coming to rest on my mound. His thumb slides down, rubbing circles around my nub, and tingles erupt. I'm about to lose it. I moan again as he leans up to capture it with his mouth. "Yes, Brooks. God, yes. I've fucking missed this cock."

"Mmm… you like that baby?"

"More. I need more."

"Not gonna last much longer, Mia." Oh Lord, everything inside me is crashing hard. My orgasm rushes down my body like a crashing sea wave, and it can happily carry me away with the tide.

"I can't Mi-" He doesn't even finish my name on his lips before his orgasm crashes into my core. Two hearts mending, becoming one. We need each other like taking the next breath. There's a lot to learn about love and life, but in this very second, I'm happy. Changed. I'm a believer in love, in Brooks' love.

We're going to be parents, and I'm sure along the way we're going to shit the bed with it, but it's worth trying because I don't want to give him up.

Nineteen

Mia

The appointment has been scheduled for the past two weeks, and my nerves are on a see-saw these days. Shortly after peeing on all those sticks, we'd gone to the doctor who confirmed with a blood test that I definitely was cooking a bun in the oven.

I hated needles; it's probably why I stopped at one tattoo on my thigh when I went through my badass goth girl phase. Not that I've left that phase, but maybe a little growing up and becoming a little more normal is due. Through all of this, I have Brooks to thank.

He's there every time I wake up to pray to the porcelain god, which I've started calling Tiffany, every time I want food, the multiple times I just need him in the middle of the night when I rub against him so frantically just to get rid of the ache. I'm constantly horny, I know it's shocking. So freaking horny all the time, well, except when I'm puking.

We've been sitting in the waiting room for fifteen minutes now, and I've got ants in my pants. My knee bounces up and down with the beat of the music playing softly overhead. Every woman or couple that walks through that door looks like they would make amazing parents. They're dressed in normal clothes and have normal hair colors.

These couples look like they genuinely have their shit together, and then there's me. Pink, purple, and blue hair in my black clothing and combat boots. Definitely winning every single creepy mom award. A hand squeezes my knee lightly to stop it from bouncing. My eyes find Brooks, and a smile crosses his perfect lips. A smile just for me, dimples showing.

"Hey, get out of your head. It's going to be just fine, Pixie."

"I know… I'm just…"

He leans over and kisses my forehead, resting there for a minute longer than necessary. "I know… me too. It's going to be okay, though. Everything is going to be fine. Just a little bit longer before we get to see our little miracle in there." His hand reaches over and rubs my still flat tummy. I love it when his big palm covers me. The amount of love he shows in one simple gesture overwhelms my hormones and I get sappy eyed.

The door opens, and we all look up, waiting to be the next name called. "Mia Preston." I sit there for longer than I need to. Brooks slowly gets up, offering me his hand.

"It's your turn, my pixie girl. You ready to see our baby?"

Tears form in my eyes and I resist crying. For once in the last few weeks, it's a grateful feeling to be able to control that one simple instance. "Yeah, I'm ready."

He smiles at me, and I give him my best mean face. "Don't you dare laugh at me, Brooks Jansen. You're the reason I'm in this position."

Leaning over, he whispers in my ear, "I like when my little badass shows emotions, and I can't wait to practice that position more when we get home, now get your cute little ass over there." He pinches my butt, and I stick out my tongue at him.

A short huff and I walk toward the medical assistant, but a smile forms on my face anyhow. I can't help it. I'm fucking over the moon happy… until she tells me to get on the scale. I know the inevitable weight gain is coming, and I mourn my sexy figure.

Twenty minutes later, my feet are secure in those terrible stirrup contraptions. I'm scooted to the very end of the bed, where I'm sure every single part of my hoohah and ass is hanging out. I can feel a damn breeze. Brooks sneaks a peek or two and then waggles his eyebrows at me. I narrow mine in return. He's so mature—the father of my child, everyone.

The doctor is about to shove a big ass wand into my V that will probably be the most uncomfortable thing that's ever been in there and that's saying a lot.

The walls of this room are too white. Normally, I enjoy black and white, but today I want something less sterile. Something blue.

My attention turns to the little black and white screen to the right of the doctor. The doctor adjusts the wand once it's inside and taps a few keys. You can tell Dr. Morgan has been doing this doctor thing for a while. She uses a calming tone, and her mellow-ness makes me feel less on edge. I haven't smoked a good joint since I got knocked up, and I miss my weed. Or maybe just the calming effect it gives me, but I don't want to do anything that will cause harm to my child.

Brooks has come to my side since checking out my lady bits. He holds my hand firmly and squeezes, letting me know it's okay. He looks impatient as we wait to see our baby. Deep brown eyes firmly planted on the black and white screen like mine should be doing, but I can't stop taking in this image of him being excited over something we created together. He's been murmuring sweet words to me since the appointment started, knowing that he needs to calm my nerves.

He's probably the only thing that could at this point. It's been weeks since we found out I was pregnant. Ever since I came home, we decided to take it one day at a time, a step at a time. We've been learning about each other and working on more of our wish list items, but I've realized that it's not about sex with us anymore.

Maybe it never really was…

Yes, the sex is hot, but it's him that makes it so hot. It's the way he cares for me. The way he's been caring for our child who's not even born. If I had to think about it, it hasn't been about the sex for a while. It took some hard truths and a little pregnancy to make me realize it though.

Dr. Morgan clears her throat and points to the center of a circle. "There's your baby, mom and dad."

"Where?" I try squinting but my foggy eyes are heavy with unshed tears. Cue the waterworks. I start to panic, feelings crashing into every part of my body, and I shudder.

I feel a hand on my leg and look at her. "Hey, take a deep breath. I know it's a big moment, Mia, but I need you to be calm for me. Okay?" I breathe in slowly and then release it out. She smiles. "Good, Mia. That's really good." We all look back up at the monitor.

She points to a small blob in the middle of the screen. "This little blob is your baby in there."

I squint, leaning in closer. "Really? It's so small…"

Dr. Morgan rolls the machine closer, so we can get a better look. "Yep, that's your little one in there growing away."

I look up at Brooks. "That's our baby."

A tear slips down his cheek, and he wipes under his eyes. "Yeah, beautiful, it is." Seeing Brooks crying has me losing it. I feel so overwhelmed. My eyes start leaking, and there is no stopping this rainstorm.

Brooks looks over and winks. "It's okay to cry, Mia. I won't tell anyone."

I huff, "I'm not crying, you're crying."

It's a damn good thing I didn't wear makeup today because it would've definitely run down my face in black waterfalls by now. All these emotions are hounding me.

Happy tears because I'm so thankful for the bundle of joy I'm carrying. Scared out of my mind tears because I don't know if I can do this. It's when fear creeps in and tries to strangle the last breath—a hand gripping your heart. Brooks squeezes my hand, reminding me that he's still here with me.

Something that sounds close to wild horses running across the plains sounds in the room and I pause, listening. "Is that?" I whisper.

"That's your baby's heartbeat," my doctor confirms. "We've got a perfectly healthy little embryo in there, you two. Everything looks just as it should. Would you two like a picture of the baby to take with you?"

"Of course we do," I hear Brooks say, but it doesn't really register. I'm so incredibly happy right now.

"Everything looks just as it should," I repeat her words. The timeline is accurate. It matches the time Brooks and I started going at it like bunnies. She gave us the date she believes the conception happened, and I remember that night well. It was the night that I let Brooks kiss me for the first time. It really was a night of firsts for us—first kiss with Brooks. First time getting knocked up.

The doctor prints us off a couple of copies, and I can't take my eyes off Brooks. He's a ball of tears like I am. The emotions are breaking me down and exposing me bare. He finds me staring and winks at me, dimples blazing.

He leans over and whispers, "See what your kiss did to me. It just urged my manly swimmers to fight for your girls in there a little harder. You are magical. I can't believe you don't see it yet."

I play smack his shoulder. "Brooks, hush."

"I love you, Mama Mia."

"Love you too, Papa Brooksy."

Dr. Morgan is smiling when I look up, and I know she was listening in on our private convo. "Okay, you two. Congrats, we're having a baby!" She reaches into her pocket, pulling out a script pad, scribbles something, and then passes it to me. "This is the name of some over the counter prenatal vitamins. You should be able to pick it up at any pharmacy. The nurse will come in and give you some of our literature for first-time parents and websites you can browse. If anything comes up at all, you can call us. There is an emergency line in case you need to reach me. Stop at the front desk on your way out and schedule your next appointment. I'll be seeing you every month until your third trimester now. Lucky you."

I look over at Brooks as he beams down at the picture of our little blip. "It's really happening, we're having a baby."

"Yeah, we are Mia, and you're going to do great."

"But how do you know?"

"Because you're fierce. You aren't going to let anything happen to our little nugget."

The doctor clears her throat, a small smile crossing her face. "Any other questions I can answer before I go?" Heat streaks across my face, flushing me with embarrassment. I thought she'd already left the room.

Brooks looks at me shyly. I quirk an eyebrow. He turns to Dr. Morgan. "It's okay if we… you know, right? It won't like… hurt the baby or anything?"

She laughs, and the tension of his question melts away. "Yes, you can be intimate with her. It won't hurt the baby a bit."

He looks down. "Okay, and it can't see my like…" He runs his hands over his lower body and I stifle a giggle.

"No, it can't see anything, dad. You're good."

"And… I'm not gonna like whack him or her in the head or anything if we get a little frisky with things?"

"Oh, good Lord, Brooks. Your dick doesn't go into my uterus.

The baby will be just fine when you love me hard." A blush creeps across his face, and he laughs to cover the embarrassment.

Dr. Morgan chuckles and looks at me. "Any other questions, just send me an email or call. Here's my card."

"Thank you, doctor."

She leaves the room, and I turn to Brooks. "Really, Brooks?"

"What, I kind of have a big dick, according to you... I wanted to make sure it was okay..."

"You're a goof."

"You love me."

"I do. So much."

His voice gets all low. "Do you have any idea how much that hospital gown is turning me on?"

I wink and spin around, shaking my bare ass. "Oh yeah? Sexy with my ass hanging out?"

He nods. "Mmmhmm... I think it would look better on the floor if I do say so myself."

"I like it when you go all dark and naughty on me, Brooks. It's so hot."

"You know what's hot? You standing there all knocked up with my baby inside you. It makes me want to do very, very dirty things to you. Like inspect every single birthmark and freckle that runs across your skin with my lips. Lick every inch of skin until I'm sure that I've tasted all of you."

I drop my robe, bare naked in front of him and his eyes trail every dip and curve of my body. "How about this? Does this make it hot...?"

I don't even get the word hotter out before he's all over me—kissing me, running his hands up and down my body, making me ache for him. "Need you, Mia."

"Well, come get me, big boy." My hands find his belt buckle when there's a knock on the door. We fly apart like we've caught fire, and Brooks turns so he can push his raging boner down. I bend, grabbing the robe and draping it over my shoulders.

The door opens a crack. "Everything okay here?"

Brooks grunts behind me, clearly disappointed, and holds me in front of him. I'm assuming he doesn't want to share how turned on he is with the nurse. "Yeah, come on in," I call out.

"So, Dr. Morgan wanted me to give you some pamphlets and website links for any questions you may have. I think she already gave you the prenatal information and her card, but if not, it's in the packet as well. Anything else you two need before you go?"

I look back at Brooks and he winks. "No, I think we're good."

"Awesome. Don't forget to stop by the front desk on your way out."

"Oh, we won't," Brooks pipes up. She grins at us one more time, and with a congrats, she's gone.

I go to grab my clothes from the chair, but Brooks beats me to it. "Let me help you."

"Weren't you the one who just wanted to ravish me in the doctor's office?"

Dimples light up his face. "Hasn't changed, but the faster I can get you clothed… the faster I can get you in the privacy of our home to do any number of naughty things with you."

A yawn takes over, and I cover my mouth with my hand. "Ahhh."

He chuckles. "Right after you take a nap. You were up kind of early today."

"I couldn't sleep."

Leaning down, he holds out my panties for me to step into. He pulls them slowly up my legs, and my libido goes on a rampage. Apparently, my pre-pregnant horny was nothing compared to now…

He pulls them the last bit up over my ass and smacks it, then kisses my front. I love it when his lips are on my body. Pulling back, he lifts my bra. The black lace tickles my sensitive nipples, and I can't help but let out a giggle.

As he turns me to get the back clasped, he kisses my shoulder and my neck. Each kiss, another zap to my already tingly skin from him, just being this close to me. I'm losing it, about to ask him to strip and do me right on the floor... but I figure someone else would knock on the door and interrupt us again... I won't do that to Brooks and his raging boner.

Lifting my arms, he slides my cat graphic tee shirt over my head and bends to get my leggings, but I tsk him. "Oh no, you let me put those on myself."

I make a big deal of bending over slowly while biting my lip and looking over my shoulder at him. I slip each leg over my feet and pull up ever so slowly, making sure he sees every single movement. A low moan comes from Brooks' throat as he stands stoking himself behind me. "Problem?" I wink.

"You're being a tease, Mia. You remember what happens when bad girls tease? They get spanked."

"Oooo, you gonna go all bossy on me, Brooksy?"

"You're working your way up to not being allowed to come later. Add in that you left me high and dry after getting me all worked up last night, and it's looking like a long afternoon of build-up and let down for you."

I raise my hand to my chest, faking shock. "You wouldn't..."

"Keep teasing, and we'll see."

"Ya know, you were such a sweet little innocent thing a couple months ago..."

He winks at me. "I'd say by the way you're squirming, you definitely prefer the new and improved Brooks."

Damn, he's good. That was about the sexiest, un-strip tease I've ever had in my life. He leaned in and kissed me once before picking up my bag and turning to leave. The kiss left me in a lust induced haze, and my brain was simply puttering along. I think I can. I think I can.

He helps me put on my winter jacket and gloves. The cold has chosen to stick around, and that means the holidays will be coming soon. I hate the holidays.

Every single holiday growing up made me bitter. Thanksgiving was always a fight. Christmas was just another day where you didn't get presents, and my parents would yet again fight. I didn't look forward to them this year, but maybe with Brooks, it would be different. Soon, we would have a child to spoil on the holidays, and I needed to get over my hatred for them.

He looked back over his shoulder as he walked purposefully toward the door. "You coming, Mia?"

"Not yet, but I hope to be soon."

"Let's get going then. Good orgasms are being wasted as we speak…"

We walk down the hall together, his arm around my waist and mine around his. I think to myself that we may just be alright.

Twenty

Mia

It's been weeks since we got to see our little nugget for the first time on that black and white screen in Dr. Morgan's office. I've seen her twice since then, just for monthly exams and check-ups. The holidays have come and gone, leaving me in disbelief that it's New Years'.

Since I found out about the baby, I'd called Rising Tides and asked them to postpone my showing. I had too many other things going on without worrying about an art show too. Worrying about anything is not a good idea for the baby. I've fallen so hard in love with this little one, and it isn't even born yet.

I hope one day soon I'll be able to feel the first kick of our child. I'm consumed with overwhelming emotions during the first trimester. Spending most of it reading every book, I can get my hands on and then terrifying myself with every bad thing that might happen between now and the birth.

I wake Brooks up time and time again when my brain won't shut off with the questions constantly battering it. I'll be the first to admit the fear of the unknown scares me.

Scared I'll do something wrong.

Scared something will happen, and I'll lose that tiny little life that Brooks and I created.

Scared that I'd turn into my mother and rely on drugs to chase the feelings away.

Brooks always manages to calm me and make me believe we'll be better than our parents are.

We started talking about baby names, but without knowing if it's a girl or boy, it kind of leaves us standing still. All that changes today.

We're about to do the ultrasound that tells us if our little bundle is a girl or a boy. Dr. Morgan offered to do a genetic test at week 12 to determine the gender, but Brooks wanted to wait. Something about being together when we found out the gender.

The first couple of times after we'd seen my OB, he'd treated me with princess hands during sex. He wouldn't give me rough, worrying that he may hurt the baby or me in some way. I'd finally sat him down one night and told him that if he planned on not getting laid for the next year, then he needed to up his game... and up his game he did.

My love for Brooks grows daily. It's a constant in this life. Knowing that his love will never ebb or flow, it's steady.

He wakes up and holds my hair as I puke my morning away, then he'll make me a Rooibos tea and give me saltines, we'll talk about everything we'd read the night before while I work on my paintings, generally followed by a quickie, and then he'd leave for the day if he's scheduled to work.

We've become domestic, and for some reason, it doesn't bother me.

At night he comes home, and I go to work.

On nights that I don't work, we catch up on whatever show we've been binging on Netflix, and he'll rub my feet. I'm spoiled with this whole foot rubbing thing. Brooks even makes it his mission while grocery shopping to make sure I'm fully stocked up on dill pickles, ice cream, lays, and chocolate sauce.

When this crazy train started months ago, I never thought I'd be here now. Pregnant and barefoot in the kitchen with the love of my life.

Brooks has applied with a trade school to build on his desire to own a woodworking company. He wants to get a better job, and once the baby is here, we'll be making quite a few changes.

Today, we're back in the same room I was in for my eight-week appointment all those weeks ago. Luckily, no detestable stirrups this time. Dr. Morgan says we should be able to tell the sex with a non-uterine ultrasound, and that makes me gleeful. Just thinking about that probe makes my V cringe.

I don another one of those fashion gowns the nurse provides me. It rests against my bump, while a blanket covers my lower half. Score for being able to keep on my underwear.

The door opens, and the doctor walks in. "Mia, Brooks, how's momma doing today?"

"Good, anxious to find out what we're having," I blurt out first.

"Alright, well, let's get the ultrasound up and see what we can see." She sits down on the stool beside me, getting the machine up and running. Cool gel hits my belly, a vast difference in temperature from my skin. As she trails the wand over my stomach, my eyes are glued to the black and white screen, waiting. Brooks squeezes my hand, but I won't pull my eyes away, so I just squeeze back. I want to see as much of my baby as I can.

The wand moves over my stomach effortlessly thanks to the

gel, and she presses down slightly. The blip on the screen no longer looks like a blip. There are arms and legs, even toes and fingers. The baby's heartbeat thumps loudly throughout the room, and its music to my ears every time I hear it. It calms me that he or she has a strong heartbeat. Dr. Morgan makes a face at the screen, moves the wand again, another weird look. "Well, that's interesting."

My heartbeat shatters. Every bad thing I've read in the books comes to the forefront in my brain. I swallow audibly. I sneak a peek at Brooks, and his face looks pale. We've talked about all the things that could go wrong, so I'm sure his brain is scrambling to make sense too.

Getting up the courage, I ask, "What, what is it? What's wrong?"

A smile crosses her lips before she points to the screen. I'm not sure what she's looking at. "It appears there are two babies in there."

"There are what?" Brooks whispers to my side.

"You're having twins…"

"Twins…" It's all that slips out between his lips before he hits the ground, hard.

"Brooks!" I yell, catching Dr. Morgan's attention.

"Nurse!" Dr. Morgan calls out to no one in particular before the door opens, and one of the nurses I've seen before pops in. "We've lost Mr. Jansen to some exciting news." She points to Brooks on the floor.

"Brooks!" I'm in a panic. He just passed out and I can't move, I'm frozen in place as the nurse moves to help him.

Dr. Morgan grabs a hold of my hands, making me look at her. "Mia, I'm going to need you to stay calm. He's going to be just fine. Deep breath in, deep breath out." She breathes along with me and it seems to be helping. "I need you to calm down for the babies."

"Babies…" My brain still hasn't wrapped its head around the

fact that not only am I having one, but I'm having two. Two tiny babies.

"You and Brooks are going to be just fine." I shake my head, trying to speak. "You will. Look, he's waking up now. Just blacked out for a minute. Susan is going to help him into that chair." I watch as the nurse pulls a chair up to the bed and helps him sit down.

Looking up at me, his brow furrows. "What happened?"

Susan leans over to speak with him face to face. "Brooks, you fainted. I'm going to need you to sit here for a couple minutes and just relax."

Eyes still on me, he continues, "Did she say twins?"

"Yep, there's two in there. Way to go, dude. You didn't just knock me up, you pulled out all the stops."

He chuckles and I can't help but laugh.

"So… You want to know the sex today, right?" Dr. Morgan pulls our attention back to the screen.

Brooks speaks up before my mouth even opens. "Yes!"

"Well, if you look right here… baby number one is a little boy." I look up at Brooks as he looks closer and squints. "Is that his…"

"Yes," she confirms. "That's a penis."

"Look at that, Mia. Takes after his dad in the package department." I throw him a scowl.

"Brooks, behave," I admonish. He wiggles his eyebrows at me and winks. This man. I look back at the screen and emotions overwhelm me. What about the other baby?

She moves the wand around again, and baby number two appears. "Looks like baby number two is a little girl. A boy and a girl. How precious."

Not only am I having one baby, we're having two. I've secretly been hoping for a little boy, and it's the first time I admit it to myself, but I'm kind of excited for the possibility of a little girl too.

She continues moving the wand over my belly to get a better

view of them. Hitting the keys a couple of times as she snaps photos. "You have two perfectly healthy little ones on the way."

Tears invade my eyes. My blurry eyes find Brooks, and my heart can't help but beat faster. He wipes under his eyes, the emotions getting to him too. Each time we have another appointment, it seems more real. His dark chocolate eyes burn bright with love as he looks at me. He leans down, kissing my forehead. "You're doing so great, Mama Mia."

"I couldn't have done it without you." It's the truth. Had I not decided to give this I try, I probably wouldn't have Brooks by my side. The thought of that is just agonizingly painful. Our family just doubled in size with one tiny ultrasound. Isn't it funny how life works?

We've started setting up the nursery at this point. I gave up my room because I haven't slept in it in months. Brooks' room became our room. The nursery is being done in a theme of wood, black, blue, purple, and grey. I'm painting a mural on the wall across from where the cribs will sit.

Looking over my shoulder from where I'm working on the mural, I spot Brooks leaning against the doorway watching me. He takes up most of the doorway, and I can't but admire the man who's captured this crazy heart of mine.

"You get a camera yet?"

"No need."

"Oh yeah? Why's that?"

"I've got you forever now, it'll last longer than any photo I could take of you. Plus, there's no way I could erase you from my mind. You're perfect."

"Charmer…"

"Uh huh. Mind if I try?" He nods to the mural.

"What? You want to paint?"

"I'd love to try it."

"Okay, well, come on over." I watch as he walks across the room in all his manly glory. How did I get stuck with such a hottie? "Take this…" He grabs the paintbrush from my hand. "Now, paint along this line here." I point where I want him to start, and he pushes the brush to the wall leaving behind a streak of purple.

"Like this?" He looks to me for approval, and I can't help but smile. Leaning around him, I watch as he continues to paint strokes onto the wall.

"It's perfect."

"You know… you should probably be limited the amount of time you paint these days. I don't want you or our babies inhaling too many fumes."

"That's sweet, Brooks, but do I need to remind you of your stick figure drawing capabilities? Plus, it's pretty much done anyhow."

He chuckles, shaking his head. "Oh yeah, wanna see about my painting abilities?"

"Brooks…" I warn.

"What? I just want to show you how good I really am…" Not paying enough attention, I miss all the signs of what he's about to do until I feel the bristles of the brush glide over my left cheek, leaving behind cold, wet paint.

"You did not…"

"Oh, but I did." He laughs at the look of shock on my face, and I take the minute to grab paint from the easel and smear it across his own face.

His eyes widen as he realizes what I've just done. "Oh, now you're going to get it."

I giggle and try to run away, but Brooks snatches me into him.

Hands pressed softly to my bulging belly. "Got you," he whispers into my ear as he smears the paint I spread on him just a few minutes ago onto me again. "I'm never letting you go."

"You better not." I smile. Yes, I've become that hypocritical girl. The one who didn't believe in love is now head over heels in it. I blame Brooks and his swoony ways. See, I told you... Brainwashing.

We step back and look at what we've created. A teepee, grey with black, blue, and purple patterns. Blue for Brooks. Black for me. Purple for our newest additions.

Right above where one baby will sleep, over the crib, hangs a wooden circle with the name Wesley Greyson in big, bold black and white letters. Above the other hangs a second wooden circle with the name Piper Brielle in big, bold black and purple letters.

A knock on the front door stops us. "That must be the cribs." The white and black Aztec patterned carpet showed up yesterday and goes perfectly with the hardwood floors. Everything's coming together, and all we need are both cribs and dressers to complete the look.

A child's play teepee has been erected in the corner to go with the theme. Lantern lights hang proudly—one on each side of where the cribs will go. Willie and Charlie from the bar chipped in together and purchased me a rocker for the corner of the room. Black in color to go with the rest.

Brooks opens the door, and the guy delivering both cribs is Wyatt, the guy that started this all. I smile at the funny memories surrounding this moment. He smiles a knowing smile after looking to my stomach. My bump is on full display these days. Maternity pants my new way of life.

"Hey, man," Brooks says, lending his hand out to shake with his old roomie.

"Hey, stranger. I see things are going well for you these days."

Brooks looks back and smiles at me. "Sure are."

"Seems like some congrats are in order."

"Thanks."

He looks down at the package he laid against the door. "Crib?"

"Cribs. Twins."

"Wow, congrats you two."

"Thank you." I can't help but love the dimples that peek out with Brooks' smile.

Handing over the box, he nods. "Well, I'll leave you to it. May the force be with you. I've heard those are beasts to put together."

Brooks chuckles. "See Mia, Star Wars. It's a thing." I wrinkle my nose. I still to this day, can't get into Star Wars. Every other thing we watch together is something we both enjoy, but not that.

Closing the door, he picks up the boxes and heads back to Wesley and Piper's nursery. It's weird calling them by their names even though they aren't here yet, but not too much longer—several more weeks, hopefully.

As soon as we open the box to the first crib, it becomes clear what Wyatt said. So many tiny intricate pieces. "Um…Mia. We have an issue. These instructions are all in Spanish."

I throw my hand to my chest and fake gasp. "You don't know Spanish?! The audacity!" He looks at me, mouth agape like he isn't even sure how to respond to me. That's the case most days. Gotta keep him on his toes, right?

"Flip it over, Brooks. Is there an English version on the other side?"

"Yep, right. Got it." He takes a few minutes before looking over again. "Hey, do you think it'd be sexy if I learned Spanish as a second language?"

"Only if you learn the dirtiest words…"

"My naughty little girl."

"Mmmhmm, and this naughty little pixie brain is thinking the dirtiest things about you right now and very well might need a shower."

"Shower is too dangerous to bang you like I want to, baby. I'm pro-bed these days."

I stick out my bottom lip in a pout. "No fair. I like naughty shower sex."

He groans, probably thinking about how hot it was the last time we'd had shower sex. So...hot. When I first started getting my baby bump, I'd protested that I was getting too fat for sex. I was only getting bigger. I wondered if at some point he was going to stop finding me attractive, but he was insatiable. He never wanted to stop. It was almost as if my being pregnant made him want it more.

He picks me up and carries me to our room. Ripping my leggings from my body, he doesn't even seem apologetic. Next comes my shirt. He can't wait to get me naked. I've taken on a zero-tolerance policy on wearing underwear, and a bra these days seems to be taxing unless I'm going to work or out.

"Mmhmm. I like it when you don't wear underthings."

I shake my head at him. "Underthings, Brooks, really? I thought we were past this phase."

He shrugs, followed by a wink. "They will always be underthings, Mia. But they're very sexy underthings."

The cribs forgotten, Brooks does what he does best. He makes me forget that a world exists outside of the two of us. We move as one as we make love that night. It's poetic watching our shadows paint the walls, much like my brush painting a canvas. We're still painting the canvas of our life, one stroke at a time.

Twenty-One

Brooks

Zara and Macy talked me into letting them throw Mia a surprise baby shower. Knowing her answer would've been hell no had they asked, they decided to go ahead and do it, consequences be damned.

Eddie shut down Topsy Turvy at three this afternoon and kicked everyone out. The guests for the baby shower will be arriving soon, and they need to get everything cleaned and set up beforehand.

She may hate me for keeping this from her. Mia isn't a fan of surprises or change—in fact, she loathes it, but if her best friends want to throw a party for her, far be it for me to get in the middle of it. I'll deal with whatever comes my way. Hopefully, it'll be Mia...

I find her sitting in the rocking chair in the nursery rubbing her belly. She's glowing, and I can't help but appreciate it. She's all baby and she's gorgeous. Every time I see her these days, she just looks so perfect. To me, she's always been perfect, perfectly imperfect to me. Looking up, she sees me and smiles. "Hey, Brooksy. I'm still finding it so hard to believe that our little ones will be here in less than a month's time. Heck, I can't believe it's almost been a year since we moved in together. I'm so not ready."

"You're going to do just fine, Mia. I believe in you, in us. It's a great big world, and we have our whole lives ahead of us. I wouldn't want to do this journey with anyone but you."

A tear slides down her cheek, and she swipes it away quickly.

"Hey," I say softly. "What are the tears for now?"

"I guess I'm just emotional. When I was a kid, my mom was the best mom. She seemed like the perfect person. Like she had it all together because that's what she let me see as a child. She had me fooled into thinking that the world was okay."

Another tear slips down her cheek. "She was strong, brave. I thought she was invincible, but she hid her true self. Inside she was breaking down. It started slowly, but bit by bit, her true colors started to show. She cracked a little every day and the only person that knew it was her. Until it was too much, and then little by little, it crept into her daily life. My heart aches knowing that she'll never meet her grandchildren, but I also can't allow myself to feel bad about it either because I won't put anyone through what I went through. I hate that the person she became will never get to meet her grandchildren or have an impact on their lives."

I reach out, letting my fingers slip down her arm. "No child should have to see their mom turn into a drug addict, Mia. It's not fair to you."

"I know. Just... so many emotions going on up here today." She points to her head, and I understand that well. I often wonder the same thing. How would my parents feel about not knowing their grandchildren, but I've always come back to the same conclusion. They disowned me, so they don't get a choice in the matter and I'd never raise a child how I grew up.

"Well, then let me take you somewhere. Let me do something nice for you. Do you trust me?"

She smiles the smile she only gives to me. A twinkle of light in her bright blue eyes. "You know I do."

"Okay, then." I walk back into the living room, grabbing her purse. She meets me at the door to the nursery and quirks her eyebrows. "Where are we going?"

"Me to know, Mia. You to find out. Now hurry. We don't want to miss it." Handing her her purse, I kiss the top of her head.

I'm so deeply in love with this woman. I can't believe that it's summer already. I go to help her down the stairs, and she gives me the look. The I-can-do-it-myself look.

"You know I don't need help, right?" *Sassy girl.*

"You also know I'm going to help you whether you complain or not, right? You're eight months pregnant, Mia. Your safety is my main concern right now." Down ten steps to the sidewalk, through the door, and we're ready. I open the car door and help her in before jogging to my own side and jumping in. I've brought a tie with me to cover her eyes, and when I pull it out, a smirk runs across her face. Yep, she remembers this tie well. Or more like, how I blindfolded her and then loved her into submission a couple nights ago.

"A blindfold, really?"

"Yep, you said you trusted me. We're doing this." She holds still as I reach over from the driver's seat and loosely tie it around her head, making sure random hairs don't get caught in the knot. "Can you see anything?" I say, waving my hand in front of her face.

"No, but I can feel things just fine." She reaches over and runs her fingers along the outside of my pants right over where my dick rests.

"Hey, play nice, or I'll have to bend you over my knee later."

"Promise?" She smiles.

"Naughty… always so very naughty." I know the possibility of bending her over my knee these days is non-existent. Her belly is too big, and I miss making love to her and looking into those beautiful sapphire eyes.

Pulling up to the bar a couple minutes later, she looks over at me. I can't see her eyes, but I know she's wondering why it's only been a couple minutes since we started driving. Grabbing my phone from my pocket, I text the group text Zara, that Macy added me to, letting them know we're outside.

Zara: *About damn time, what were you doing? And if you tell me I was sitting around waiting for you two to finish going at it, I'm gonna smack you.*
Me: *No, Mia was a little sad. I was trying to comfort her.*
Zara: *So you comforted her with your dick. Real suave, Brooks. *winking emoji* *
Me: *Be in soon, behave.*
Zara: *Never.*

"You ready, Mia?" I ask softly, and she nods. "Stay here, I'll come around and grab you."

"Good, I can't see you so…"

"Don't be saucy…"

She fake pouts for a second, but then a smile peeks through. "Okay."

I get out and run around the car, opening her door. Giving her my hands, I help her stand up from the car. "Can you take this blindfold off now?"

"Nope, wait til we get inside."

"Okay."

Mia

I hear whispers and movements as soon as we walk through the door. The familiar smell of stale beer clues me in on where we are, and it makes me wonder why he's chosen the bar. I can't see anything because he hasn't taken the damn blindfold off yet, and it's driving me crazy, but the rest of my senses are working just fine. I hear the whispers. I feel his strong hand as it holds me.

"Brooks…"

"Yes, Pixie?"

"Why are we at Topsy Turvy?"

The lights turn on, and suddenly I can see everything. Brooks removes his tie, and in front of me stands Zara and Macy smiling like Cheshire cats. "What's going on, bishes?"

"We're throwing you a baby shower! SURPRISE!" Everyone joins in for the surprise part. I'm in shock. I'd wondered if they were planning something. Macy and Zara don't normally talk, but she stopped into the bar a couple of times in the last month. Macy never comes to Topsy Turvy, not since Trevor.

As my eyes roam over everyone here, I realize that every single one of these people has become our family over the last couple of years. Eddie, the bar owner, stands to the side with Willie and Charlie.

Zara dragged Donatello with her. He's a silver fox, so he has to be close to his late thirties. *Hawt, girl.* I think to myself, remembering her telling me about what he'd made her do for him at the club. I've seen him once or twice in the bar, but he's more up close in this intimate setting.

Trevor stands with his arm wrapped around Macy, smiling. Trevor's parents, Lucille and Maxwell, stand off to the side looking on. I can't tell if it's a legit smile or if they just have gas. You can never tell with those two. They're a weird couple.

A couple of servers from the bar are there—Sidney and Serena. Wyatt and another girl stand to the side. This must be the infamous Kaylen. Behind everyone, gifts are lined up across the bar—everything in little boy and girl colors. Brooks must have spilled the beans about the colors we'd chosen—gifts in blues, purples, greys, and black. I sneak a quick, narrowed eye at Brooks, and he winks.

"You…"

"Me?"

He put his hands up in defense.

"How did you?"

He shakes his head and nods at his co-conspirators. He'd happily throw them under the bus, and I'm sure it was technically their idea… He looks so happy tonight. The smile on his face spreads the whole way to his eyes. It's real, I see the love when he looks at me. The spark of life in his eyes when he talks to our babies. Hard to believe that a few months ago, I thought love was just a myth.

"Zara and Macy practically held me at gunpoint and made sure I followed their demands. Don't blame me. Blame them for sure."

Arms crossed in front of her, she sticks out her hip. "Uh huh."

We clink our glasses together and take a sip of sparkling grape juice. I miss my liquor but going without is worth it. Now that I have this wonderful reason not to drink. Eddie grabs some beers for the guys from the bar, and everyone else seems to be hanging out, mingling with each other. I'm sure Brooks is thrilled about the beer. He hasn't been drinking on my account, and I feel bad that he's missing out because of me. Even though he told me it doesn't bother him.

"I think this is the first time I've been in a bar and not had alcohol. It's weird, Mia. Super weeeirrrrd." Zara stretches out the word making Macy and I giggle.

"Oh hush, it's not that bad. If I've had to do without for almost nine months, I think you can survive one teeny tiny night. Plus, I believe you were the ones who planned this little ordeal…"

"Brooks had a part in this too. He wanted to do something nice for you. That man is a total goner for you, Mia. There is nothing he wouldn't do to make you smile, to make you happy forever. You found a good one, finally, AND he's sexy as hell, girl." My eyes drift to where my man is standing with Wyatt, Charlie, Donatello, and Willie. Our eyes lock at the same time so effortlessly. He winks, and my heart beats just a little bit faster. A tiny foot kicks my gut, and I wince. A look of concern mars his face and he mouths, *you okay?*

I smile back. Baby is kicking. He raises an eyebrow as if he has no idea what I'm saying, then excuses himself from the guys.

Quiet catcalls leave Zara's mouth as she turns to watch him walk our way and the blush that crosses Brooks' face is absolutely priceless. I'm pretty sure she still makes him uncomfortable.

He walks up to me and leans down to kiss my head. His breath sending light touches against my ear as he whispers. "Did you ask me to go fishing?"

I groan. "Good Lord, man, we're gonna have to work on your lip reading...let's think this through, shall we? Have I ever mentioned going fishing before? Can you picture me hooking and gutting a fish?"

He laughs. "That's an excellent point you have."

"The babies are kicking, Brooks. A tiny little foot... oomph. There he goes again." He lays his hand gently on my baby bump and smiles when the one of the babies kicks again. His eyes twinkle deep brown every time it happens. It's one of those priceless moments we won't have again, unless we have more kids, which we haven't even discussed yet. "How do you know who's kicking?"

"I don't. I'm just guessing."

"You guys are so adorable, it's sickening. Hold my non-alcoholic drink while I politely barf, Macy." Zara jests smirking at my other best friend.

Donatello walks up behind Zara, slips a hand lightly into her hair, and pulls her head toward him. "Do I hear you being a bad girl over here?"

She smirks. "Uh huh. You planning to do something about it, big man?"

"I should give you something for that mouth of yours, but I'm guessing this party is a little more appropriate than that so…" He looks up, his eyes meeting Brooks. "You guys got a bathroom or stockroom around here. Apparently, my lady needs to learn some manners."

Brooks tilts his head with a smile toward the hallway. "Bathrooms that way. Make sure you lock the door."

One nod is all Don gives Brooks. Zara puts her hand into Don's outstretched one, and they leave us watching them walk away.

I'm feeling all sorts of hot and bothered just thinking about the few things he'd said. I want bossy Brooks again. He hasn't been bossy with me for a while, and I hope that I can talk him into it later. He does owe me after springing this little shindig after all.

Macy stands up. "Okay, everyone—gifts or games?"

"Gifts!" everyone shouts back. I'm thankful. I'd heard of the games played at these events and am horrified at the idea of them. Like melting candy pieces and putting them in diapers for people to identify… who does that?

Macy pulls two chairs in front of the bar helps me as I sit down even though I protest. I understand the reason. I'm the size of a barn, and I'm front heavy. Brooks helps her move the gifts to the floor beside me so I can easily reach them. He stands beside me as I open the first couple of gifts. It's annoying me, and I need him to be on my level.

"Brooks, want to sit down?"

"Nah, I think I'm good here."

"Brooks, I think you should sit down."

"Seriously, I don't mind standing."

"If you do not sit down, I will go pregnancy crazy on your ass… do you really want to see that?"

I watch as he slowly walks over to the chair and sits down, arms out in defense as if I'm a wild animal ready and poised to take him out.

"Okay, I'm sitting. Happy?"

"Tickled pink."

By the end of all the presents and then games. Yeah, so much for thinking I was getting out of that situation. I'm ready to pass the crap out. I've never been so tired as I am being pregnant. Then again, carrying extra weight around on the front for eight months and constantly feeling like you're going to tip forward and sink like the titanic doesn't help much either.

Most of the guests help clean up all the wrapping paper, and Eddie sticks around to help load the gifts into the back of his truck and bring them to the apartment. They won't fit in my Miata without multiple trips. It's nice seeing everyone, and I appreciate all the love they showed for Wesley and Piper. They're going to be two spoiled little kiddos for sure. We say our goodbyes, thanking them for the gifts.

Macy drops down in the chair next to me and huffs. "I didn't realize how much work went into coordinating one of these things…"

I reach over and give her a hug. "Thank you for doing this."

A tear sneaks its way down my cheek, and she smiles. "There's the girl with feelings. I like her. You should bring her out more."

"If you tell anyone, I will cut you."

"And there's the Mia I know and love." I stick my tongue out at her, but I'm so thankful for her. After college, I'd stuck around for Macy. She needed me after her mom died, and then again when her dad died. We're best friends, and that's something you just can't replace.

I rub my hand over my belly, feeling Wesley and Piper moving around again. "So when are you and Trevor planning on having a horde?"

"Well, first off, we are not aliens, so no horde."

"You sure about that? Trevor is so strait-laced that I sometimes wonder if he's even breathing. Like I want to legit poke him just to make sure he flinches."

"Mean…"

"Truth."

"He's not that bad. He just… doesn't understand the concept of fun at times. He grew up with Lucille and Maxwell…"

"That explains a lot. She smiled at me earlier, and I couldn't tell if it was a legit smile. She'd had too much Botox, she was constipated, or just had really bad gas…"

Macy bends over laughing and I can't help but join her.

"I have that same problem sometimes… figuring out if she's smiling, that is. Not the whole gas part."

"I can imagine. But seriously, though, I thought you wanted kids right away after you got married?" I lean over and bump her with my shoulder.

She shrugs. "I did… but I'm still in school and helping with the shelter part-time. Trevor's running the shelter. We don't really have time right now to settle and do the whole baby thing. But I do kinda have baby fever… like I can't wait for Wesley and Piper to get here so I can love all over their cute little squishy faces." She moves her fingers up like she's squishing something.

"Did you just talk about my children like a dog's floppy cheeks? You have serious issues."

"Hey, they may be chunky, you don't know…"

"Compared my sweet bundles of joy to a dog and then called them fat. Winning friends right now, Macy. Winning friends…"

"Hey! That is for whacking me along the backside of my head and calling me dumb when I didn't realize how bad Trevor had it for me!"

"Fine, I'll let it slide."

She nods. "Thank you. I don't know if I'll ever be ready for kids. It seems like just yesterday we were in college and now you're having not one, but two babies. I mean, it's insane."

I rub my belly. "Yeah, I didn't think I was ready either. Most days, I'm still scared shitless. But you see that man over there?" I point to Brooks, and he waves at us. "He's the reason I can do this, and I can't imagine having it any other way. Doing it with anyone but him."

"Did he ask you to marry him again yet?"

"Nope, I think he's scared now."

"Well, you did kind of freak out on him and run..."

"I know, but I've been giving him hints, Macy. Leaving things up on the computer that say bride or obviously watching movies with brides in them, and he's still not getting it."

"Honey, boys are dumb. Sometimes you need to go Bam Bam Flintstone on their butts until they get it."

She looks at my hair and then smiles. "Have I told you how good motherhood looks on you? I love that you let your hair go back to its normal color. I always thought you looked pretty as a strawberry blonde."

"Don't get used to it. Dr. Morgan had strict orders that I couldn't dye it until after my first trimester, and then I just kind of forgot to get it redone. Once these babies are out, though, it's blue, pink, and purple for me again."

Macys hands reach over, and I feel her fingers weave through my hair. "Why not just leave it the way it is, though? It's so pretty. Plus, it is so silky and smooth. I could totally, totally just sit here and pet you all day."

"Haha, like the day I got to pet a penis? I wanted to stroke it all day long."

"That's what she said!" she teases.

I laugh, but then remember my reasoning for wanting to

remain a cotton candy color, haired lady. "Because Macy, this strawberry blonde is the old me. It's fighting parents, smoking, and fucking boys who broke my heart. But blue, purple, and pink… it's the new me. The bold, confident woman who fell in love with a man and who's having his children. This cotton candy color hair kind of brought me my very own happily ever after."

"I get it, Mia. It's you now. The post family drama you. The grown-up, I've got my shit together, and I'm having a twins with the man of my dreams, you."

"Exactly."

I look down at myself. "You know what else I like about this pregnancy? This rack. I mean look at my boobs, Macy. Look at them. They're huge."

"I'm sure Brooks is enjoying the perks of that."

"Oh, he totally is! Let's just say this whole pregnancy, I haven't really been able to keep my grabby little hands off him. He's just so damn sexy, and then you take off all those clothes and I'm a total goner. Like put a dick in me, and I'm done."

"Interesting twist on the stick a fork in me quote…"

"Isn't it, though? Totally thought of it and ran that sucker hard."

My mind travels back to Brooks, making love to me last night. The scratchy ends of his beard, rubbing me raw and leaving marks across my thighs and between my legs. He's always so enthusiastic when he makes love to me with his tongue, going over every inch of my skin, making sure no spot goes untouched by his love. A smile crosses my lips, and I squirm in my seat.

Out of the corner of my eye I catch Brooks walking toward us. A small box in his hand. The same box I wondered about when he first moved in. When he gets to us, he pulls over a chair in front of me.

"Where have you been?" I ask curiously.

"Had to run home for my gift for you tonight."

"And you waited until everyone left?"

"Yep, this is a special gift, and I didn't want to share it with everyone."

Macy gets up and tries to excuse herself. "You don't have to leave, Macy. You can stay."

She looks to Brooks, and he nods in agreement. "Okay." Sitting back down, she crosses her legs, placing her hands folded over them, waiting.

I open the box on my lap and look inside. Wooden toys, baby shoes, and other random baby items greet me. "What is all this?"

"I've been saving this stuff for when I had my own little one, and now I want to share it with you. The wooden toys I made when I was younger and didn't have any other entertainment than a knife and a piece of wood. A horse, since they were my favorite animals when I was growing up. I'd sit and watch them frolic around and play when I was a boy. I never got to actually ride them. I was told I was there to help where needed, and riding horses never came into play. So I watched them from afar, admiring them. Much like I admired you."

"It's true you were quite the stalker…"

"Hey now, I never stood outside your apartment like a creeper, I just admired you from across the bar, hoping that one day you'd grace me with your presence."

"That's almost sweet."

"It's true. The day you asked if I wanted to move in with you, I almost passed out. I was scared to death that you were going to chew my ass up and spit me out."

"I was not like that."

Macy took that moment to laugh. I raise my eyebrow. "Why are you laughing?"

"Well, it's true. You do have a tendency to throw off this leave me alone, or I'll cut you vibe sometimes. I don't mind it, but to an outsider, I could see it being intimidating. You know when she first mentioned you, Brooks, she wouldn't shut the hell up about how hot you were and how you had a nice package, right?"

Brooks laughs, his eyes finding mine. "Oh, really?"

"Yep and looks like I was right all along. Looks good, smells good, has a pretty package."

He harrumphs. "My package is big and manly, not pretty, never pretty. Mia, do you remember what I promised you in the car earlier if you didn't behave?"

I feign ignorance. "Um, no. Care to remind me?"

He shakes his head and then leans in, hot breath against my skin. "I will spank you. And you will like it." I take in a big whoosh of air. Damn.

Trevor walks up behind Macy. "Alright, Mace. Eddie and I got everything loaded into the truck. You ready to go? Got an early morning at the shelter, and you have classes."

"Sure do." She stands up, and I slowly follow suit. "Guess that's goodnight for me. I am so proud of you, Mia. You're going to be a great mom. I can't wait to meet your little ones in a few short weeks."

"Thank you for all this, Macy."

"You're welcome, mama. I wanted you to know how much we all cared about you."

Eddie follows us back to the apartment, and Brooks helps bring in all the gifts from our friends. Not expecting a baby shower has me feeling so many things with how many gifts we received tonight. The love is overflowing for Wesley and Piper.

Onesies, a double stroller, car seats, bottles, milk pumps, bibs, identical high chairs, and so many other gifts litter our apartment. Where we have room for all of this stuff is beyond me, but I don't want to give up this place. It's my home for years, where I feel the most comfortable in the whole world.

"Thanks so much for helping us bring all this stuff home, Eddie," I say with a sleepy yawn.

"No problem at all, Mia. I don't mind a bit."

"Alright, I'll get outta your hair. See you in the morning, Brooks." And with that, he's gone. Finally, some alone time with my man.

"Geez, I'm beat! This mama needs some serious beauty sleep time."

"You're beautiful enough."

"I'm still sleepy, Brooksy."

He comes over and gives me a hug, kissing my head. "Go to bed, Pixie girl. I'll get this all into the nursery, then come and join you."

The room is dark, and I'm hot. It's now the middle of summer and thank goodness I spent most of my pregnancy in the cold because I could not handle it now. I'm glad Brooks isn't joining me now, or else I'd be hot for sure. He's a death by cuddles kinda cuddler, and I wouldn't be able to breathe.

"Hey, Brooks. Can you turn down the AC for a little while? I'm hot."

"Sure thing, Mia."

I hear the rustle of the air kicking on and know that I'll be feeling much better shortly.

I shred my leggings, shirt, and bra and slip under the cool covers. This mattress Brooks got has some sort of cooling technology that helps me from burning up all night long.

Just as sleep is taking me under, I hear footsteps. The sheet rustles behind me, and the mattress dips. Brooks slips in front of me but stays on his own side.

Thank God.

His cologne's heady scent worships my nostrils, and I breathe it in deeply. He's taken off his shirt too because I can feel the heat radiating off his body. My fingers trail along his chest and play with the little bit of hair that runs across it. He lifts his hand, cupping my cheek, and kissing me on the lips. Heat shoots through me, but the desire for sleep is too overwhelming.

We lay there in silence for a few minutes longer. His steady beating heart is like a lullaby drifting me off to dreamland. He's claimed me, heart and soul. He may not be perfect, but he's everything good and pure in a man. He's not perfect by any means, but our imperfections mar together perfectly.

Epilogue

Brooks

"I don't think I can do this!" she screams at me, squeezing the life out of my hand as she pushes.

"You're doing great, Mia. You're almost done. Just a little bit more." I wipe a washcloth over her forehead, trying to get some of the sweat on her brow.

"Why are you rubbing my head like a dog?"

"You're sweating, my beautiful girl."

She glares at me. "Don't call me that. Ever again. In fact, let's go with never. I'm not beautiful right now. I'm gross."

I shake my head. "You don't mean that Mia."

She swears like a sailor again and squeezes my already dying hand. "That goes for your dick too. I never want to see your amazingly large dick. I thought it ruined me, instead, it's your children. Murdering me slowly from the inside out and I hate you."

"Okay, hate me, Mia. As long as you push, you can hate me as long as you want to."

"Good, because I really, really want to murder you right now… with a sharpened pencil, because a gun would be too painless."

Okay, I think to myself. The crazy is in the building. I don't react to her lashing out. I know she's in a great deal of pain. She refused an epidural, and I'm fairly positive that she's regretting that decision very much right now.

"Get it out of me. It's splitting me in half!" she's yelling again as our doctor smiles and looks up at me.

"You're doing great, Mia. Only a couple more pushes, and baby number one will be here with us."

"Are you sure I can't have that epidural? It sounds really good right about now…"

"Yes, I'm sure, Mia. One more big push. You're so close."

Mia grits her teeth and pushes one more time, and the sweetest sound hits my ears. A loud, piercing scream. Mia falls back onto the bed, heaving and breathing heavily.

I lean over to kiss her, giving her every single praise I can think of because she's literally pushed a baby out of her V, as she likes to call it, and there's still one to go. I'm so damn proud of her.

"You have a beautiful baby boy, " Dr. Morgan announces with a smile. My heart only grows as I watch the nurse take our little guy over to the table and wipe him clean. His lungs are definitely fully developed because he hasn't stopped screaming since he came out.

"You have a very healthy little guy here. Looks like he's eighteen inches and six pounds, one ounce. And very good lungs. My, oh my." She smiles.

"Okay, Mia. We've got one more baby in there who wants to meet you."

"I don't think I can do this, Dr. M." She adamantly shakes her head.

"You're strong, Mia. You're the strongest person I know. You can do this," I say to her in a low voice.

She nods her head, a sheen of sweat on her forehead slipping down her chest. "Okay, okay."

A couple more minutes of pushing and a second shrieking cry pierces through the air. "A beautiful baby girl."

The nurse does the same thing with our baby girl. Taking her over to the table to clean her off. She's not screaming like her brother, but she did cry a little. "Another very healthy little girl. She's seventeen inches and five pounds, eight ounces. She's adorable, you two."

I thought my heart couldn't take anymore, but it beats furiously within me, a happy melody. The melody of hope. Of new beginnings. Of a furious love that can't be taken away. Our little girl is swept away to be cleaned up a little before the nurse looks up and asks the question I've been waiting for since we got here earlier today.

"Do you want to hold them?"

I nod yes at the same time, Mia says yes. She looks exhausted. Sweat coats her hair, and her face is flushed from pushing. Her breathing has calmed slightly, but it's still heavier than normal. The nurse swaddles our little bundles up and is walking them over to Mia, instructing her to lift the gown so they can have skin to skin bonding time. They're placed gently on her chest, and tears stream down her face. Mia looks up at me. "We did it, babe. They're here, and they're beautiful."

"You did it, Pixie. I'm so damn proud and happy right now."

She raises her hand and runs a finger along his chubby little cheeks, cooing softly to our twins. My heart beats wildly in my chest, my pulse strong with love for all three of them. At this moment, my life is perfect. I lean over and kiss his blonde peach fuzz head, followed by her dark fuzz head. "Welcome to the world, Wesley Greyson and Piper Brielle. We're your mom and dad."

"Which last name do you want to use, Mia?"

"Jansen."

"Are you sure?"

"Well, I'm hoping that someday soon we'll all be Jansen's." She smiles a teary smile and looks back at the bundles of joy in her arms.

"I like the sound of that. Well then, welcome to the world, Wesley Greyson and Piper Brielle Jansen. We love you so much, little ones." I run my forefinger over Wesley's hand, and he reaches out to latch onto me. My heart melts. I'm absolutely done for with one simple touch. There I go again, collecting tiny moments of treasure along my lifetime. Each time I experience something new and exciting, I'm reminded that I knew nothing when I first asked if I could breathe without a heartbeat.

"They're perfect."

I look at her. "Just like you."

"No, just like us. Two perfectly imperfect creatures making a perfectly imperfect, awkward, and topsy turvy life together."

I'd gone in search of tea early the next morning. It proved a success after I finally found the cafeteria. I open the door to our hospital room, and Mia's soft snores welcome me. I look over to the babies and watch as their little arms and legs move within the swaddle they're wrapped up in.

It was a rough night for Mia. She'd slept lightly, waking every time Wesley or Piper moved. The nurse had shown her how to get each baby to latch onto her, and it'd taken a few times for them to get the hang of it, but my kiddos are smart cookies. I glide using soft steps across the floor to my chair beside the bed and sit down.

Flowers litter the room, painting each table in bright colors.

The floral scent mixes with the sterile smells of a typical hospital room, making it almost bearable. Most have accompanying balloons and cards that say "Congrats," "It's a girl," or "It's a boy." A few stuffed animals are scattered throughout as well.

All of our friends sent their well wishes. Macy and Trevor. Zara and Don. Trevor's parents. It still hurt not being able to tell my parents that I was finally happy and exactly where I'm meant to be, but I chose this life. I chose to walk away. Best damn decision I've ever made.

Don, as I'd taken to calling him, came back a little later on without Zara, and we chatted for a while, catching up on everything that's happened since he left. I still find it hard to believe he owns a sex club, but he's doing what he wants to do, same as me.

Tears blur my vision as I look at my sleeping girlfriend and the gift she's given me in Wesley and Piper.

I'm exhausted. Every time Mia was up, I was up. Sleep calls to me, but I can't pry my eyes away from my precious family in front of me. My eyes trail over Mia. She stopped dying her hair once Dr. Morgan told her she couldn't in the first trimester. It's a silky strawberry blonde color. It fits her, but I much prefer her rainbow-colored glory. It's much more her. She stirs when I reach out to hold her hand, and sapphire blue eyes meet mine. "Shhh, go to sleep, my Pixie girl. I'm just gonna sit here and rock our little ones."

She nods, and her eyes flutter shut again at my command. Sleep takes her soon enough, and her soft breathing tells me she's out. The tea I'm holding may be cold by the time she wakes up, but I know where the source is now so I can get it for her whenever.

The babies start cooing, and I'm drawn to them. Lifting them out of the hospital edition cribs, I return to my seat and start swaying slowly, my motions putting them back to sleep. The nurse suggested that I take off my shirt and let both babies' bond with me, skin to skin like they did with Mia yesterday, but we'll do it later.

Right now, I just want to hold these little miracles in front of me. I lean over and kiss Wesley and then Piper's forehead softly like I do to their mom. It's become second nature to me.

Mia's eyes drift open again, and she groans. "Do you know what that does for me?"

"What does?"

"You sitting there looking so manly holding our children in your arms?" she purrs. It's been a while since we've had sex, and I miss it but I wouldn't change this for the world. The way Mia is looking at me right now makes me want to strip naked and do dirty things to her, but I resist. I don't need to be thinking about anything like that with the little ones right in front of me. That's indecent.

"Stop ogling, Mia."

"I can't help it. It's like the worst best mommy porno right now."

"Six long agonizing weeks, Mia. No sexy time until then."

"We can do other stuff though." She wiggles her eyebrows at me.

"You need to sleep, ma'am. You'll need all the rest you can get, so take it while you can. If you behave and do as you're told, I may show you my cock later."

"Oooo, how about you send me a dick pic? That was on our list, and we never got to it. We still have so many things we haven't tried yet."

"Mia…" I warn her.

"I know, I know. Sleep."

She goes to close her eyes again and then sighs. "Brooks?"

"Yeah?"

"I'm sorry about all the mean and hurtful things that potentially came out of my mouth yesterday."

"Already forgiven. I expected nothing less. You were incredibly brave foregoing that epidural."

"I was a moron."

"You're amazing. Just remember that for next time."

"There will be no more next time for a very long time."

"Just to be clear, are we talking about another baby or sex? Because I have an issue with the no more sex thing…"

"Oh, loads and loads of sex, Brooks. You can't get out of that one. Even when I'm old and gray, I'll still be asking to ride you like a stripper pole."

I chuckle a hearty laugh, quickly quieting when I remember the sleeping babies.

"Go to sleep, my sexy lady. We need some baby daddy bonding time."

She grumbles but complies with my request. Seconds later, she relaxes back into her pillow and hits dreamland.

I look down at my children. Wesley's blonde hair sticks out like he's been having a really bad hair day, and I can't help but laugh. I wondered what he would look like when he was finally here. He reminds me of his mom. Cute little nose, blue eyes, blonde peach fuzz, but I see me in him too, especially in those little dimples. Leaning down, I bring my lips to his little forehead and plant a kiss, inhaling his baby scent—the scent of new life, of miracles.

Piper, however, is a stark contrast to her brother. Her hair is darker like mine, and everything's in place. She already has a frown marring her perfect little face and I hope that doesn't speak of what's to come. I see alot of Mia in her facial features and smile. It's still hard to believe that now we have twins. Two little ones to care for instead of just one. It means double of everything, but I'm ready for all of it because I finally got the girl.

Piper starts to fall asleep, and I stand up slowly and return her to the hospital crib. I just want to hold my little boy and look at those cute blue eyes.

Sitting back down, I allow my finger to run slowly down his soft skin and a little hand reaches out to grab my pinkie. Something explodes in my chest, and a hole I didn't even know existed seals itself tightly. Everything in this single moment has made me feel whole, complete. Each phase of this relationship with Mia has given me something more. The touch of my children has given my life so much more meaning than I could ever imagine. I'm collecting all of these memories and storing them in my mind.

For the second time in my life, I feel an intense connection. I knew from the moment Mia's eyes met mine that she was it for me, and I feel it the same way when I look at these sweet babies.

Is it too soon to admit that my life is way too fulfilling? Gorgeous girlfriend that I hope will someday be my wife, a beautiful baby boy who is peacefully cooing in my arms, holding my pinkie finger, and a cute little girl fast asleep in her crib. My hope is that they never experience being unloved or feeling unwanted. My hope is that they grow up strong and knowing that they're the best thing that's ever happened to Mia and I. Neither may have been planned, but they're little six pound blessings.

We sit there for what seems like hours before I hear Mia stir again. Little mister gets grumpy, and I wonder if he needs a diaper change. I smell him and grimace... yep, that's a new diaper needed for sure. Without trying to wake Mia up, I walk him over to the table and start changing his diaper. I pull back the front flap and am met with a urinating baby. Pee is going all over me, and I'm trying to cover it like a water valve that won't shut off. I hear laughter behind me and look over to find Mia watching.

"Isn't he magical?"

"Magical isn't the specific word I was thinking, no," I grumble, frustrated. "How much pee does this kid have in there?"

She shakes her head. "Welcome to parenthood, Brooksy."

"Gahh... let's hope there's a shower in here. Thank God I brought another set of clothes." I hadn't planned on getting peed on, but I threw in an extra set just in case.

I finish changing the diaper, and Mia asks to hold Wesley. I wrap him up and walk him over to her. Watching as she unlatches her hospital gown and allows him to latch on. I should probably give them privacy, but I can't stop watching this intimate moment before me.

"Lucky guy."

"Brooks..."

"What? I miss booby time, and now I won't get it for a while."

"Believe me, it's not as pleasant as it looks..."

"I'll take your word for it."

Walking over, I lean down to my baby girl again and kiss her forehead. "Look at us, Mia. Hardcore adulting. We did it. You did it. We have the most beautiful little gifts in the world."

"Was it all worth it?"

"It was always worth it. You, Wesley, and Piper will always be more than just worth it to me. You're everything I've ever dreamed of and more."

Extra Epilogue

Mia

The gallery buzzes with enthusiasm. A lot of people came tonight just to see my work. For so many years, I kept my most precious works hidden from the world; it's nice to see them lined against the walls, hearing people talk about them like masterpieces. Each swirl, line, or circle just another worry of my past blending into the canvas of my life.

I'd lived many lives through each of these paintings, being transported from one place to another just with the simple stroke of a brush. Almost as if each stroke was washing yet another sin from my body. Making me forget the past and the horrible people that came with it.

It'd been ten months since I'd had Wesley and Piper. Brooks and I had fallen into a pattern every day, and we're enjoying every second of our little ones growing up. It's hard to believe that our twins will be a year old in just two months. They'd come with us tonight, but Macy and Trevor offered to watch both babies so I could mingle with my guests.

Hip hop music plays softly in the background, and I sway to it from where I stand. Brooks comes up behind me, kissing my bare shoulder. "Here's to you, Mia." He holds out a bright pink drink in his hand.

"What's this?"

"Well, I had the caterers make the new drink I've been working on for the bar. It's called... The Topsy Turvy."

"Mmm... it looks amazing, what's in it?"

"A little grenadine, orange liqueur, a dash of simple syrup, sweetened lime juice, and Código 1530 Rosa Tequila."

"You know what tequila does to me, right?"

"I like what tequila does to you." He winks at me, and I can't help but smile.

"So, why the celebration juice?"

"You mean, you don't know? You've almost sold out, Mia."

My eyebrows raise. "Really? People actually want to buy my pieces?"

"Yes, really. I told you they were amazing from day one. You just needed a little nudge in the right direction."

"Thank you, Brooks. Really... for everything. Making me believe in love. Believing in me when I was fighting the one thing I didn't know I needed. Letting me run, but always remembering to pull me back. Loving me in our crazy, unconventional way."

"I think it should be the other way around. I should be thanking you."

The corners of my lips tip up into a smile. "Thanking me for what?"

I notice that all of our friends have started gathering around us, and I wonder if this is finally the moment that Brooks is going to make good on his promise. Macy and Trevor bring over a sleeping Wesley and Piper. I smile. I love them to pieces. No matter how many sleepless nights or diaper changes we have along the way.

My attention turns back to Brooks.

"Thank you for asking a guy you didn't know very well to move in. Giving me a chance to prove to you that I'm not like every other guy before me. For giving me the key to unlock your past and let me into that beautiful heart of yours. For allowing me to love you and for loving me back. For allowing me to raise our incredible twins with you. For making me a father. Words will never truly express how incredible our journey has been, and I can't wait to see where it takes us next."

My eyes start to water. The man in front of me came crashing into my life like a wrecking ball and spun everything I knew upside down. A gasp grows amongst the crowd, and my heart stirs loudly against my chest. Pounding to be let out so it can pour itself out to the man standing in front of me.

"Mia," he whispers before dropping down to one knee. "Be my wife. My partner. My love. Through schooling, art shows, the bar, and everything in between, I want to be with you and no one else until my dying breath. I want to have a house full of kids. I want to make you the happiest girl alive."

The tears try to drown my eyes as they flow out and down my cheeks. A smile broadens my face, and I nod. "Yes. Yes. YES!" He opens a small ring box, and the ring is perfect—a solitary sapphire surrounded by tiny diamonds lining the outside of the whole ring.

He stands up and kisses me like I'd just made his whole entire year. See, the thing about Brooks and I is this... we may be weird. We may be awkward. Hell, this whole thing started out as a roommate agreement and morphed into a sex bucket list.

The truth is... our love might be a little topsy turvy, but it's our kinda love, and I wouldn't have it any other way.

THE END

Topsy Turvy Signature Drink Recipe:

- 2 oz Codigo 1530 Rosa Tequila
- 1 oz Grenadine
- ½ oz Orange liqueur
- 1 oz Lime Juice
- Simple Syrup to taste

Other Titles

Written in the Sand

Catch up today:

"Written in the Sand is quite an emotional ride! From page one, the captivating storyline takes off and leads me on an unforgettable journey. Such an inspirational romance about moving forward from destruction and finding that special someone to share forever with."* —
USA *Today* Bestselling Author, Harloe Rae

I always believed my happily ever after came with the words "I do." I'd been happy once. In love. Until one night changed everything. Changed us. The love of my life, or so I thought, had become my own worst nightmare.

So here I am...

Back in Moonshine Springs. A place I wouldn't return to unless absolutely necessary. But that's not the biggest shock. Waiting for me with open arms and a safe place to stay is my high school best friend's brother, Beau. He's told me I'm his, but starting over isn't as easy as creating a new happily ever after. My past isn't done with me and soon enough, bleeds into my present.
My name is Cassidy Mae and this is my chance to begin again...

This book contains some scenes of domestic and graphic violence, sexual scenes, and mature themes. Please be aware these may cause triggers for the reader.

Melting Wynter

Catch up today:

Weston Croix

Okay, so I might have a few playboy like tendencies. That tends to happen when you fall in love and don't end up with the happily ever after of your dreams. I built a wall around my heart and decided to have a little fun instead.

Now, I've found myself falling for the ice queen herself. Did I mention that she's also my editor-in-chief?

She's not interested in me or being an us, but when our best friends start dating, we can no longer escape our insecurities or the fire burning between us.

I guess I'm just going to have to turn up the heat and melt her heart.

Wynter Carlisle

I've got the perfect job, an apartment in NYC's elite 425 Madison high rise and life as I know is great.

If there's one thing I've learned over the years, it's that people are fickle and love isn't always permanent. I'm the only one I can always count on, well except for my best friend Addison.

I had a plan to protect my heart. That was, until Weston—the cocky columnist who works for me…in more ways than one.

Can we really break down our own barriers or will our destiny go up in flames? We're about to find out.

After all, 425 Madison is the perfect place to fall in love!

Second Chance Rescue

Catch up today:

The plan was simple. The results are anything but…

I've lost too much to even think about opening my heart to anyone again. Grief consumed my life, and all I wanted was to be left alone so I could drown my sorrows while trying to find a sliver of relief at the bottom of a bottle.

But my father saw right through me, throwing me a curveball I never saw coming. Go back to working at our family's law firm, or take a wife. If I don't, I can kiss my inheritance goodbye.

Luckily, I have another card up my sleeve—and her name is Macy. She's shy, sweet, with curves in all the right places. She's also the perfect solution to my problem *if* I can convince her that what I'm proposing will end up benefiting us both.

It's easy. She needs money, and I need a wife. It's a win-win situation.

The way I see it, it's just another business transaction. No commitment.

No strings. Zero complications. What could possibly go wrong?

*This is a Stand-Alone Novel with No Cliffhangers, and a guaranteed

HEA*

Acknowledgments

Hopefully if you're reading this it means you made it to the end! I hope the journey was worth it. Mia has been on my mind for the last year and I've added and erased so many times that I questioned if she would ever make an appearance in the world. I AM SO GLAD she did. I fell in love with Brooks and Mia. Their story. I hope you loved them too! That being said... book number four published! I can't hardly wrap my head around it. I've wanted to quit this book so many times, but I'm glad I didn't.

This year? Man, it's honestly been a tough one. We're all trying to persevere and do the absolute best that we can with what we've been given. It's been a struggle and I want to tell you... it's okay to not be okay. Just take one day at a time, one breath at a time and we'll get there. I have to remind myself that often these days. That being said... I want to give a huge thank you to YOU for picking up this book in these challenging times to just read my words. You have zero idea how much it means to me. You are the reason I write! I could shout it from the top of the empire state building and it wouldn't be enough... THANK YOU, THANK YOU!

To my husband, you've been such a stronghold in my author and regular life. You pick me up when I'm down. You tell me I can do it when I tell you continually that I have no clue what the hell I'm doing. You encourage me to write even when I want to crawl into a ball and just sleep to drown out the world. You make me laugh in the stupidest ways. You're my favorite road trip buddy and sometimes your ideas for my books are outlandish, yet brilliant. I would rather be drunk in love with you than any other being in this universe. You my guy and for that I'm ever grateful.

To, Sarah… words cannot express how much appreciation and admiration for you. You always seem to know when I need an encouraging word or a laugh. Your friendship is one of my true favorites. Without this amazing book community, I wouldn't have met you and that would've been an utter shame! Thank you for making life more exciting and hilarious.

To Jill… Thank you isn't enough for how I feel about our friendship. You're always there with words of wisdom and a kind thought when I need it most. You'll never know how much you truly matter to me.

To Ally… thank you for stressing out over my books just as much as I do. For continuing to push me to be better, to do better. For giving all the encouraging words even when I don't want to hear them. I appreciate you so much!

I'm forever grateful that I found Talia at Book Cover Kingdom. I wish I could say we've been together since my first book, but… better late than never, right? You make kickass covers and graphics and for that you've got me as long as this author life takes me. I'm always excited to work on new projects and I'm so thankful for your friendship! You are a sweet soul and I hope that never changes! I can't wait to see what we do next and I'M SO IN LOVE WITH MIA'S COVER!!! I'm SO GLAD I didn't make you wait til 2021 to show off this gorgeous thing!!!!

A HUGE thank you to Stacey with Champagne Book Design for making this formatting look so epic! I love your creativity and how you effortlessly find the perfection of images! Without your help, my book would not be half as pretty! I have a new appreciation for all the work it takes to format novels these days after purchasing Vellum myself earlier this year. What I can do isn't half as pretty or professional as your stuff. So, thank you. For being patient with me and for always fitting me in! Your work doesn't go unnoticed and I just want you to know how important you are in this process!

To Jill, Ally, Norma, Rose, Amanda, JoAnna, Carolina—thank you so much for everything you do! The sharing, the encouragement, the belief that I can write books time and time again when I question myself. The writing community needs more amazing people like you. The reviews, the messages, the inspiration, everything—you mean the world to me and I can't shout it enough. You took a chance on me with Second Chance Rescue, Written in the Sand... and here with are... a year later and YOU'RE STILL HERE!!!! There are so many more of you included in this thank you, but I'd write a book with just your names! You know who you are!

This year I met two amazing ladies, Aubree and Lauren, with Forever Write PR. You two took a chance on a young writer and made a dream come true (writing for the 425 Madison series). You've helped me so much over these last few months and I feel like thank you doesn't even cover how I feel. From book tours to social media calendar help, amazon category help, and everything in between... THANK YOU!!! You make releases so easy and that is something that's magical!

To my beta readers—Rose, Sarah, Rachel, and Norma—Thank you so much for making Topsy Turvy Kinda Love even better than it was at the beginning. Your notes, encouragement, questions, and overall support is something I could never replace in a million years. Each one of you is so dear to me and I'm glad we've become book world friends!

To my author friends, new and old—Gabrielle, Eliza, Julie, Leigh L., Rachel, Becca, Ashton, Anna, and Gail. You ladies are so encouraging and inspire me to write all the things! I'm so thankful for each and every one of you, even though we don't talk on the daily! It's always nice to pick up where we left off!

My review team is some of the best readers I've ever met. Your endless love of my words and your continual want to read them inspires me to write more and you guys... the stories I have brewing right now may be some of my best yet!

Thank you to Jenny for taking the time to edit my book. For fixing all my comma's and periods, haha. I know there were so many! You are so very appreciated!

Thank you to Yvette for proofreading this beauty! Thank you for fitting me in and understanding when I had to tweak my schedule up. THANK YOU, THANK YOU!

A huge thank you to Carlos and Fede at Codigo 1530 for allowing me to use your tequila name in this novel. If any of my readers are looking for an amazing tequila... this is going to be your jam! I had one too many trying it out and man, it's GOOD!

To my reader group, Zoey's Lit Ink Lovers... you guys are the reason for the words I write. Thank you for all the comments, suggestions, playing along with my silly polls, and offering suggestions and thoughts. A big thank you to Jill for picking out the name Piper Brielle for our little girl! The polls I do in my group make such a difference and I definitely take them into consideration in my books. So, thank you from the bottom of my heart for continuing to stick around and be the best readers and some of the best friends a girl could ask for in this lifetime!

About the Author

Zoey Drake is a hopeless romantic with a serious Chipotle addiction. When she isn't searching for her next book boyfriend, she's writing him. Although she has West Virginia roots, she currently resides in Ohio with her husband and rescue dog, Sir Cooper Ryder Mess.

Join her Facebook readers group, Zoey's Lit Ink Lovers, at www.facebook.com/groups/zoeyslitinklovers

Stay Connected

Zoey loves interacting with readers, so don't be afraid to reach out and say hey!
Want to find out the latest news and what's next for Z?

Social Media Links:

Bookbub (Zoey): www.bookbub.com/profile/zoey-drake

Amazon (Zoey): bit.ly/ZDrakeZon

Goodreads Zoey Drake Profile: bit.ly/ZDrakeGR

Instagram: www.instagram.com/simply_zoey_drake

Facebook: www.facebook.com/zdrakebooks

Twitter: twitter.com/ZoeyDrake17

Made in the USA
Monee, IL
19 July 2021